D0342283

HOW TO
FALL

HOW TO FALL

JANE CASEY

ST. MARTIN'S GRIFFIN
New York

HOW TO FALL. Copyright © 2013 by Jane Casey. All rights reserved. Printed in the United States of America. For information, address St. Martin's Press, 175 Fifth Avenue, New York, N.Y. 10010.

www.stmartins.com

Designed by Steven Seighman

Library of Congress Cataloging-in-Publication Data

Casey, Jane (Jane E.)
    How to fall / Jane Casey. — First U.S. edition.
        pages cm. — (Jess Tennant mysteries ; 1)
    ISBN 978-1-250-04065-7 (hardcover)
    ISBN 978-1-4668-3625-9 (e-book)
    [1. Death—Fiction.   2. Cousins—Fiction.   3. Family life—England—Fiction.
4. England—Fiction.   5. Mystery and detective stories.]   I. Title.

    PZ7.C267836How 2014
    [Fic]—dc23

                                                                    2014010052

St. Martin's Griffin books may be purchased for educational, business, or promotional use. For information on bulk purchases, please contact Macmillan Corporate and Premium Sales Department at 1-800-221-7945, extension 5442, or write specialmarkets@macmillan.com.

Originally published in Great Britain by Corgi Books, an imprint of Random House Children's Publishers UK, a Random House Group Company

First U.S. Edition: August 2014

10 9 8 7 6 5 4 3 2 1

For Rachel Petty, the ideal reader

HOW TO
FALL

F reya ran.

It wasn't a night for running, and the woods weren't the best place for it. The full moon cast enough light to make it easy to see in the open, but under the trees it was one shade above pitch dark, and Freya was running blind. Rogue branches caught at her clothes, whipped her skin, barred her path. The ground under her feet was uneven, pitted with hollows and ridged with roots, and more than once she stumbled.

But Freya still ran.

She had long since lost the path, but she knew where she was going. The sound of the sea was louder than the leaves that rustled around her, louder than the voices in her head. *Slut. Bitch. Freak.* Voices she couldn't outrun.

She made herself go faster, sobbing under her breath as her feet flew. Between the trees ahead of her, she could see light. Space. Air. She threw herself toward it as if it was her only hope, as if it was her last chance. The trees thinned at the edge of the wood, spaced further apart, and she slowed a little as she dodged between the final two that stood between her and open ground. The sea spread out before her, the moon streaking a path across the waves, scattering light as the water rippled. The waves crashed against the cliff below. High tide, or close to it. Still hurrying but moving more carefully, she picked her way across the headland, skirting the thick gorse bushes that covered it, heading for the highest point of land where she knew there was a bench. In front of it, the ground fell away, the cliff face sheer down to the water. She could see every detail of it when she closed her eyes; she knew it as well as she knew her own face. It was terrifying.

But it was the only way this could end.

The bench rose up before her, sooner than she had expected, and she clung to the back of it for a moment. The weathered wood was reassuringly familiar under her hands, the paint flaking a little as she touched it. She let go of it reluctantly, stepping around it, stopping for a second to concentrate as she stood just in front of it. Ten steps from the bench to the edge of the cliff. Eight steps to the left.

And then jump.

She thought for a second that the bench was shaking, but it was her legs trembling uncontrollably. Exhaustion, because of her run. But more than that. Fear.

Suddenly aware of herself again, she could feel every bruise aching, every graze stinging. A line across her neck burned and she touched it, running her fingers along it, feeling the raised skin that would look red and raw if she could see it.

Slowly, deliberately, she took a deep breath. She was out of choices. There was nowhere else to go.

Ten steps. Eight steps. Jump.

Easy.

The voices had fallen away. The only sound was the water below, and the beating of her heart. She stared at the horizon, and moved.

Five steps.

She couldn't do it.

Three more.

She faltered, stopped.

Two more.

The edge.

In front of her, the sea, the sky, the stars. Behind her—she twisted to look—the dark mass of the woods. Nothing moved.

Impossible to go on. Impossible to go back.

Freya . . .

A whisper, barely audible. Her heart pounded, thudding in her ears. She looked around warily, trying to pick out where the voice had come from. Trying to work out if it was real.

Freya . . .

She was so tired. So tired of being afraid. So tired of running. But she couldn't jump.

The voice hissed again, commanding, demanding. *Freya . . .*

And something touched her shoulder. She stepped away from it without thinking.

The world tilted and swung, the moon spinning in the sky, the waves rushing up to meet her.

And then there was silence.

1

As a place to spend the summer, Port Sentinel probably had its good points, but it was doing a good job of hiding them. I trudged down Fore Street, the main and only street in town, feeling the rain soak into my jeans. It had been pouring since the night before, when my mother and I arrived in the middle of a thunderstorm and unloaded all our belongings in a serious cloudburst, running from the car to the holiday cottage in total hysterics. It would take weeks for everything to dry out completely.

When I woke the following morning to steady drizzle the weather pretty much matched my mood. The sky was an ominous shade of gray that suggested there was plenty more rain to come. There was no TV in our rented cottage, or access to the internet, and I had lasted through four chapters of the witless romantic novel I'd found on a shelf before I gave up. Just because the hero was a ruggedly handsome cowboy, I didn't see why it gave him the right to be so rude all the time.

Plus the heroine was a twit. I couldn't even be bothered to flick to the end to make sure they really did live happily ever after. I grabbed my jacket (rainproof, hooded, essential accessory for a summer holiday in England) and went to find Mum.

She was in her bedroom, I discovered, lying on the bed, staring at the ceiling.

"Are you OK?"

"Fine. This is called relaxing. I'm relaxing."

"You sound as if you're trying to convince yourself."

She grabbed a pillow and threw it at me. "Leave me alone."

"What? I'm just saying, you don't look relaxed."

"I'm trying. This is a holiday, after all."

A holiday *she* had decided we were going to take. Molly Tennant, née Cole, returning to her roots accompanied by her teenage daughter, Jess, after an absence of many years and a bitter divorce. Because there was absolutely no chance of *that* being awkward. I didn't bother with I-told-you-so. "I'm going out for a wander. Do you want to come?"

She shook her head.

"You're going to have to leave the house sometime."

"Not yet, though."

"Mum . . ."

"I'm building up to it."

"I'll leave you to it, then. I'll be back soon."

Which was no word of a lie, because it wasn't as if it was going to take a long time to look around. Port Sentinel wasn't a one-horse town, but that was only because they'd upgraded the horse to a Range Rover for the sake of the out-of-towners who owned holiday homes there. The locals probably had to share a three-legged donkey, but they were very much less important than the bankers and brokers who'd built large houses all the way across the hill above the town. They were all at least five times the size of the tiny fishermen's cottages and pastel-painted terraced houses that had once been the only buildings in Port Sentinel, before it became fashionable. Huge picture windows stared out blankly at the view, reflecting nothing but gray skies and the gravel-colored sea. It would be pretty if the sun ever came out, I admitted grudgingly. Very grudgingly after I had stepped off the pavement into a puddle and soaked my right foot. Very grudgingly indeed after a blonde in a four-wheel drive had come within inches of mowing me down as she sped down the road, huge sunglasses firmly in place despite the weather.

Fore Street was small and narrow, the old buildings leaning against one another drunkenly when you looked above the shopfronts. Half the shops were little boutiques and designer outlets too exclusive for me to consider visiting, even to get out of the rain. The other half consisted of a fairly random collection of teashops, charity shops, junk shops, and we-sell-everything mini-markets wreathed in brightly colored displays of plastic beach toys. They took up most of the narrow pavement. Passing one, I pushed an inflatable whale out of my way and collided with a girl who had been hidden behind it, heading in the opposite direction.

"Sorry." I wasn't, in fact; it was at least as much her fault as mine. But instead of apologizing in return as I had expected, the girl stared at me for a long moment from under her dripping umbrella. I had plenty of time to notice very perfect mascara standing out like stars around her wide eyes, and the serious diamond studs in her ears, and the expensively highlighted hair, and the white skinny jeans, and the sky-high wedges, and the pale-pink polo shirt she was wearing with the collar flipped up, and the Burberry mini-trench that had cost more than my entire wardrobe put together. She looked far more rattled than a near-miss should have made her—stunned, in fact. Alarmed. Panicked. And as a cascade of raindrops fell between us, I realized the hand that held the umbrella was shaking. Rainy it might have been, but it wasn't cold. Not even a little bit.

She stepped sideways eventually, still staring, and I walked on, wondering if she had just never seen anyone in frayed jeans and battered trainers on Fore Street before. I wasn't wearing makeup, either. *Call the fashion police, quick.*

I probably wouldn't have thought much more about it if it hadn't been for two things. One was the old lady who opened a shop door right in front of me a minute later so I caught sight of the street behind me reflected in the glass—including a perfect view of the girl standing under her umbrella, still gazing in my direction, now on her mobile phone, talking urgently. The other was the fact that three other people stopped to gawp at me in the space of the next three minutes: two girls on the other side of the road who nudged each other as soon as they spotted me, and a middle-aged woman who peered at me short-sightedly and started to wave, then dropped her hand and hurried on. I knew I was blushing, which was annoying in itself. If this was what it was like to be a celebrity I'd be quite happy to remain obscure forever.

But I was never going to be obscure in a small town like Port Sentinel. It was one of the many reasons why I hadn't been thrilled to hear we were spending the summer there. I had waited to tackle Mum until we were actually in the car, halfway down the motorway, London not even a brown smudge in the rear-view mirror any more. I'd read in a parenting book Mum had borrowed from the library that the car was the ideal place for awkward conversations with teenagers; I didn't see why that shouldn't work just as well the other way round. (If you're wondering why I was reading a parenting book, all I'll say is: knowledge is power. I like to spot the psychological trickery well in advance. And if you're wondering why Mum was reading a parenting book, so was I.)

"The thing I don't understand," I had said carefully, "is why now."

"Sorry?" My mother, who is neither deaf nor stupid, played for time.

"Why now? You haven't gone near Port Sentinel or your family since before I was born, and suddenly we're spending the summer there. Which, by the way, you didn't even discuss with me."

"There was nothing to discuss, Jess." She kept her eyes on the motorway and her knuckles were white as she gripped the steering wheel. That didn't mean anything; she was a nervous driver at the best of times. But I knew I was making her tense.

Which was no reason to stop.

"I was sort of looking forward to spending the summer in London. You know, with my friends. And with Dad," I added.

"I seem to recall someone complaining about their friends being away. Isn't Lauren in France?"

"Staying with a family in Provence. Her mum is completely obsessed with her being fluent in French by the end of the holidays." Lauren had moaned about having to go, right up to the moment when she realized the family included an exceptionally hot nineteen-year-old named Raoul. Raoul, who was tall, dark, and handsome—and knew it. Raoul, who spent his life lounging around half naked or in the pool. She had only been there for three days but already I'd been e-mailed seven pictures of him snapped with her phone, and if she thought he hadn't noticed her stalking him she was quite wrong. Raoul posing casually by the fridge in boxers, drinking milk straight out of the carton (which, yuck—but it hadn't put Lauren off). Raoul standing on a diving board, six-pack on display. Raoul soaking wet, his tan like caramel, glancing casually at Lauren at just the moment she happened to be taking his picture. Five more and I'd have enough for a calendar.

"And Ella's in the States."

"In a giant camper van, with her whole family, on the trip of a lifetime." I shook my head. "I don't think everyone's going to make it back alive."

"That's a long time to be stuck in the same vehicle together. I could barely face the drive down to Devon."

"Yes, and why exactly are we going?"

"That again."

"You didn't answer me the first time."

"Is this teenage rebellion kicking in at last?" Mum shot me a sidelong look, amused.

"Oh, you'll know when it's teenage rebellion, I promise you. This isn't it. I just want to know why we packed up everything we own so we could spend six weeks in the back end of nowhere."

A shrug. "Family stuff."

Very informative.

"What about Dad?"

"What about him?"

"Doesn't he mind us being away for that long?"

"Well, your father doesn't care where I go, or with whom." Another sidelong look; she had picked up on the note of hurt I hadn't quite managed to keep out of my voice. "And I did ask him about your visits, Jess, but he's really busy at the moment and he said he'd catch up with you when we get back."

"Busy with work or with Martine?"

"I didn't ask. But I imagine with both."

I rolled my eyes. "Grim."

"Martine seems a very nice person."

"Mum, you don't have to like everyone. Especially not Dad's new girlfriend."

"We're divorced. He can do what he likes. And so can I."

She spoke lightly but I wasn't fooled. It had been a tough couple of years since they broke up. Or rather, since Dad had left her. Mum had married young and stayed young, so when Dad left, she struggled to cope. We'd both had to do a lot of growing up in a hurry. There were days when I felt as if *I* was the one who should be looking after *her*.

"OK. So if you're going to start acting like Dad, I can expect you to turn up with a twenty-four-year-old lover one of these days."

She laughed. "I don't really go for younger men."

"Maybe you should. Maybe that's the mistake we've been making. Younger men must be easier to push around."

Mum's eyes were full of sympathy. "Oh, Jess. Are you still upset about Conrad?"

"Never mention that name to me again."

"OK. I won't. But just so you know, I never liked him. I thought you could do better."

"If only you'd said."

"You wouldn't have paid any attention."

She was right. It was my turn to go silent. I stared out of the window. I couldn't think about Conrad without wanting to curl up in a ball, which wasn't really possible in the front seat of Mum's Nissan Micra. I didn't like to think about how I'd fallen for Conrad. He was tall and thin, with high cheekbones, amazing hair, and a dreamy, distracted air that had intrigued me. I had imagined it was because he was deep in thought but actually he was just vacant, his brain in neutral most of the time. He was artistic, or so he said. He wrote poetry, even. Really, really bad poetry, as I'd discovered almost immediately. No matter how much I wanted to believe he was The One, the poetry had always worried me.

All that, and I'd thought I was in love. Right up until the moment I'd arrived late at a party, wandered in, and found him sitting on top of Karen Seagram, one hand burrowing in her top as if he'd lost his keys, with his tongue stuck in her mouth. To which I had said, "Rather her than me, Conrad. You kiss like a goat eating a jam sandwich through a letterbox."

I'd walked out with my head high, thinking, *Never let them see you cry*. But in private I'd done more than my share of crying.

I shook my head, trying to dislodge the image, and returned to my original point. "What family stuff?"

"You're not going to drop it, are you?"

"Nope."

"You're so stubborn. I think you get it from your father."

"That's fighting talk."

"You do get some things from him, you know."

"Name three."

"You're argumentative. Stubborn, as I said before. And you're tough."

I hadn't been expecting that. "Tough?"

"Not in a bad way. Just—you're not like me. You don't back down. You stand up for yourself."

"If I have to. But I'm not sure I like being described as 'tough.'"

"Call it strength of character, then."

"That's better."

"Proving my point . . ." Mum murmured, more or less to herself. Then she sighed. "Look, it's been a difficult year. You know about Freya."

"Of course." Freya, my cousin, born not long after me, dead since last summer. I had never met her. The news of her death had been strangely shocking—strange, because I had never thought about her, beyond knowing her name. Strange because I had felt a sharp sense of loss for something I had never known I was missing. "I hadn't realized it was a year ago already."

"In a couple of weeks." Mum's hands tightened on the wheel and she didn't look at me as she said, "When it happened I was already in touch with Tilly."

"You didn't tell me that." Tilly, Mum's twin sister. Freya's mother.

She wriggled. "I didn't want to tell you about it because I wasn't sure what was going to happen. We were just getting to know one another again. It takes time to build up a relationship after being out of touch for so long."

"Eighteen years."

A nod. "From right after I got engaged to your father until the day the divorce papers came through."

"Because she didn't like Dad."

"Not much. But I didn't listen."

"Which is why you didn't bother to warn me about Conrad," I guessed.

"One of the reasons. It didn't seem worth it. When you're in love, reason goes out the window. And I loved your father very much."

"We all make mistakes," I said kindly.

"It wasn't a mistake. If I hadn't married him, I wouldn't have you."

"Thanks. For the gift of life, I mean."

"You're welcome. Tilly was nice enough not to say *I told you so*, and she and Jack invited us to come and stay last year. But then Freya died."

"It was an accident, wasn't it?"

"As far as I know."

"Not suicide or something."

The car lurched as Mum yanked the wheel, irritated. "Jess, I'm serious. Do not even *suggest* something like that to Tilly. Promise me."

"I was just asking," I said, wounded.

"You can't ask. It would be too hurtful."

"Because they don't want to think Freya killed herself."

"Exactly."

"Don't they want to know the truth, though?"

"Not necessarily."

I thought about that for a couple of miles. I could understand that if Freya had chosen to end her life, it would be hard to bear. I'd still have wanted to know for sure, though. And it was weird to think that she'd been the same age as me, and now she was gone.

"So why are we going to see them now?"

"I want to go home," Mum said simply. "I want to see the old places. I want to see my sister and get to know my niece and nephews, and I want you to have a family."

"I *have* a family."

"You have your father, his current girlfriend, and me. That's not enough."

I was frowning. "If you were in touch with Tilly when Freya died, why didn't you go to see her then?"

"It wasn't the right time."

"Why not?"

Mum looked at me before she answered, as if she was considering what to say and how to say it. "Because you would have come with me."

"So? I know Tilly didn't like Dad, but I'm not that much like him."

"Mm."

"What else?"

"Is my handbag on your side of the car?"

"Don't change the subject."

"I'm not." Mum glanced at me again. "Seriously, Jess—look inside my bag, in the zipped pocket."

I found the bag wedged behind my left foot and dragged it onto my lap with some difficulty, since the front of the car was crammed, as was the back seat and the boot. We did not travel light. "What am I looking for?"

"Tilly sent me a photo of the family. I think you should see what Freya looked like."

As she said it, I unzipped the pocket. My fingertips brushed against a stiff bit of paper and I slid it out, careful not to bend the edges. It was a family photograph of six people sitting on a grassy slope. Two adults, one the image of Mum, the other tall and fair, superficially like Dad. The sisters had a type, it seemed. Two girls, two boys. Two older, two younger.

"Hugo was the eldest. Then Freya. Then Petra. Then Tom."

Tom with a football under his arm and a scowl on his face, as if he wanted to go and play instead of posing for a picture. He was maybe ten, a couple of years younger than Petra. She sat with one sandal off, bare brown legs crossed in front of her, still childish but not for much longer. Hugo, as dark as I am fair, a year older than me and broodingly attractive. And Freya, I guessed. Freya, who was blond, like me. Who had the same shape of face as me, the same pointed chin. The same slanting blue eyes. The same mouth.

The same. Top to toe. The dead girl and I could have been twins.

I looked up. "Mum . . ."

"Don't worry. I sent Tilly pictures of you. She knows what to expect."

But everyone else wouldn't, I thought, feeling distinctly uncomfortable.

So it wasn't really surprising, all things considered, that people on Fore Street were acting as if they'd seen a ghost. As far as they were concerned, Freya was back from the dead.

Awkward wasn't the word.

I lasted another ten steps before yet another person did a double take, this time an elderly man carrying a battered golf umbrella. He stopped in his tracks, the better to stare at me. I dived without thinking into the nearest shop, without even checking to see what it sold, looking for a place to hide. The dovecot smell of dusty old books met me and I smiled to myself as I pushed my hood back. A proper secondhand bookshop. Exactly what I had been looking for.

It wasn't a large shop but every inch of available space was shelved and a pair of bookcases ran down the middle of the room so that it was divided into three narrow aisles. Stacks of hardbacks teetered on the floor, waiting for a gap to appear in the row upon row of books, faded and worn and thoroughly enticing. The expensive ones were in glass cases nearest the door, the collector's items in tooled leather or wrapped in the original dust jackets. Not for me. I wandered down the middle aisle, passing gardening and theology, politics and fishing—nothing that would tempt me to stop. There was a desk near the back with a cash register on it, but no sign of the person who was reading—I leaned over to look at the hardback that was lying on the desk—*Classic Cars of the 1970s*. Interesting stuff.

Or perhaps not.

Behind the desk, a sign on a frankly dangerous-looking spiral staircase promised that the fun stuff like contemporary fiction was upstairs. I put my hand on the banister, prepared to risk the narrow treads for the sake of something decent to read, then stopped. Quick footsteps overhead: someone moving toward the stairs. I stood back to let them come down. I wasn't superstitious about passing people on the stairs—there just wasn't room for two on the death spiral.

The owner of the feet rattled down the steps at top speed, a mug of coffee in one hand, a stack of books balanced precariously in the other, and it was my turn to stare. He was very much not the fuddy-duddy bookshop owner I had expected, lean in jeans and a T-shirt. He was seventeen or eighteen, tall, with dark hair. Straight nose. Broad shoulders. *Oh, hello . . .*

He half glanced at me, his eyes startlingly gray against his tan, then did a classic double take and almost slipped. He swore as the books slid to the floor, but managed not to spill his coffee, which impressed me. I might have wondered what his problem was if he hadn't been giving me the look I was starting to expect: shock mixed with suspicion. And what looked like— but surely couldn't have been—fear . . .

"Are you OK?"

"Fine." He didn't look at me again as he set his mug down on the desk and turned to rescue the books he'd dropped.

"Sorry." I picked up the paperback that had fallen at my feet—*To Kill a Mockingbird*—and handed it to him.

"Why are you sorry?" He concentrated on flattening the pages that had creased when the book fell.

"Because I startled you."

He didn't bother to deny it. "No harm done."

"Harper Lee is looking a bit battered," I observed.

A glance at the back of the book, then the gray eyes met mine again. He looked amused and I wondered if I had imagined him going pale under his tan when he saw me first. "She wasn't exactly pristine before."

There was absolutely no reason for me to blush, but I did it anyway. To cover it, I said, at random, "I was just going upstairs."

"Be my guest."

I started up the staircase, acutely conscious that he was watching me. I risked a look down from near the top, and felt a jolt of surprise that was halfway to disappointment. He was sitting down with his back to me, already absorbed in his book. And why not? I was just another customer.

Even so, I wandered around the upstairs room as the floor creaked, dithering about which book to choose from the thousands that lined the walls. It wasn't that I wanted to impress him, I promised myself. But romance was out. Crime didn't seem to strike the right note either. Distracted, I found myself wishing I knew more about Freya. Had she been an intellectual? Did she read novels? Did she read anything at all? The room was large, with a pair of sagging leather armchairs in the middle and dormer windows that looked out on the wet street below. A door in the corner was marked PRIVATE; that would be where he had made his coffee, I thought, and then wondered why I cared. I went as far as one of the windows, stepping up on a low shelf to peer out at the street. As I turned away, I half saw myself reflected in the glass and looked again—a ghost version of me, shadows for eyes, washed-out skin, and hair that hung in straggling tails. A drowned me. They had found Freya in the sea, I recalled, with a shiver that surprised me, then made me laugh. I was getting to be as bad as everyone else in Port Sentinel, as edgy about nothing, about a coincidental resemblance. I turned the shiver into a shrug and jumped down off the shelf, careless of the noise I made. I was there to buy a book, after all, not wallow in creepiness. And I still didn't have a clue what to choose.

In the end, a cheap paperback edition of *Cold Comfort Farm* came to the rescue. I knew the title but not what it was about, and levered it off a crowded shelf to have a look. Sitting in one of the armchairs, I lost track of time as I read the first few pages, and then a few more. I hadn't expected it to be funny, but it was. I made myself stop reading eventually, checked I could afford it, and went back down the stairs with the grace and dexterity of a three-toed sloth. The boy could run down if he liked. I didn't mind sacrificing speed if it meant I wouldn't make a fool of myself by falling. I was so busy concentrating on looking nonchalant that I didn't notice the boy was gone until I put my book down on the desk. In his place sat a balding middle-aged man in a tweed jacket, the bookshop owner of my imagination. He didn't crack a smile as I handed him two pound coins, tossing them into the till with something approaching disdain.

Taking my book, I hesitated for a second, then plunged. "Where did your assistant go?"

"Who? Oh—Will. He was just looking after the shop for me for half an hour. We're not busy today. As usual."

My book was not going to make the difference between profit and loss, it seemed. I slunk out, hiding it under my jacket to protect it from the rain that was still falling. At least I had found out the boy's name, if nothing else. It suited him, I thought. *Will.*

And as if I had summoned him, he fell into step beside me. "I think we need to talk."

2

Too startled to protest, I allowed myself to be steered toward a small coffee shop on the other side of the street from the bookshop. It was dark, with sticky oil-cloth coverings on the tables and a seriously no-frills approach to décor, but it smelled of freshly baked cakes and good coffee, and almost all the tables were full. Will pulled back a chair to let an old lady out, then nicked the table she had just left, to one side of the window.

An elderly waitress bustled up before I had finished unzipping my jacket, her eyes locked on her notepad. "What are you having?"

I didn't dare ask for time to look at a menu. "Just a black coffee."

"Same for me," Will said.

Her head snapped up at the sound of his voice and she beamed at him. "I didn't see it was you, my darling. We've got a lovely chocolate cake today."

"Not right now, Dot. I'm still full from breakfast."

"I don't believe it. A growing boy like you needs to eat. I'll bring you a small piece. On the house. With two forks." As she said the last bit, she turned to me and winked. I felt rather than saw the shock hit her, amusement fading instantly to doubtful confusion. I busied myself with rummaging in my bag, looking for absolutely nothing, until she had moved away.

"You'd better get used to that." He hadn't missed it, then. I didn't think the gray eyes would miss much. "It's a small town. And everyone knew Freya."

It helped that he had said her name first. "Freya was my cousin."

"That almost explains the resemblance."

"I didn't know." I was fiddling with the end of my ponytail, I realized, and made myself stop. "My mum and her mum are identical twins. And my dad looks quite like Jack. They have the same coloring, anyway."

He was looking at me intently, studying my face. "It's uncanny."

"It's genetic."

I saw him react to the sharp-edged comment but only because I happened to be staring at his mouth when the corner of it curved upward. Instead of responding directly, he said, "You don't sound like her."

"Because I grew up in London?"

"Because of the things you say, more." He didn't explain what he meant, and I didn't want to ask until I had a better idea of him, and how well he had known my cousin. Quite well, I thought. Maybe very. But he was asking, "Didn't you ever meet her?"

I shook my head. "Mum's the black sheep of the family, so this is my first trip. We're staying for the summer."

"I'll sort out the welcome banners. But I'll need to know your name."

"Oh! Sorry. I forgot. I'm Jess Tennant."

"Jess." He repeated it, as if it sounded strange to him, as if he needed to learn it. I wondered for a second if I had found another halfwit—a matching pair with Conrad—but that didn't fit with the steady appraisal I was getting. I wondered what he was thinking, and then remembered with a rush of embarrassment that I wasn't supposed to know what he was called.

"And you are?"

"I'm Will Henderson. I live near the Leonards," he added with a half-smile.

The Leonards. My cousins. "I haven't met them yet."

The half-smile widened to a proper grin. "It's an experience."

"I can't wait."

"You might not have to. Hugo and Petra are around today. I think they went down to the harbor."

I leaned back in my seat, unable to keep the dismay off my face.

Will raised his eyebrows. "What's wrong?"

"You mean apart from having a whole family I've never met? What about looking exactly like their dead sister?"

There was a clunk as Dot dumped my cup in front of me. She had to have heard the last bit, and I stared down at my coffee as she gave Will his and set the cake between us. I was afraid to see the expression on her face. Without missing a beat Will engaged her in conversation about business and the tourist season and what she'd done at the weekend while I wished the window opened wide enough to let me escape. After what seemed like forever, she creaked off.

"It's OK. She's gone." Will sounded amused.

I gave him a filthy look. "Is it any wonder I'm on edge?"

He relented. "Don't be. You don't need to be."

"Oh really?"

"Really. Word will get around pretty quickly that you're her cousin."

"But until then I'd better get used to the staring and whispering."

"It won't be that bad."

"You think?" I fiddled with my cup. "You had a pretty strong reaction when you saw me."

"I slipped."

I really wanted to take him at his word, but I couldn't. "I bet you could go up and down those stairs a million times a day carrying a hundred books, blindfolded, and you'd never put a foot wrong. I know what I saw. You were freaked out."

"Not me." He looked interested. "What do you mean by everyone else?"

"Take your pick. Pretty much everyone in here has had a look at me since we came in. Some of them are still staring. The girl in the corner hasn't noticed me yet, but it's only a matter of time."

"There's no need to be paranoid. You're just not used to the small-town atmosphere."

"It's not paranoia. And I'm not so sure it's a small-town thing either." He looked skeptical and I added, "Before you suggest it, I'm not imagining it."

"I wouldn't dream of it." He spun his cup on its saucer. "You can't be surprised about the staring. Given what happened."

I leaned across the table, lowering my voice. "That's the thing. I don't *know* what happened. Everyone hints but no one actually says it."

"People don't like to talk about that sort of thing."

"I get that. But I also have the feeling I've come in halfway through the story and I'm never going to catch up. And I want to know more about Freya."

"What do you want to know?"

I hesitated, thinking of what Mum had said about not asking questions in case I hurt someone's feelings. But Will wasn't part of Freya's family. And he was basically offering to tell me all about it. I couldn't let that opportunity go.

"Were you friends with her?"

"Of course." He looked wary, as if he didn't like where I was steering the conversation.

"Were you more than friends?"

His eyebrows shot up. "Direct, aren't you?"

I held my nerve. "You haven't answered the question."

"We didn't go out."

That didn't mean he hadn't had feelings for her, or her for him, but I didn't have it in me to push any further. "Right."

"If it's any help, you needn't worry. No one's going to confuse the two of you for long."

"What's that supposed to mean?" I demanded.

"Freya was Freya and you aren't. Simple as that."

I was more interested in finding out about my cousin than in snapping back, but he was as irritating as nettle stings on bare legs. "What was she like?"

He shook his head. "I can't sum her up. She was herself."

"Very helpful."

"Sorry."

I had a sudden urge to make him uneasy, to set him on edge again, to shake him and see what fell out.

"Right. Let's start at the other end."

"What do you mean?"

"I want to know how she died."

"Can't help with that either." From one second to the next, his eyes had gone the color of steel. *Back off.*

Torture wouldn't have got me to admit it, but it was the first time I'd felt scared since I arrived in Port Sentinel. I had the impression that I was wading confidently into dangerous waters, that I would soon be well out of my depth. Which was clearly ridiculous.

"You must know."

"Why do you care?"

I shrugged. "I don't have the full story and I don't want to put my foot in it when I meet my cousins for the first time. This is the kind of thing I should know."

Whether he agreed with that or not, he answered me, but his jaw was tight with tension. "She fell off a cliff."

"Fell? Or jumped?"

He drank his coffee, not answering.

"Was she suicidal? Did Freya want to die?"

"I don't think I can answer that."

"Can't? Or *won't*?" The irritation was back and it made my voice sharp. I leaned forward. "Come on, Will. It's not difficult. Did she kill herself? Or was she pushed?"

"Are you looking for trouble, Jess?"

"I'm just trying to find out what happened to my cousin. Why should that cause trouble?"

"Because there are people who might not like you asking questions about Freya."

"Including you?"

He shook his head, as if I was a fly buzzing at him. "Just leave it alone."

"I'm not afraid of trouble."

"Maybe you should be."

I didn't feel scared any more. I was too angry. "Is that a threat?"

He laughed, a degree of self-possession returning. "Hardly. Call it friendly advice."

"You can call it what you like. I'm more than capable of making up my own mind about that sort of thing."

"You really are surprisingly feisty. I mean that as a compliment," he added quickly.

I ignored the second part, though I could tell I was blushing. "Why are you surprised? Wasn't Freya?"

"No. Not really. But she had principles. She was the sort of person who stood up for what was right. She didn't back down if she believed in something."

"Me neither."

"I have no doubt." He looked out of the window, then pushed the untouched cake toward me as he stood up. "If you want to meet your cousins, now's your chance."

Before I could say anything else, the café door swung open. Without saying good-bye, Will went across to greet a boy I recognized as Hugo. He was frowning, his expression lightening as he saw Will. The two of them spoke for a moment, their voices low, Hugo looking over Will's shoulder at me as he listened. No surprise. No shock. Hugo, at least, was prepared. I wished I felt the same way.

"I'm getting soaked." The voice was shrill and came from behind Hugo, who stepped back to allow Petra inside. I would have known her immediately even though her hair was longer and her face thinner than in the photograph. Her hair was a lighter brown than Hugo's, sun-bleached around the front where curls frizzed, fighting free of their clips. She shook water off her bright yellow raincoat and yanked it off, revealing a purple T-shirt and green trousers. I blinked, feeling suddenly drab in my faded gray sweatshirt and ancient jeans.

"Oh my God." Petra had spotted me straight away, and her voice cut through the hum of conversation in the café, making people turn to look at her, at me. "You're here. Hugo, she's here."

She didn't wait for him to answer but dodged through the tables to get to where I was sitting. I was braced for her to hug me but she stopped short once she was within reach, as if she had suddenly realized that I was a stranger, even if we were related. Even if I did look unsettlingly familiar. Seeing me wouldn't be easy for her, or anyone who had loved Freya, and I realized it was up to me to set her at her ease if I could.

I smiled. "You must be Petra."

"And you're Jess." A smile spread across her face, wider than the one I had managed. Uncomplicated welcome, for once. "We wondered if we'd see you in town."

"You knew we were here?"

"Mum said." A faint shadow of doubt. "Is *your* mother here?"

My mother was hiding in our cottage, trying to come to

terms with something I didn't fully understand. I settled for, "She's around and about."

As I spoke, I noticed Will walking past the window, head down against the rain. He didn't look at me, but then again, he hadn't since he'd stood up to go. I wondered if he'd got what he wanted. I thought he might have got more than he bargained for.

In contrast to Petra, Hugo made his way toward me at a saunter. He stood shoulder to shoulder with his sister, gazing down at me with a mocking smile on his face. I wasn't sure whether I was invited to share the joke or whether I *was* the joke.

"Hello, cousin. Fancy meeting you here. We thought we'd see you at the house tomorrow."

"Are we invited?"

"For tea. I'm making scones." Petra was round-eyed with excitement.

Hugo snorted. "Don't worry. There'll be plenty of other stuff to eat."

"Don't be mean!" She elbowed him hard in the stomach. I watched, amused and very slightly wistful. This was family life, up close.

Hugo gave Petra a shove in the direction of the empty chair. "Sit there and shut up."

She stared at the cake. "Are you eating that?"

"All yours."

She dug into it enthusiastically, the cake oozing chocolate fudge sauce that smeared around her mouth. Hugo found a spare chair at a nearby table and drew it up beside me. He stared at his sister in horror as he sat down.

"Did it fight back?"

"Shut up." The words were indistinct and she sprayed crumbs as she said them. "I didn't have time for breakfast."

"Nor did I." He glanced at me. "Jess thinks you're revolting."

"No, I don't." I handed Petra a napkin. "I just can't imagine eating chocolate cake for breakfast, that's all."

Hugo had started in on the cake from the other end and was making quick, neat progress. "Sorry. We're not that refined."

"I'm not refined."

"Sophisticated, then."

"Hardly." I looked at him, curious. "What did Will say to you?"

"Hello."

"And? What else?"

"That's not really any of your business. It was nothing to do with you, anyway."

The second sentence was delivered with such fluency that I was pretty sure it was a lie. How could it be true? I wasn't actually offended; I would have been shocked if he'd told me what they had discussed. I just wanted to make sure that Hugo knew I was aware they'd talked about me. I stared at him without saying anything until the tips of his ears turned red.

"What?"

"Nothing. Just trying to work out if you're always rude or if I'm getting special treatment."

"He's always rude," Petra said promptly.

Hugo grinned, looking far less hostile. It was as if I'd passed a test. "No special treatment. Not for one of the family."

"I feel honored."

"Naturally."

The two of us looked at each other with matching amusement. A draw, I thought. Time for a ceasefire.

"How do you know Will Henderson?" Petra tilted her head to one side. "I've only just realized you were here with him."

"We just got talking. In the bookshop. He wanted to know who I was."

Petra sighed. "He's lovely."

"Not this again." Hugo threw his fork down on the empty plate where it clattered. To me, he said, "Petra's got a crush on Will."

"I do not!"

"Of course you do. But it's never going to happen. He's too old for you."

"I'm very mature for my age."

"No, you're not." The words were harsh but Hugo spoke quite gently. "He's never going to notice you, Petra."

"He said he lives near you," I interjected, seeing Petra's eyes glistening with hurt.

"Over the back wall. He used to climb into our garden all the time."

"Why doesn't he come round any more?" I asked. It was an idle question designed to distract Petra from her grievances and I regretted it as soon as I'd said it. The reason was obvious, and painful. Hugo's voice was matter-of-fact, though, when he answered.

"Because of Freya."

"Were they close?"

He held up crossed fingers. "Like that."

I wasn't surprised to hear it. Will had been looking for something when he talked to me, something he had been missing. And I had a fairly shrewd idea that I had failed to provide it.

"You said it was because of Freya, but Will stopped coming round *before* she—" Petra stopped short of saying the next word. *Died.*

Her brother shook his head. "You're deluded. He was always in our house." To me, he said, "We used to have an open-door policy. All sorts of waifs and strays catered for, entertained, and sheltered for very reasonable rates. But then, after what happened, Mum didn't want other people around much."

"I can imagine."

"Nope. You can't." He leaned back in his chair, seeming to be relaxed despite the subject under discussion. "Don't worry. Things are better now."

"Much better." Petra rubbed a wet finger across the plate to pick up the last traces of chocolate. "Almost normal. Except that Will hasn't come back yet."

"I wouldn't have thought he qualified as a waif or a stray. He seemed pretty self-possessed to me."

"He's a mate," Hugo said shortly, throwing a glare in Petra's direction that stopped her from saying whatever she had been about to. "He's part of the family."

Like me, I thought. But his membership was by invitation. And mine could be revoked if my mother and their mother didn't start getting on again. The stakes were high; I could sort of see why Mum was hiding in her bedroom rather than getting on with seeing her twin.

Petra bit her lip. "You mustn't think we've forgotten about Freya just because things are getting back to normal."

"Of course I don't." I was genuinely shocked at the idea.

"It's just that you can't stop living because someone you love dies."

"And it's not what Freya would have wanted." Hugo's face was expressionless. "If she'd stopped to think about the rest of us for a second before she did her swan-dive off the edge of the cliff."

"Hugo!"

I ignored Petra's protest. Hugo, for one, wasn't going to keel over if I talked about his sister, and I was going to take advantage of that. "So you think it was deliberate?"

"I don't know. No one knows. But that's what they say."

"Do they? Why would she have wanted to kill herself?"

"She didn't have a reason," Petra said. "She didn't do it deliberately. She just fell."

"She had no reason to be there in the first place. Not at that time of night." Hugo sighed. "Don't get into the middle of this discussion if you know what's good for you, Jess. It goes round and round and never stops. We just have the questions. Freya was the one with the answers, and she's not much into talking these days."

"I don't want to upset anyone." I was feeling uncomfortable again, upset by the misery in Petra's eyes when she talked about her sister, and Hugo's brittle composure that was just about keeping the lid on simmering rage, as far as I could see. "I'm sorry for asking about it. I just wanted to know."

"You're not the only one." Hugo gave me a rueful smile. "We're all in the dark. Except Freya, who's bathing in perpetual light somewhere beyond the third rainbow on the left."

"No one knows what happened," Petra said. "Not for sure."

"That's the hardest part, especially for Mum and Dad. Everyone assumed she'd killed herself. They made out that she'd been unhappy and no one had noticed, which made Mum miserable. Like she'd neglected her duty."

"You didn't think she'd been unhappy."

"No. The opposite." Hugo looked very slightly shamefaced. "But I don't think I'd have noticed unless she'd been seriously upset. I didn't spend a lot of time worrying about how she was feeling."

"She was fine, though." Petra patted his arm. "There was nothing to notice. She was just the same as normal. Except— except that I thought she was happier than usual before it happened. And she looked so beautiful. Like she was lit up from inside."

"If you say so." Hugo sounded dubious. "The haircut wasn't a good idea."

"Oh, but that wasn't—" Petra stopped herself, then smiled at me. This time, the smile didn't quite reach her eyes. "We shouldn't be going on about Freya. We should be asking about *you*."

"I'm not interesting."

"You are to us," she said simply. "Tell us about London. Where do you live?"

There was no way to avoid talking about myself for a while; I owed it to them, really, as they'd been so open with me. Right up to the point where the barriers had come clanging down. Petra had very definitely not wanted to talk about Freya anymore—there was something she didn't want to think about, or discuss with me, at any rate. I chattered on, paying attention with about ten percent of my brain to what I was saying as Petra hung on my every word. The rest of my mind was concentrating on what I'd heard that morning about my cousin and her tragic, mysterious death. Words came into my head, unbidden. *Secrets. Rumors. Lies.*

Words that should have warned me to stay out of it. Leave the dead in peace. Let sleeping dangers lie.

I just didn't have enough sense to walk away.

3

I was actually quite glad of the rain on the short walk back to the cottage. It gave me an excuse to pull my hood forward and duck my head so no one noticed me. Although they probably did and I didn't notice them. That somehow made it easier.

Mum was in the kitchen when I got back. I hung up my anorak to let it drip in the hall, smelling toast on the wind. Breakfast for her, lunch for me.

"Well, what did you find?" she called.

"Hugo and Petra."

A clatter of plates answered me. Mum poked her head out of the kitchen door. "Seriously?"

"Oh yes."

"How was that?"

"Fine. They were really nice." Which didn't go very far toward conveying Hugo's fairly astringent personality, or Petra's mixture of friendliness and sudden reserve.

"What did you talk about?"

"This and that." I relented. "Everything, really. Things to do in Port Sentinel when it isn't raining. What it's like to live in London. The fact that we're invited for tea tomorrow."

Mum put her hand to her mouth. "I completely forgot to tell you. Sorry, Jess."

"Are you looking forward to it?"

"Of course." She looked surprised. "Why wouldn't I be?"

"Because you're nervous about seeing your sister and meeting her family, maybe?"

She flapped a hand at me and disappeared back into the kitchen, saying, "Don't be silly."

I followed. "So why did you spend the morning hiding under the covers?"

"I didn't." She blushed scarlet. It was easy to see where that particular tendency of mine came from. "I was just having a lie-in. It's not exactly picture-taking weather."

I raised my eyebrows. The weather didn't usually stop Mum from taking pictures, if she was in the mood to do it. She was a born photographer.

"I bet there are really moody pictures you could take of the seaside in bad weather. Black-and-white shots."

"No doubt there are. But I prefer color."

"Excuses, excuses." I nicked a piece of toast off her plate. "You *are* going to take your camera out while we're down here, aren't you?"

"Try and stop me," she said lightly, as if she wasn't so lacking in confidence that more often than not it stayed in her bag.

"And you *are* going to leave the house?"

"Jess, I had one morning to myself. One. Why is that such a big deal?"

"Because after eighteen years, I would have thought you would be desperate to look around your old haunts." I frowned at her. "What haven't you told me? Why are you in hiding?"

"I am not in hiding. We're here for weeks and weeks, remember? There will be plenty of time to explore in better weather. Now eat your lunch." A plate spun across the table toward me and I grabbed it, and the toast that had been on it, before both fell on the floor.

"I don't like mysteries."

"Well, don't go looking for them, then."

My second warning of the day. I nibbled the toast in silence, thinking about it. What people had said. What they hadn't said. Whether I should just spend the summer hanging out on the beach instead of asking questions and not getting any answers.

Maybe if I'd been a better swimmer, I'd have made a different decision.

I was lying on the sofa, two chapters from the end of *Cold Comfort Farm,* when there was a knock on the door.

"Are you expecting a visitor?"

Mum shook her head, looking wary. I rolled off the sofa and went to answer it, discovering a girl about my age standing on the doorstep, a small, curvy girl with bone-straight dark hair and very long eyelashes. She was wearing a fashion-student outfit: a white crocheted shift dress over leggings and a stripy top, lace-up boy shoes, a denim jacket, and a straw hat.

I would have looked as if I had sleepwalked into an Oxfam shop and dressed myself before I woke up. On her, it sort of worked. She stared at me with eyes as round as marbles.

"Wow. I mean, seriously. Wow. You have to be Jess."

"Can I help you?"

"I'm Darcy." Her hand shot out and I shook it, admiring the five different shades of varnish on her nails. Gray, coral, teal, yellow, mint-green. "I was Freya's best, best friend."

"Oh, right."

"Petra told me you were here." She laughed, a completely joyous gurgle that made me smile too, more or less in spite of myself. "No one is going to believe this until they see you. I mean, *I* didn't believe it."

A creak behind me was Mum coming to look over my shoulder. She had to have heard what Darcy was saying, which made me meanly pleased. *This is what I'm going to have to put up with all summer. Happy now?*

"I'm Jess's mother."

"It's nice to meet you, Mrs. Tennant." She had the surname right and everything. She'd done her homework, I thought. Another handshake and no hint of shyness about it. She had a parent-charming smile that made Mum melt.

"Jess, aren't you going to invite Darcy in?"

"No, because the cottage isn't big enough for three."

"I came round to see if Jess wanted to come for a walk, Mrs. Tennant. Is that OK?"

"Fine by me." I could hear the relief in Mum's voice. *Jess is making friends. This holiday isn't going to be a disaster.*

"Give me two minutes to get ready." I squinted at the sky. "Has it stopped raining?"

"Half an hour ago. The forecast is good for this evening too, so you won't need your jacket, if that's it." She was staring at the anorak on its hook with complete, unfeigned horror. It was more practical than stylish, as I would have been the first to admit. I almost wanted to wear it anyway, just to tease her, but the temperature had climbed as the weather improved and I really didn't need it.

I ran upstairs and changed into a long-sleeved top that was lighter than my sweatshirt. A quick look in the mirror confirmed that my plait had come loose, ends of hair poking out at all angles. I pulled the elastic off the end, ran my fingers down the length of it and shook it out over my shoulders. It had enough of a natural wave not to need any more attention apart from a quick brush. Also, I really couldn't be bothered to do more. What I was looking forward to was a conversation with someone who wasn't overburdened with dark secrets. Darcy seemed to be about as deep as a puddle, and more or less as transparent.

Her jaw dropped as I rattled back down the stairs. "How did you have time to do your hair?"

"I didn't really do anything to it."

"You have magic hair." She nodded wisely. "Many long for it. Few are gifted with it."

"Oh, come off it." I looked in the hall mirror. "It's just hanging there."

"Like a shampoo ad." She sighed. "Do you know how long it would take me to make my hair look remotely like that? I mean, just getting it straight like this is a battle. Forget volume and waves."

"I'm willing to bet you take a while getting ready to go out."

"What gives you that idea?"

"Not sure. Maybe the manicure."

She looked down at it briefly, then waggled her fingers at me. "Don't you love it, though? Seriously?"

"I seriously do," I said truthfully, stepping out onto the pavement and pulling the door closed behind me. "Where are we going?"

"The seafront." She said it as if it was the obvious choice.

"I didn't make it that far this morning. I just went down Fore Street."

"OK, well, then you don't know anything about Port Sentinel. Basically, there's the seafront where the beach is, and then there's a hill, and then, on the other side of that, there's the harbor. The seafront is where you go. The harbor is where you go to look at boats." She pulled a face at the very idea. "Have you even seen the beach?"

"Nope. But it was raining this morning. I doubt it would have been looking its best."

"Oh, OK. I forgot. Well, it's not massive, but it's *such* a nice beach. It's good for swimming because it's sheltered and the water's pretty shallow. And we don't have day-trippers much because there isn't a lot of parking nearby, so it doesn't get too busy."

"Is everyone in this town on the tourist board's payroll? Petra was telling me what a great place it was to stay too."

Darcy stopped walking and stared up at me soulfully, one hand on my arm. "We just want to make sure you have a good time. It's so sad that you've never been down before."

"It just didn't work out that way." I wasn't sure how much of the family history Darcy knew, but she didn't strike me as being particularly discreet. If she didn't know the details, I wasn't going to tell her.

"But you missed out on getting to know Freya."

"What was she like?" I was hoping for a straight answer for once.

"Where to start? Well, she was funny. She was seriously clever. She was really into art and design, which totally isn't a surprise because of her mum being an artist—oh, but you know that."

I did, but only vaguely. "What sort of artist?"

"Animal portraits." Darcy looked surprised when I laughed. "No, she's really good. She captures their souls."

"If they *have* souls."

"Oh my God, don't say that to Tilly. I don't know that she'd forgive you for thinking they don't."

"Right. No theological discussions. I'll try to remember that."

"Anyway, the animal portraits just pay the bills. You should ask her if you can have a look at her studio when you're at the house. It's fascinating. She does amazing things with watercolors."

"Are you into art too?"

A vigorous nod. "And fashion. But don't ask me where that comes from. I mean, my mum dresses in high-waisted jeans and loafers. My dad thinks Jack Vettriano is the greatest living artist, a genius." She mimed throwing up. "Tilly is the real thing. And so was Freya. She had an amazing eye."

"Did she paint?"

"Oh yeah. All the time. She was so good. She did everything—landscapes, portraits, pencil drawings. She was just working out what she could do, you know? Working out her own style. We were going to go to art college together." Darcy's face suddenly looked pinched, and I realized she was trying not to cry. When she spoke again, though, she was back to being perky. "What about you?"

"I'm more of a reader. I do like art, but I'm not creative in that way."

"Oh." Darcy shook her head. "I don't know why I expected you to be arty."

"Don't you?" I laughed, not minding. There was something so straightforward about Darcy, so open and direct, that I couldn't take offense. "Tell me more about Freya. What else did she like?"

We went down through the town, taking short cuts across cobbled yards and alleys so narrow we walked single file, while Darcy told me about Freya. She liked poetry—the Romantics, particularly—and long walks, and swimming. She liked films and would watch anything, in any language, including horror films and slapstick comedies. She liked surprisingly hard-edge rock music and mountain biking and eating things she'd baked herself, although she had a tendency to experiment unwisely with the ingredients. She liked vintage clothes and wearing her hair loose (I tucked mine behind my ears, suddenly self-conscious) and pretty shoes. She didn't like branded clothes. She didn't like surfing. She didn't like reality TV. She read novels, but only occasionally. Darcy brought her to life for me and I listened, enthralled, unable to resist measuring myself up against Freya, as everyone else surely would. I would have loved to meet her, I found myself thinking. She was real, when Darcy talked about her. She was interesting, and complicated, and talented. Her absence was a loss—to me and everyone else who'd never met her as well as to those who had loved her.

I was thinking about working the conversation around to how Freya died when Darcy turned right and gestured expansively. "The seafront."

In spite of what I'd been told, I was expecting the traditional English seaside—amusement arcades, ice-cream shops, and depressing little hotels that had seen better days. In Port Sentinel, however, the beach had a wide green park behind the promenade, overlooked by rows of Victorian houses. Some of them were hotels, it was true, but they were freshly painted and had flourishing palm trees in front of them. Two pink-and-white refreshment stands stood at either end of the park, looking very 1930s. The beach was flawless yellow sand that stretched across a small bay cradled by the hills, the sides high enough to shelter it from the wind that often blew along that stretch of coast.

"Which is why this place is so great," Darcy explained. "On the other side of that headland, the wind is pretty constant so if you're into sailing you can usually catch a breeze. There's another beach for the surfers that faces west and gets serious waves. This one is just for posing. And swimming," she added, looking slightly dubious. I didn't imagine she did much swimming. Too risky for her hair, for one thing.

She was leading me along the promenade, toward a knot of young people who were occupying a few benches set close together, or sitting on the grass between them. There were maybe twenty of them. Three or four were perched on the balustrade that ran beside the path, an ornate wrought-iron construction.

I hung back. "Darcy, what are you doing?"

"I want to introduce you to everyone." She grabbed my hand and pulled me after her. "Come on. Don't be shy."

"Who's everyone?" I pinned a smile on my face, trying to look confident and as if I was prepared for what was happening. A couple of people had started to look in our direction. More heads were turning every minute. I didn't have to look closely to identify their expressions; I knew what I would see.

"Everyone who is worth knowing in Port Sentinel." Darcy shot me a mischievous look. "You might as well get it over with in one go."

I was slowing down a little, dragging my feet as the distance narrowed between us and the group on the seafront. "Oh, so this is for my own good."

"Of course. And because no one would believe it if they didn't see it." She grinned. "Just have fun with it."

As we neared them, I started to pick out the different groups that made up the crowd. Five or six in black, with tons of eyeliner—the usual emo gang. The ones on the balustrade and on the grass nearby were young, male, and fit, wearing chinos or board shorts and bright T-shirts from achingly trendy surf brands. The rest were girls, clones of the one I'd encountered on Fore Street that morning, wearing tight clothes in ice-cream colors to show off their expensive-looking tans and impeccable figures. I tweaked a lock of hair over my shoulder so I could fiddle with it, just to have something to do with my hands, and said the first thing that came into my head.

"Is Will Henderson here?"

"Not a chance," Darcy said, sounding definite. "Why do you ask? How do you know Will?"

"He's practically the only person I've met so far. Apart from Petra and Hugo."

"They won't be here either. This isn't their sort of place."

"Is it *your* sort of place?"

It was a casual question but she stopped walking and looked tense. "What do you mean?"

"Nothing. I just wondered."

"These are my friends. Of course it's my sort of place."

"Oh. I just would have thought—since you were Freya's best friend—if Will and Hugo and Petra wouldn't fit in, did Freya?" I was genuinely confused, and Darcy's reaction really didn't help.

She glared at me. "She was popular. Everyone liked her."

"So these were her friends too?"

"Um . . ." Darcy started walking again, her pace quickening so I had to hurry to catch up, and then we were close enough for one of the girls to detach herself from her little clique and call Darcy's name.

"Hi, Natasha." To me, she murmured, "Natasha Watkins."

"What have you got there?" Natasha was staring. She didn't look surprised, but she didn't look the slightest bit friendly either.

"This is Jess. She's a cousin of the Leonards. From London."

"How long are you staying?" Natasha demanded.

"All summer," I said blandly, enjoying the panicky widening of her eyes as she took in the bad news. "I can't wait to get to know everyone."

She shot a look over her shoulder and I followed the direction of her gaze to see a fair-haired, tanned boy standing on top of the balustrade, balancing on the narrow rail without apparent effort as he watched us. When I made eye contact with him, he grinned widely, frank interest on his face.

"Who's that? He's cute." It was true, but I said it to get a reaction from Natasha. And got one.

"Back off, Jess," she hissed. "Stay away from him if you know what's good for you."

"But he looks so nice." I grinned back at him, then turned to Natasha. "He's not your boyfriend, is he?"

I could see her struggling with herself. Eventually, she said, "Not formally. Not yet. But we're a couple."

"Oh, right. So you want to be his girlfriend but he doesn't do commitment."

The color had risen in her cheeks and her fists were clenched by her sides. Which meant I'd been right on the money. "You don't know us. You don't know the first thing about us."

"If there is an *us*," I said quietly. "From where I'm standing it's just you and him."

Natasha's eyes were narrow. "Don't think you can do better than me at being a bitch."

"Who's being bitchy?" I caught Darcy's eye. She was looking anguished. I hated to back away from a fight, but there was a time and a place for that kind of thing. "Look, I'm going to be here for the next few weeks. Let's agree to stay out of each other's way. I won't bother you if you don't bother me."

"And you'll stay away from Ryan?"

"Is that his name?" I looked over at him again, in time to see him execute a perfect somersault to dismount from the balustrade, landing with his arms outstretched to receive a round of applause. He was so absolutely not my type, and so completely easy on the eye. "I can't promise that."

"You'll be nothing," Natasha spat. "If I say so, no one will talk to you. No one will even look at you."

"That's a shame. Your friends look so interesting." They were gathered together like a flock of flamingos, wary expressions on their faces, their two or three brain cells working overtime to process the little scene that was taking place in front of them. I couldn't help myself. I really hated bullies. "I'll have to find some other way to kill time. I've always wanted to learn to surf. Hey, does Ryan surf? Do you think he could teach me?"

"I'm warning you—" Natasha began.

"I'm only joking," I said, cutting her off. "I've never even spoken to Ryan and I sincerely doubt he's interested in teaching me to surf. You really need to get a grip."

"You're not like her," Natasha said softly. "You look like her, but you're not like her."

"You mean Freya?" I looked at Darcy, then back at Natasha. "What does she have to do with anything?"

Darcy pulled on my sleeve. "Let's just go, Jess."

Before I could respond, Ryan sauntered across to where we were standing. "Hey. Introduce us, Nats."

"This is Jess," Natasha ground out between clenched teeth. "She's Freya's cousin."

"I should have known. You look just like her." His eyes were all over me, lingering on my body, my mouth. I felt my poise begin to crumble, a blush spreading over my face. Bitchy girls I could manage; I wasn't so sure I could cope with Ryan. He grinned down at me. "Must be weird, being here."

"It can be."

He dropped an arm around my shoulders and guided me away from Darcy and his not-quite girlfriend. I didn't dare look back at her to see how she was taking it. Not well, I could imagine. "I'm Ryan. Ryan Denton. Come and meet the others."

I went, of course. I couldn't see a way to refuse without causing offense, and besides, Ryan didn't seem like the type to take no for an answer. His confidence was rock-solid, bordering on arrogance. It reminded me of Will, except that Will's self-possession was overlaid with reserve and Ryan's was the opposite. I smiled and waved and tried to remember whether Dylan was the lanky one with bad skin or the short one wearing a rugby shirt. Alfie and Rory, who were brothers. Chris, who wore glasses. Serena, Daisy, Claudia, Bex, Victoria: the names were different but the girls were interchangeable. They mumbled hellos without meeting my eyes, conscious of Natasha's furious glare, I guessed. Ryan ignored it, and so did I.

What did catch my attention was a snatch of whispered conversation I half heard when my back was turned to them.

"I don't like it. What if she finds out?"

"Finds out what? We didn't do anything."

And then a third voice, hissing like a snake: "Shut up. Just shut up. Not here."

I couldn't pin down who was talking—I wasn't even sure if I'd imagined it. But what I thought I'd heard was enough to make me properly uneasy. And fun though it was to twist Natasha's tail by flirting with Ryan, I could see by Darcy's expression that it was time to put a stop to it.

"I'm going to have to go." I ducked out from under Ryan's arm. "Thanks for showing me around."

"Don't leave. Not yet," he protested.

"I've got to. See you around." I didn't wait for him to reply, dodging through the crowd to where Darcy was standing. "Let's go."

She grabbed my arm as we walked away. "Oh my God. That was amazing."

"What was?"

"You weren't even remotely scared of Natasha."

"I've met people like her before. Besides, what's to be scared of? She's ninety percent hairspray and fake tan. The other ten is pure venom."

Darcy giggled, but with her hand over her mouth, as if she was afraid of being caught laughing at her. "Ryan totally likes you."

"I doubt that. He likes playing games with Natasha. I was just convenient."

"Yeah . . ." Darcy said slowly, not sounding convinced. "But you don't know that he was obsessed with Freya."

"Oh."

"Exactly."

"Which explains Natasha's attitude."

"I suppose so."

"How did Freya feel about Ryan? Did she like him?"

"Everyone likes Ryan. But she wasn't interested in him in that way."

"Natasha must have been relieved."

"Not really. It made it worse. Ryan likes to win. He doesn't like being second-best to anyone."

"I can imagine," I said soberly, and when Darcy started to chatter about fashion again, I went along with it, without even thinking to ask who Freya had preferred.

It wasn't until much later, when I was lying in bed, that I had time to consider it—along with about a million questions I had about Freya. It really bothered me that no one could tell me what had happened. If I hadn't looked like her, maybe I wouldn't have cared so much. But the reactions I'd had from just about everyone—that mixture of guilt and fear—made me think that there was more to the story than the tragic-accident line Mum had taken. I tried to imagine myself in her place. If I was gone, and no one knew why, I'd have wanted someone to find out the truth. I'd have *expected* it. And if no one else wanted to do it, that left the field clear for me.

Which was fine. But if Freya hadn't killed herself, and it hadn't been an accident, that left one thing: murder. And if it turned out to be murder, whoever killed her would be extremely keen for me to keep my nose out of it. I flipped my pillow over and tried to get comfortable. I didn't want to admit it to myself, but I was scared. And I would stay scared, I thought, until I knew the truth of what had happened, which made it even more important to keep going, no matter who I upset or what I found out.

So far, all I'd discovered was that just about everyone I'd met in Port Sentinel had something to hide.

4

Welcome to Sandhayes. I'd offer to show you around, but I'm sure you still remember where everything is."

As greetings went it was on the half-hearted side, all the more so because it was delivered in Hugo's mocking drawl. He was leaning on the gatepost on one side of the drive, his arms folded. I recognized Tom from the photograph. He sat on top of the other gatepost, kicking his heels against it. His knees were filthy and his shoes were falling apart. His fringe was long, hanging into his eyes, and he was looking sulky, which seemed to be his default expression.

"Mum, this is Hugo. Hugo, this is my mother."

"It's uncanny. You're the living image of my mother." He grinned at her. "But you know that too."

"It's been a while." Mum looked up at the house, shading her eyes. "The place looks the same. Maybe a touch more ivy and a few more slates missing off the roof."

"Nothing changes here." Hugo detached himself from the gatepost and grabbed his brother's shirt, pulling him off the other one without any warning so he went sprawling across the drive. "Come on. Everyone's waiting."

I followed them across the sparse gravel, still looking at the house. It was the family home, a rambling Victorian villa where Mum had grown up, and a place I'd always wanted to visit. The name suggested the seaside, but you had to stand in a particular place in one bedroom at the top of the house to have any chance of seeing the sea, Mum had warned me, especially since Port Sentinel had been developed for holiday homes. The house was tucked away in a residential street halfway up the hill, and if it wasn't the smartest house on the road it had the most character, in spite of the overgrown garden and peeling paintwork.

"Molly!" The exclamation came from inside the house. Mum hurled herself through the front door in response and I picked up speed to be in time to see the sisters wrapping their arms around each other in the middle of the hall. The house was cool and gloomy, piled high with clutter and probably not quite clean if you could see the details—there were curls of blue dust under the bench at one side of the hall, and a really handsome cobweb hung off the ceiling light—but it was grand all the same. I tried not to think like my father, who was a fan of contemporary style. His attitude to houses was: the cleaner and newer the better. No wonder he hadn't exactly fitted in with Mum's family. Instead, I concentrated on the touching reunion in front of me. It was beyond strange to see a version of my mother in a long velvet skirt and embroidered blouse, considering Mum was wearing jeans and a leather jacket. Tilly's hair was longer than Mum's too, and threaded with silver. She wasn't wearing makeup and her skin was rather weathered, but her smile was lovely.

The next minute she opened her eyes and saw me standing behind Mum, and the smile slid off her face, to be replaced by something much more grim. It must have been a shock for her to see me, even though she was forewarned, and I experienced a moment of complete and total embarrassment before Tilly's good humor reasserted itself.

"Jess, I'm staring at you. I'm sorry." It was my turn for a big hug, one that smelled of roses and squeezed all the breath out of my lungs. "You have to forgive me. I'd seen pictures but the reality is different."

"Don't worry," I said feebly. "I don't mind. It must be weird."

"*Weird* is the word." She laughed, but she held onto my shoulders for a second, scanning my face. "You know, there's plenty of your father in you now that I come to look at you. It's just the initial impression that's . . . interesting."

"If you say so." I decided not to tell her about literally turning heads all the way down Fore Street, or the reaction I'd got from Natasha and her coven.

"Mum, I'm hungry." Tom came to the rescue in a particularly whiny way. "Can we have cake now?"

"Of course we can. Sorry, Jess. Sorry, Molly. I'm forgetting my manners. Come in, come in."

Mum didn't make it two steps before she'd ground to a halt to exclaim over the new stair carpet. There was going to be a lot of that, I thought, given that she hadn't been in the house for almost twenty years. I followed Hugo and Tom through a door at the back of the hall on the basis that they were at least likely to lead me in the general direction of food, and found myself in a low-ceilinged kitchen with a table laid in the middle of it.

"I hope you ate before you came," Hugo said, scanning the table without enthusiasm. "I did warn you."

"Shut up, Hugo," came from behind him, where a red-faced Petra was struggling to carry a giant teapot. Her tongue was poking out as she concentrated on not spilling any tea and I was almost as relieved as she was when she set it down with a crash on the table. "You haven't done anything for today, so you don't get to criticize."

"It's women's work," Hugo said gravely. "And you volunteered to do it. Never volunteer."

"I wanted things to be nice for Jess and Aunt Molly."

"Define nice. They'll be lucky if they make it out of here without food poisoning."

"It all looks lovely." I smiled at Petra.

"She's being polite. It looks chaotic."

Hugo was hard on Petra as only an older brother could be, but there was a certain truth in what he said. The kitchen was warm but ramshackle, with peach walls and bright yellow woodwork that had chipped badly. A sagging dresser in one corner was almost invisible under the weight of clutter on it: plates and cups, opened letters, a dog brush bristling with white hairs. There was an Aga, but it was ancient and streaked with unidentifiable ooze in places. I wouldn't have known what to do if someone had told me to cook on it. It looked as if it might be seconds from exploding.

"It's beautiful," I said. "Lots of character." If I said it firmly enough it might drown out my dad's voice, which was murmuring horror in my ear.

A vase in the middle of the table had a straggle of garden flowers wedged in it, and Petra gave it an uncertain half-turn. "Does this look OK?"

"Perfect," I said quickly. "Did you arrange them?"

She nodded. "To welcome your mum."

"She'll appreciate it." I made a mental note to try to tip Mum off about them. She would say something nice to Petra if she knew. "Everything looks fantastic."

It was the truth, though there was a definite haphazard quality to the table. A vast sponge cake oozed jam over the edge of its plate, and none of the cups seemed to match. Two platters of sandwiches teetered at either end of the table; Tilly believed in catering in bulk. A basket of scones sat near the middle, flanked with jam and cream. They were scorched black around the edges and lopsided, but I would have to eat at least one, I realized, because they were clearly Petra's handiwork.

"We just wanted everything to be perfect." Petra went round the table lifting up the back of each chair in turn. I had no idea why she was tilting the chairs until there were two thumps, one after the other, and a pair of furious tabbies oozed out from under the tablecloth. They glowered at me and made for the back door.

"Warming the chairs?"

"Waiting for a chance to get at the cream. The fat one's Aristotle. The thin one is Diogenes. Don't worry about remembering their names, because they don't." Hugo strolled over and opened the door so they could make their escape into the garden. "Go on. Scram."

The sound of voices behind me made me turn round, and there was Mum talking at the same time as Tilly, both of them in fits of giggles, and my uncle Jack behind them. He was very like Dad in appearance, more so in person than in his photograph, but his features were gentler, his face long and kind. He gave me a smile of genuine welcome and urged me to sit down on one of the chairs that I knew had been occupied by the cats. I refused to even think about the cat hair on the cushion, or how it would look once transferred to my jeans. No one in this family would mind about that kind of thing.

Tom appeared out of nowhere to take his place at the table, and suddenly everyone was sitting down, all talking at once. I caught Mum's eye and found myself laughing with her. There were only seven of us but it sounded like thirty magpies squabbling. And I couldn't remember the last time I'd sat down to eat with six other people. I let the noise wash around me and helped myself to one of Petra's scones, conscious of her sitting beside me and watching every mouthful I took. It wasn't as bad as I had feared. The burned bits definitely added something.

Hugo lounged with an elbow on the back of an empty chair beside him, grinning at something that amused him and wolfing down the sandwiches two at a time. There was a plate and a cup and saucer in front of the empty chair, ready to be used. I looked around, wondering who was missing. I wasn't the only one.

"Should we have started? Who else is coming?" Mum's question fell into a rare silence and none of the Leonards rushed to answer it. I suddenly thought of Freya, who would never be home again, who might have a place at the table even so.

"It's there for anyone who needs it," Tilly said at last. "I always have room for anyone who might want to join us."

"It's usually Will," Tom said around a mouthful of cake.

"Will?" Mum looked at Tilly with raised eyebrows.

"Henderson. He lives in the house over the back wall." She pointed in the general direction.

"Henderson. As in—"

"Yes." I wasn't imagining it—Tilly cut Mum off before she could say anything more. And I definitely wasn't imagining the wave of color that swept into my mother's face.

"Oh. That's nice," she managed.

"He hasn't been here for a while," Jack said, frowning. "Have you seen him, Hugo?"

"Yesterday."

"Everything all right at home? How's his mum?"

"I didn't ask." Hugo folded another sandwich into his mouth and chewed it slowly.

"Hugo, you're useless," his mother scolded. To Jack, she said, "I should go round. I could make a lasagne or something."

"Is there . . . a problem?"

It was the question I had wanted to ask, but Mum did it for me.

"Not really. Who needs tea?" Tilly said it brightly, in a tone that didn't allow for any further discussion from anyone. She interrupted whatever Petra was trying to say with a brisk, "Jess, you aren't eating."

"I am," I protested.

"Tilly, don't change the subject." The two sisters glared at each other across the table and I hadn't the least idea why. From the nonplussed expression Hugo and Petra wore, they didn't know either. Jack concentrated on cutting large slices of cake, one eye half closed as he measured them out. Tom was eating as if someone was about to call time and take his plate away, and I doubted he was aware of any tension at all in the room.

"There's nothing to tell you."

"Really?" Mum picked up her teacup and paused to ask, "How is Dan these days?" before she buried her face in it. It was a useful way to hide what she was feeling.

"Working hard." Tilly looked down the table. "Jack, can you put more water in the teapot? It's nearly empty."

"Is he still a policeman?" Mum asked, sounding ultra-casual and not convincing in the slightest.

"He's an inspector," Hugo said. "The most senior officer around here."

Mum put her cup down again. "He's done well."

"And you've been gone a long time," Tilly snapped. I stared at her, then at my mother. It had seemed like such a neutral remark. I was, of course, too curious to let it go at that. More curious than wise, as usual.

"Who is Dan?"

"Will's dad," Petra said.

"Did you know him, Mum? Before?"

She smiled at me vaguely and gave a little shrug. "I knew everyone in Port Sentinel, Jess. It was that sort of place. It's probably not like that any more."

"Changed a lot," Jack said from his position by the kettle. "Too many blow-ins."

I wasn't going to be diverted. "So why are you asking about him in particular?"

"I'm not. Just catching up on other people's news." She met Tilly's eyes across the table. "As your aunt said, I've been away a long time."

I'd have thought that was a safe bet for most awkward conversational moment of the day, but Petra managed to surpass it about ten minutes later.

"Jess, do you want to see Freya's bedroom?"

I choked on my cake, spewing crumbs.

"Why would you ask her that?" Tilly was regarding her younger daughter with interest rather than outrage.

"Jess wanted to know about Freya—what she was like. I thought she might like to see her room." To me, she said, "It hasn't changed at all. It's just as she left it."

It was my turn to go red. "I'm sorry, Tilly. I wasn't prying. I was just curious about Freya, that's all."

"Of course you were curious. It's only natural." She sighed. "Such a shame you never got a chance to meet her. But having a look at her room will give you some idea of how she was. I hadn't the heart to change anything."

"I'd have done the same—left it all as she had it." Mum reached across the table and took her hand, their previous spat forgotten.

Tilly looked sheepish. "Well, I say I left everything. I did tidy up a bit."

"Mouldy cereal bowls under the bed didn't go with her image as perfect dead daughter." Hugo took a huge bite of cake, ignoring the glare from his mother and Mum's gasp of shock.

I grinned at him, knowing he was pleased to have got a reaction.

"Shall we go?" Petra pushed her chair back, suddenly keen to leave.

I nodded. "Absolutely."

"Don't make a mess of the place." It was a knee-jerk maternal nag but I gave it the eye-roll it deserved. What she thought I was going to do, I didn't know. Jump on the bed, maybe. Draw on the walls. It seemed to me parents' perception of their children froze at about two or three years old, and they never grew out of the "put your coat on it's cold" warnings after that. Mum probably couldn't help it, but that didn't mean I had to be gracious about it.

Freya's room was on the top floor, in the attic, and Petra took the stairs three at a time. I panted behind her, not even attempting to keep up. She kept up a running commentary on the rooms we were passing (". . . and that's Tom's but I wouldn't go in because it always stinks of feet and farts. He really is filthy. This is Hugo's room but I'm not allowed to open the door so you'll have to get him to show you. It's very boring. All books. Mum and Dad are in that one. They've got the biggest room but it's the coldest too, so no one minds.")

We stopped off at Petra's own room on the floor below Freya's and I toured it solemnly, admiring the collection of dolls that she'd had for years. She was too old for them now, she admitted, and had customized most of them with new haircuts, different outfits and some fairly savage makeup. It was a Leonard habit, I was starting to realize. Why settle for the default option when you can make a thing your own?

Another flight of stairs, this time complete with dust, as if to prove no one came up here any more. Freya's quest for originality had led her to paint her door dark blue and stencil stars in gold leaf all over it.

"She used the wrong kind of paint," Petra said dismissively, sliding a nail under a loose flake and flicking it away. "It looked OK just after she did it, but I told her it wouldn't last. And the gold leaf started to come off about a day later, even though she sprayed it."

"*Nothing gold can stay.*"

"Huh?"

"It's from a poem by Robert Frost." I was aware that I sounded a touch too intellectual for my own good. "I think the point of it is that perfection never lasts."

"I don't know anything about poetry." Petra was regarding me with something approaching awe.

I grinned. "Nor do I. I got it from a novel. It just always stayed in my head, for some reason."

"I like it." She turned the handle and flung open the door. "Here you go. Let's play *Through the Keyhole*. Who would live in a room like this?"

The short answer was: someone very lucky indeed. It was a big space, with windows on two sides overlooking different aspects of the garden. There was a window-seat at one of them and I would have loved to curl up there with a book for an hour or two. A fat velvet hippo sat there now, a much-rubbed toy. Petra went over and picked it up, cuddling it against her.

"Was that Freya's favorite?"

"Mm." She pressed her nose against the top of its head. "Mr. Bobo. He used to smell of her but it's worn off now."

"Where did the name come from?"

"She couldn't say hippo when she got him."

"I should have worked that out, really." The room was tidy, the small bookcase arranged alphabetically and packed with children's classics. *The Secret Garden. A Little Princess. Little House on the Prairie.* There were art books too, and biographies of female painters like Gwen John and Mainie Jellett. Her school books were stacked on the bottom shelf, probably where she'd left them. There was nothing on the desk at all, but the notice board above it was covered—last year's calendar featuring maybe-ironic pictures of kittens, flyers for events that had long since taken place, scraps of material, glow-in-the-dark stars, and a handful of art postcards that ranged from Degas to Renoir via the Pre-Raphaelites. There was one on its own in the corner, half obscured by a leaflet for a band night, and I recognized the heavy gold leaf of Klimt's *The Kiss.* I unpinned it and looked at the other side. A scrawl I could barely read, in black ink: *Thinking of you.* I pulled a face.

"Don't you like it?"

"The painting?" I turned it over again and looked at it. "Not really. It just looks awkward. He's kissing her but she's turning away. It should be romantic, but it isn't."

"Freya didn't like it either," Petra said. So that was one thing we had in common. I stood for a moment looking at the postcard. She hadn't liked it and she'd pinned it up. *Thinking of you* . . . Was it from the boy who was better-than-Ryan? And if so, why hadn't he signed it?

Whatever about paintings, a quick peek in the wardrobe confirmed that Freya and I had had very different taste in clothes.

"She liked vintage stuff." Petra pulled out a hanger and

showed me a gauzy seventies dress with tiny buttons all the way up to the neck, patterned in maroon and gold. "She made this sort of thing look fabulous."

"I bet." I took it from her to look at it, then hung it back on the rail, not remotely tempted to try it on. It would not have looked fabulous on me—of that I was quite sure.

The wall behind the bed was the most interesting thing in the room. It was essentially a gallery. "Did she do all this?"

"Yeah." Petra came to stand beside me, appraising the pictures with a critical eye. "They're not bad."

"They're amazing." Freya had worked in different media, equally competently in each as far as I could see, and I was taken with a series of self-portraits in pencil. It was a style that could easily have been moodily self-indulgent, but there was something about the eyes that suggested a sense of humor, an irony that wouldn't allow her to go completely over the top. She had done watercolors too—landscapes and still-life paintings rather than portraits. I lingered over three of the landscapes—windblown bushes riding a Dartmoor hillside, the sea whipping around some rocks at the foot of a headland, a lovely woodland scene that glowed with light. I thought they were remarkable.

The photographs were black and white for the most part. Hugo scowling over the top of a book, and Tilly painting, her face tense with concentration. A close-up of hands grimy with something like engine grease was pin-sharp, technically excellent, and somehow tender. So much talent. So much life to live.

"What a waste."

"I know." Petra sat down on the edge of the bed. "These aren't sad paintings, are they? These aren't the sort of thing you'd do if you were depressed."

"Were they the last things she did?"

"Some of them. She changed this wall around all the time." Petra lay back and stared at the ceiling. "There are some paintings in the studio that she was planning to put up, and there's a sketchpad somewhere with more drawings in it that would have been from right before it happened. She never got a chance to sort them."

"That's sad."

"That's what makes me sure it was an accident." She was still looking at the ceiling, not at me. Almost to herself, she said, "You'd want your best work to be on display. Your legacy. You wouldn't want to be judged on old material."

I had seen a sketchpad on the bookcase. I went over and pulled it out. "Is this it?"

"Let me see?" Petra sat up, leaning on one elbow as she flipped through the pages, treating me to a quick slideshow of the contents. Half-finished drawings, lists, scribbles, a fragment of poetry . . . it flashed past too quickly for me to examine each page closely, but I got the idea. Freya's sketchbook had been like a diary, and if anything was going to give me an insight into how she'd been feeling before she died, the sketchbook would.

Petra was shaking her head. "Not this one. This is an old one. It's from three years ago." She showed me the date on the cover, neatly inscribed in pencil. Freya had been methodical about her work, I thought.

"Where would the last one be?"

"I don't know. The studio, maybe."

"I'd like to see it."

"So would I." She flopped back on the bed. "I think Freya

would have wanted us to see it too. She would have wanted people to look at it. She'd never have just thrown herself off the cliff without thinking about that kind of thing."

"So you think she'd have prepared better?"

"Definitely. She'd have dressed for it as well. She was wearing a summer dress, pretty but not dramatic. I know she'd have wanted something spectacular if she was going to kill herself."

"Maybe it wasn't planned. Maybe it was a spur-of-the-moment decision."

"Maybe." Petra still didn't look at me.

I went over to the window and knelt on the seat. The back garden stretched away behind the house, lush with summer growth and pleasantly disorganized. At the bottom of the garden there was a long wooden building with big skylights let into the roof.

"What's the super-shed for?"

"Mum's studio. That's probably where you'd find the last things Freya was working on. She used to go down there and paint while Mum was doing other stuff."

"Is your mum working much at the moment?"

"She's not taking on any new commissions. She finished off the ones she was working on, though, when it happened. She can paint—she just says she doesn't want to." Petra looked tired, all of a sudden, and too old for her years. Worry would do that to you.

"So she's not doing her own things, either?"

"Bits and pieces, I think. How do you know about her work?"

"Darcy said it was amazing."

That *did* get her attention. "When did you meet Darcy?"

"Yesterday afternoon. She came to the cottage to see me in person. I think she was just curious."

"That would fit." Petra looked oddly disapproving. "Did she say anything about Freya?"

"Lots. I only asked what she was like."

She managed a weak smile. "Darcy likes to talk."

I couldn't work out why Petra sounded so unenthusiastic about her sister's best friend. I had thought she was on the ditzy side, but basically well intentioned. "She didn't say anything mean, you know. She was a big fan of Freya's."

Petra bit her lip. "Did she say anything about why they argued?"

I had the uneasy sensation of standing on what you think is solid ground and feeling it start to slip away beneath you. "No. She didn't mention an argument."

"It was the week before Freya died. I'm not sure what it was about, but I know they hadn't made up."

"It must have been a bad one if you knew about it."

"It was. Freya and Darcy were really close. They used to see each other every day. Freya didn't have a mobile—well, she did, but she lost it so often Mum wouldn't replace it. Darcy phoned the house instead, first thing in the morning and last thing at night. Dad hated her tying up the phone for hours on end. He couldn't understand how they could spend the day together and still have anything left to talk about."

"I got that from my dad when he still lived with us." One major reason why I hadn't minded too much about him moving out.

"They were proper friends. And then, nothing. From one day to the next."

"Freya didn't tell you anything about it?"

Petra shook her head. "I didn't dare to ask."

"And you haven't asked Darcy about it since Freya fell?"

"I don't know her that well. I'm just Freya's annoying little sister. She never bothered with me. But she seems interested in you. *You* could find out."

"I could try." I could add it to the list of things I wanted to find out—the list that was getting longer, not shorter, the more I found out about Freya. It bothered me that no one knew what had happened to her. It didn't seem right.

I looked back out at the garden, at the trees that half screened the house behind the studio so I could only see that it was painted white and was on the small side compared to the Leonards' house. The studio squatted at the end of the garden, the windows dark, the door shut. It looked deserted. Untouched for many months. Forgotten.

I could stop, I thought. I could let Freya fade away into the past. Leave the door locked. Let the questions remain unanswered. Forget.

Yeah. There was never really any chance *that* was going to happen.

5

I made my way down the garden alone, the key to the studio clutched in one hand. It was starting to drizzle again, the sky dark with the promise of real rain, and soon. The ground was waterlogged already. My feet slid on the muddy path—more of a track, really—and I wished I had brought my anorak.

Tilly had been perfectly happy for me to go and look at her workplace.

Mum was more perplexed. "Why do you want to go there?"

"Just curious, I suppose."

She frowned. "It's where your aunt works."

"You make it sound like an office. It's a bit more interesting than that." I saw Mum wince and wished I'd put it differently. I knew she hated her job. She worked as a secretary for an elderly solicitor who was easing into retirement gradually and spent the summer at his holiday home in Florida. Working for him wasn't difficult and having the summer off was a nice perk, but it was boring, and badly paid, and I knew she would have loved to try making a living as a photographer if she'd thought she was good enough. Dad had never encouraged her—quite the opposite—so she'd settled for second best. But it had to be hard on Mum to see her sister doing something creative for a living, something she loved.

Still, I *did* want to see the studio. I looked at Tilly. "You don't mind, do you?"

"No. Not at all."

"Don't touch anything." Mum was using her extra-threatening tone of voice. "Don't play with anything." Exactly as if I was three. To Petra, Mum said, "You can keep an eye on her."

"I'm not going. Seen it before." The break from the table seemed to have done Petra's appetite a world of good; she was hoovering up the remaining sandwiches as if she was taking part in an eating contest.

"I don't think she'll come to any harm in the studio," Jack said, smiling at me over Mum's head. "The kids go down there unsupervised all the time. Or they used to."

"And I'm not working on anything at the moment." Tilly sounded matter-of-fact about it rather than tragic. "So there's really no problem with Jess going wherever she likes."

"Freya's stuff is on the right, in the corner. It's all still there, Mum, isn't it?" Petra wasn't looking at her mother when she asked, so she missed the way Tilly's expression tightened, even though she answered calmly.

"It's all there. Almost as she left it." And she was smiling as she added, "Just a bit tidier."

The grass had grown up in front of the studio door, tall

and lush. Weeds and nettles were threaded through it. I trod it all down so I could get at the door, wondering how long it had been since anyone else had been there. The key turned at the first time of asking, much to my surprise, but it was a modern lock that was well oiled and the door was solid. Mum was right: it was where Tilly worked, and far more organized than the house was. It was immaculate, the floor swept clean, the art materials filed away, the paintings arranged in racks. There were several big plan chests and I slid open a few drawers, feeling highly self-conscious about snooping. They turned out to contain drawings—preparatory sketches mainly. I couldn't help being impressed by the sketches Tilly did to prepare for the proper portraits—fast ones that were nothing more than a few lines but captured the essence of a basset hound's humpy back, or more detailed ones that she had worked on, shading in the delicate feathering of a cat's fur around its eyes. I could see she was good at what she did, professional and dedicated in equal measure, and it was a lot better than the greetings-card cutesiness I had been expecting. Tilly's own artwork was interesting too, but not as appealing to me, basically because I wasn't sure I got it. Darcy had been reverent about her watercolors but I didn't really know why they were supposed to be good. Mum's artiness was something else that had passed me by. I had inherited Dad's logic instead, which seemed a fair trade.

The room smelled of paint and varnish—the classic artist's studio—but there was a stale quality to the air. I was glad I had left the door open to allow the fresh green smell of damp earth and crushed grass to fill the space. The main thing that made it a bit different from the usual studio, at least in my eyes, was the collection of dog beds stacked up against one wall beside a basket full of toys of various shapes and sizes. On a high shelf, I spotted jars of Bonios and cat treats, and as I walked across the room I kicked a jangling ball that skittered away into the corner. Catering for the clientele, I supposed.

I was really there to see Freya's paintings, I reminded myself, turning toward the right side of the studio where Petra had said I would find them. There was a stack of canvases leaning against the wall, wrapped in an old dustsheet. I pulled the sheet away carefully and saw I had guessed correctly— Freya's signature was on the bottom of each painting. It was a scrawl, a confident F and a low, looping y the only identifiable bits, but it matched the signature on the pictures I had seen hanging in her bedroom. I wouldn't have recognized the paintings as hers otherwise. Darcy had said she was trying out new things, experimenting with her style, but these were strikingly different from one another. I flicked through the canvases: abstract paintings where the paint was plastered on in layers, a still life of a bowl with cherries in it that was as realistic as a photograph, and right at the back some studies of a half-dressed girl that I identified after a moment's confusion as Freya herself. Rationally, I knew I wasn't the subject of the paintings but there was still something unsettling about them, something uncomfortably intimate about seeing my double posing with her naked back to the viewer, piling up the great weight of her hair on her head. The colors were muted, the tones of her flesh pale and ghostly, and I could understand why Tilly had hidden them at the back of the collection. The Freya they depicted was a wraith, otherworldly, and I wondered if she had had a premonition that she was going to die young. I wondered if she had planned her own death, despite what her sister thought.

Dressing for the occasion would have drawn attention to her, and attention was presumably not what you wanted when you were planning to fling yourself off a cliff.

I was staring at one of the semi-nudes when I became aware of something—a disturbance in the air more than an actual sound. I glanced over my shoulder to see Will Henderson standing in the doorway, watching me. With a smothered exclamation I let go of the paintings I was holding so they fell back against the wall. The clatter sounded shockingly loud in the quiet studio, and my voice sounded too loud too.

"What do you think you're doing?"

"I was just about to ask you the same thing."

"You first." I started to rearrange the paintings—more for something to do than because they needed it.

"I saw you coming down the garden. I thought I'd drop in."

"Why?"

"To say hello." I raised one eyebrow, not even trying to hide that I was skeptical, and he laughed. "OK, OK. To find out what you're doing here."

"That sounds more like the truth."

"I was curious." He leaned against the doorframe and crossed his arms. "Are you looking for something?"

"Not really. Just nosing around." I didn't want to talk to him about what I was doing, I realized. I couldn't have said why that was the case, but it was true. I went for a half-truth instead. "I hadn't seen Tilly's work before. I was curious."

"Those aren't Tilly's paintings."

I looked down. "No. I know."

"Still wondering about Freya?"

There was no point in lying. "I still want to know what really happened last summer."

He didn't answer me straight away and I wished he wasn't silhouetted against the light. I couldn't see the expression on his face clearly enough to know what he was thinking.

"And what have you found?"

I shrugged. "Different people remember different things. I haven't put it all together yet."

"But you're sure you will."

There was a hint of mockery in his voice and I was instantly nettled. "Like your dad didn't?"

"What's that supposed to mean?"

"I gather he's the top cop around here. It should have been his job to find out what happened to Freya."

"He looked into it. He didn't find any evidence of foul play." Will's voice was completely neutral.

"Did you agree with that?"

"There was no evidence."

"That's not an answer. Did you agree with him?"

"My opinion doesn't matter a lot to him."

"Really? I'd like to know what you thought about it." It was my turn to fold my arms. I hoped I looked self-possessed. Determined. Not how I felt, anyway. "I'd like to know why you warned me to mind my own business when I asked you about Freya. Why would you bother with that if her death was an accident?"

"I didn't say it was."

"So you think it wasn't? Where's your money—suicide or murder?" I was meanly pleased to see him flinch, glad that I

73

could get a reaction from him. "I don't know why she'd have wanted to kill herself, but you might have a better idea."

It was almost reluctant, the way he moved away from the door. His stride was slow and measured as he came toward me. The look in his eyes was anything but friendly. "What makes you say that?"

"A shot in the dark?" I could have left it there. I probably should have left it there. "Look, I don't know you but you seem awfully tense about what happened to Freya. And you keep turning up. You really want to find out what I know, don't you? That just sounds like guilt to me."

He seemed to consider it for a moment. "Why would I be guilty?"

"You tell me."

He was still coming toward me and I took a step back, wanting to put some distance between us. The house was a long way from the studio. Too far to expect anyone to notice that I was no longer alone.

Too far for anyone to rescue me.

What had I got myself into now?

Panic was just starting to flutter beneath my ribs when Will stopped a meter away from me and squatted down to flip through the canvases. He paused on a swirling painting in apricot and yellow tones. I turned my head sideways to look at it. The painting was an abstract but I couldn't help trying to make it into something real, literal-minded as I was. It could have been a sunrise, or a sunset. Or leftover mustard on a plate.

"Not my favorites, these, but she was pleased with them," Will remarked. Art criticism. I was grateful enough for a neutral topic of conversation to join in.

"Darcy said Freya was trying new things out."

"Darcy? When did you meet her?"

"Yesterday. She was really helpful." *In a way that you aren't.*

He frowned. "Look, I'm not saying you should stay away from her, but don't trust her."

"What does that mean?"

"Just what I said."

"You can't say something like that and not explain it."

He shook his head decisively. "I'm not saying anything else about her. But don't believe everything she says."

"About Freya?"

"About anything."

"You're not her biggest fan, are you?"

"It's completely mutual." He turned back to the paintings and something about the set of his jaw told me I'd heard as much as I was going to about Darcy. I would ask her what she thought of him, I decided. Darcy was unlikely to be discreet.

While Will concentrated on the paintings I was free to stare at him, and stare I did. Up close, I could see that spots of water dappled the shoulders of his gray T-shirt and clung to his hair. I had that slightly giddy feeling you get from standing too close to someone really, truly handsome—I could appreciate that, even if I didn't like him as a person. After all, I reminded myself, Conrad had taught me a lesson. He'd been good-looking too, but the pretty face was hiding a dismal personality. *Look, but don't even think about touching . . .*

Aware that I had allowed a silence to develop, I tried to think of something sensible to say. "Did Freya talk to you about her painting?"

"Sometimes. It was important to her."

It had been important to her so she had talked to Will about it. I wondered again about how close they had been. "Do you know anything about art?"

"A little." He shrugged without looking round at me. "I've grown up beside the Leonards. I've picked up bits and pieces over the years."

"From what I gather, you're usually here a lot."

"Been asking about me?"

"Of course not," I snapped, feeling my face flame. I really hoped he wouldn't turn round—at least not until I had de-lobstered. "You just happened to be the answer to a question Mum asked."

"Your mother was asking about me." He sounded skeptical, as well he might.

"Not directly." One of these days I would stop blushing and saying stupid things. It was just a shame that it was unlikely to happen when Will Henderson was around. I took a deep breath before I went on. "Tilly laid a place for you at the table and Mum wanted to know who was supposed to sit there."

"Oh, right."

"You don't sound surprised."

"That Tilly had made sure there was room for me at the table in case I turned up?" He twisted round to grin at me with a sudden charm that was as dazzling as sunlight on water. "She always does."

"Why's that? Don't your parents feed you?" It was a flippant remark, not meant to provoke, but Will's eyes darkened and the smile disappeared. He turned back to the paintings, flicking through them without comment. I wondered if I should apologize. Since I didn't know what I'd said that was so offensive, I decided I didn't have to. And if he wanted silence, I was more than happy to oblige.

For the next minute or two, there wasn't a sound in the studio except for the drumming of the rain on the sodden earth outside and the soft thud of canvases being shifted about. I watched Will's hands as he worked through the paintings. I was a fool for hands, always, and his were close to ideal—nicely shaped, with long fingers, but strong and capable too. I frowned. They looked oddly familiar.

"Did Freya photograph you?"

He glanced up at me, surprised into making eye contact again. "How did you know that?"

"There's a picture of your hands on her bedroom wall."

"Just my hands?" The corner of his mouth slid up in the usual mocking half-smile. I was watching for it now. "And you recognized me?"

"It's a striking image," I said stiffly. "I'm pretty sure it was you. It was someone with dirty hands."

"And that made you think of me. Interesting."

"It looks like engine grease." I pointed at his leg, refusing to get flustered. "There's a smudge of something black and oily on the left knee of your jeans, and there's another black mark on the toe of your right trainer. And you were reading a book about cars yesterday in the bookshop. It looks to me as if you regularly spend quality time with some bit of machinery or other, so I think it was a fair assumption that the hands in the picture belonged to you."

Will looked down at himself and grinned. "You don't miss much, do you?"

"I'm pretty sure you don't either, even if you think it's clever to pretend to be stupid."

"That seems a touch harsh."

"Well, I'm sorry. But it's a simple question and I don't know why you're being so difficult about answering it. Did she take your picture or not?"

He relented. "Yeah. She took lots of pictures of everyone. She liked to experiment with her camera."

"But she put the picture of you on her wall . . ." I said slowly. "It meant something to her."

"What was it you said? *It's a striking image.* It took her a few goes to get the light the way she wanted it. She stuck up the pictures she liked, the ones she was proud of."

"The ones that mattered to her." I had to ask the question outright; I couldn't stand not knowing. "What was the deal with you and Freya, Will? Did she like you?"

"As a friend."

"And more than a friend."

He stood up, suddenly seeming very tall and very much too close. "You're basing this on a photo."

"I'm basing it on you not wanting to talk about her but not being able to stay away. I'm basing it on the fact that it's obvious you used to come to Sandhayes all the time, and then you stopped, around the time that Freya died—a bit before that happened, I gather, but I don't know why. I'm basing it on how close your relationship with Freya evidently was, because she talked to you about what mattered to her and you don't do that with your next-door neighbor, no matter how much time you spend with them, unless you feel pretty strongly about them."

His eyes were icy. "It must be a London thing."

"What is?"

"Your rudeness."

I glowered. "I'm not aware I was being rude."

"That says it all, doesn't it?"

"You asked why I thought you'd been in a relationship with Freya. I'm just explaining it to you. If you don't like the suggestion, tell me the truth."

Instead of answering, he went back to the pictures, flipping through another two before he stopped again. I knew what he was looking at before I looked myself; I'd been counting down toward the ones at the back. The ones of Freya in the nude. She hadn't painted anything too explicit—it was a suggestion of being naked rather than anything more obvious—but I still found myself blushing, yet again, as Will stared at Freya's body for what felt like an hour. The painting he was holding was of Freya looking away to the left. The fingertips of each hand touched the opposite shoulder so her crossed arms hid her chest from view. She looked like a Degas ballerina in her dressing room, halfway through a costume change, unaware of being watched.

I should have said nothing, but I'm not very good at keeping quiet.

"Haven't you seen them before?"

"Seen what?"

"The paintings. The self-portraits."

"I had seen them. She showed me."

I nodded as if that sounded perfectly reasonable.

"You're jumping to conclusions," Will said. "Stop it."

"I didn't say a word."

"I know what you're thinking."

"I really doubt that."

"OK, then." He turned the first picture face down and looked at the next one, which was the painting of Freya holding her hair up, her back curved in an elegant swoop. "But I suspect you're thinking I wouldn't have seen these if Freya and I hadn't been closer than friends."

"I'm sure you're going to tell me why I'm wrong about that."

Will shrugged. "Freya didn't think anything of the nudity. She'd been brought up on great works of art that happened to have naked bodies in them and she didn't think it was anything to get excited about."

I really, really wanted to ask if he'd got excited about it, but I managed not to. He was looking at the painting again, studying it, and I wished I could see more of his face, to get some idea of what he was thinking. I could hear his watch ticking, and the rain beating a steady rhythm on the roof as it gathered strength, and I had the very clear impression he had forgotten I was there. It was almost a shock when he spoke again.

"You never did answer my question. What are you looking for out here?"

"The last things Freya worked on."

He straightened up. "Why?"

"I want to know how she was feeling before she died. She was a creative person—everyone agrees on that. But so far I've been told she could have been depressed, or completely normal, or happier than she'd ever been, and no one seems to be able to decide which is true."

"And you think you'll be able to work it out if you see what she was painting."

"You don't sound convinced. Is that because you think I wouldn't know the difference?"

Will frowned. "It's not that. It's just that I don't think it's that easy to tell." He turned back to the self-portrait. "This could be anything, couldn't it? She could be feeling depressed or elated and you'd never know."

"I still think it's worth a look." I hesitated, not sure if I should be honest. "I'm not really that interested in the finished paintings. I was looking for her sketchbook. It's more likely to give me an insight into how she was feeling."

"Why do you say that?"

I pointed at the painting that was nearest me. "This would have taken her a long time, wouldn't it? She'd have been working on it for ages, and here, where anyone who knew her could see it and might ask her about it. From what I saw in her room, her sketchbook would be more like a diary—bits and pieces that occurred to her on the spur of the moment. It would be more private, I suppose."

"You could be right." Will was looking down at me and the expression on his face gave me absolutely no clue as to what he was thinking.

"So?"

"So what?"

"So do you have any idea where it might be?"

"She had hundreds." He pointed to a plan chest that stood

in the corner of the room. "You could have a look in there. That was where Freya kept her work-in-progress."

I was there before he'd finished talking, pulling out the shallow drawers one by one. It was neatly arranged, methodically organized, and I did find sketchbooks—lots of them, and all dated on the cover.

"When did she die?"

"It was the beginning of August. The fifth."

"Thanks." I was shuffling through sketchbooks. "It took her four or five weeks to finish one of these, by the looks of things. That means she probably started the last one in June."

"Sounds about right."

"But the last one I've found covers May and the start of June." I flicked through it: flowers and leaves in botanical detail, homework notes, nothing interesting. I would take it anyway, to check through it later, just in case I'd missed something. "The next one isn't here."

Will frowned. "Are you sure?"

"I've only had a quick look, but they're all in order." I shuffled through them again. "If it was here, it should be after this one. And it's not."

He didn't say anything straight away and when I turned to see what he thought, he was looking amused. "You do like your mysteries, don't you?"

"This isn't one I've invented." I pushed the drawer shut. "It should be there and it's not."

"Maybe Tilly has it."

"I'll ask her."

His expression changed from mocking amusement to serious, and he reached out to put his hand on my arm, as if to stop me from rushing in to talk to her then and there. "Go easy. She's not coping as well as all that."

"I had noticed." I moved away a little so I was out of his reach. My skin tingled where his fingers had touched me.

"You didn't know her before, though." He shook his head. "She used to be so happy. Now it's as if the light's gone out."

"It's the not knowing."

Will's expression hardened. "So you're going to find out what happened, is that it? Solve all her problems by answering the question: what happened to Freya? And once we all know the truth, we can carry on as we were."

"You sound like you disagree," I said icily.

"I do. Profoundly. I think you should leave it alone and enjoy your holiday. But I know you're not going to do that and I do want to know what you find out, so I'm planning to stick around."

"I really don't need your help." Especially when one of the things I really wanted to find out was what he was hiding, because there was definitely *something* he wasn't telling me. I just couldn't tell if it was important or not.

"Don't worry. I won't get in the way."

I narrowed my eyes. "Why were you so curious about what I was doing down here anyway? Afraid of what I might find?"

"Not me." He stretched, looking at that moment about as stressed out as a cat in a sunbeam. His T-shirt rode up to reveal a few centimeters of tanned, flat stomach. *Come on, Jess, concentrate.*

"Like I said," Will went on, "I was just curious. The same way you're just curious about what happened to your cousin."

"I don't think it's the same thing at all."

"Fine." He leaned down, his face inches from mine. "But you're not going to get rid of me."

I couldn't come up with an answer to save my life. The air between us was crackling with tension. I thought Will was going to hit me, or kiss me, or say something honest and unguarded for a change. I don't know what would have happened next if we hadn't been interrupted, but all of a sudden I became aware of footsteps getting closer and closer, rustling through the grass. Will heard them too and moved back smartly, so when my mother breezed through the door we were a couple of meters apart, and Will was concentrating on rearranging Freya's paintings.

"Jess, you've been down here forever. It's time we were going." Her eyes fell on Will, who had his back to her. "Oh. Hello."

Mum wasn't the strictest of parents but she definitely had views on her one and only daughter having alone time with strange boys, and her tone was not encouraging.

I hurried to explain. "Mum, this is—"

"Will Henderson." He turned and smiled at her, putting out his hand to shake hers as he crossed the room. "I live over the back wall."

"Oh." I could tell that was all Mum was capable of saying. She was staring at Will. The blood had drained from her face and I thought she actually might faint.

"Mum, are you OK?"

Instead of answering me, she swayed and I ran across the studio to support her. As I reached her she seemed to come back to herself.

"Don't be silly, Jess. I'm fine." She blinked a couple of times, very quickly, and obviously made a huge effort to seem composed. "Will, did you say?"

"Henderson." He was looking wary.

"I should have known who you are." She tried to smile. "You look just like your father."

"So I'm told." From the expression on Will's face it was absolutely the wrong thing to say to him. He turned to me. "I'd better go."

"I'm sure I'll see you around."

"I'm sure you will." He nodded to Mum. "Nice to meet you, Mrs. Tennant."

"And you," she said automatically. She watched him as he walked past her, and kept looking at the empty doorway after he'd gone.

"Mum. Come back."

"What?" She glanced at me for a second. "Oh. I'm fine."

"You look like you've seen a ghost."

"I sort of have," she said softly, then shook her head. "Where was I? Oh yes. It's time to go. Unless you want to stay for dinner."

"I couldn't eat another thing," I said, clutching my stomach, where Petra's scone was staging a sit-in.

"Did you find what you were looking for?"

"Not as such."

"We have an open invitation to the house, so you can come back if you want." She gave the studio the briefest of glances, then turned away. "For now, I think we should leave. I don't want us to outstay our welcome on our first visit."

I wasn't actually sure that was possible given how pleased Tilly had been to see Mum again, but I let it go. Mum had

had enough, and in truth, so had I. I followed her obediently, single file along the muddy path that cut through the unkempt lawn, the rain tapping on my head, and tried to ignore the tingle between my shoulder blades that told me I was being watched.

6

The next day I got a job.

It was all Tilly's idea, really. Work had not featured in my plans for the summer, and when my aunt turned up early the following morning with a strange old woman in tow, I wasn't inclined to be enthusiastic. Tilly didn't seem to notice.

"Jess, I wanted you to meet Sylvia Burman. She runs a charity shop in the village and she's looking for someone to help her."

"Three mornings a week," Sylvia said. "I don't open every day." She was dressed in a shapeless cardigan and skirt. The cardigan was held together halfway down her front with a safety pin, having lost most of the buttons during its long life. Her outfit involved several different shades of brown, all drab but all managing to clash with the others. Her hair was white and long, pinned to the back of her head with a tortoiseshell skewer that wasn't quite up to the job. She had a tiny, wispy voice that matched her appearance.

I tried to think of a way to say no without causing any offense. "Oh. I'm not sure—"

Tilly ignored me. "Sylvia mentioned she was looking for someone to work with her and I thought you might find it interesting."

"Really?" I tried to catch Mum's eye. *Help.*

Either she misread the signals I was trying to send her or she was determined to ruin my summer. "It's not a bad idea, Jess. Good experience for you."

"Of what?" I snapped.

"Dealing with people. Retail. That sort of thing."

I was about to explode but Sylvia got in first. "Of course, I can't pay you a lot. It is a small charity—I founded it myself—and most of the income is from the shop."

This was getting better and better. "What sort of charity is it?"

"Owls."

"Owls?"

"Rare owls." She looked like an owl herself, I thought, with her big eyes blinking behind thick-lensed glasses. "I fund a breeding program for them."

"That sounds very . . . worthy." And not particularly appealing. Owls were fine—I quite liked them, if anything—but worrying about their sex lives wasn't going to get me out of bed in the morning. I gathered myself together to say no, and had got as far as opening my mouth when Sylvia happened to mention exactly how much she was prepared to pay me. "Not a lot" in Port Sentinel meant a good deal more money than I had ever earned before.

"Is that per week?"

"Per day."

"Mornings only." I couldn't believe it. There had to be a catch.

"I say mornings but I should be more specific. About three hours altogether. I usually open between nine and one, but you don't have to be there too early." She blinked again. "We don't get many visitors before ten or so."

"What sort of thing would I have to do?"

"A bit of everything, I suppose." She looked wistful. "It's just that it's all getting beyond me. The fetching and carrying, I mean. And I like the company in the shop. There are days when it's very quiet indeed."

I could imagine. I didn't think the residents of Port Sentinel would be that keen on owls. Or charity shops, for that matter. The more I thought about it, the more I felt it wasn't the sort of place where it was fun to be poor. I could do with having some cash. I swapped my dubious expression for an employee-of-the-year smile.

"I'd love to work for you."

"Really?" Sylvia clasped her hands together. "That's wonderful. Can you start today?"

"Today?"

"Of course she can," Mum said cheerfully. "We didn't have any plans, did we, Jess?"

"No, but—" *But I'd like some time to get used to the idea.*

"Wonderful," Sylvia said again. She turned to Tilly. "Oh, I'm so glad you suggested it, Matilda. She's perfect."

"I'm still in my pajamas," I pointed out. "I'm not exactly ready for work."

"Just come to the shop when you're dressed, dear." I was

pretty sure that was as close as Sylvia ever came to cracking the whip.

"Where is it?"

"Silly me. Of course, you don't know it." Sylvia gave a little giggle. "It's halfway down Fore Street, just beside the bakery. You can't miss it. It's called Fine Feathers."

It was almost half past ten before Fine Feathers' newest employee made it to work, slinking down Fore Street while doing my best to be invisible. I was still getting more than my fair share of double takes from strangers, but I was starting to get used to it; I'd perfected my no-you-don't-know-me glare. It was more that I really didn't want to meet anyone I knew, especially since I'd made an enemy of roughly half the people I'd met so far in Port Sentinel. Natasha, for one, would make a big deal out of my new job; I could practically hear her already. Even I had to admit there was something slightly ridiculous about a charity shop devoted to owls, and I didn't feel any more enthusiastic when I found it.

It was in a brilliant location, right at the heart of the shopping area, but the bay window was dusty and the window display was half-hearted. A mannequin that was missing both hands lolled awkwardly on a wicker chair, her wig sliding off her head. The gray dress she was wearing looked as if it had come directly from Sylvia's own wardrobe. A couple of handbags sagged at the mannequin's chipped feet, along with a pair of lurid vases and a woeful hat. Most of the window was taken up with faded pictures of owls. It was impossible to see inside the shop from the street, no matter how hard I peered through the window. Forget not having many customers before ten—I was surprised anyone was ever tempted to open the door. Not having any choice about it myself, I took a deep breath and went in.

Things didn't get much better once I was inside the shop. Even before the bell had stopped jangling, my nose was itching and my eyes were streaming. Dust and mothballs made a fairly potent combination, it turned out, and I answered Sylvia's enthusiastic greeting with a barrage of sneezes.

"Don't worry. You'll get used to it." She began making her way toward me, skirting stacks of full bin liners that took up most of the space. "These are all donations. I haven't had a chance to unpack them yet."

"I'm sure you're run off your feet." I looked around as my eyes became accustomed to the light—or rather the lack of it. The impression of total chaos wasn't completely fair—there were shelves at the back of the shop loaded with bric-a-brac and books, and racks of clothes lurked on either side of me. There was even a changing room, though the curtain was hanging off the rail and the mirror was gray with dust. As I started to turn away I half saw a figure in the back room, standing against the wall, watching me, and my heart took off at a gallop. There was that feeling again—pure fear, ballooning out of nowhere. I refused to acknowledge it but some part of me knew because of Freya I could be blundering into danger with every step I took, so I was beyond jumpy. And that made me even more determined not to be intimidated. I wiped my sweaty hands on my jeans, took a deep breath and faced the figure squarely, meeting her unwavering gaze. It didn't take me long to realize that this was one staring competition I wasn't going to win.

"Are you all right, dear?" Sylvia was looking concerned.

"I thought there was someone in the back room, but it's just a mannequin."

She peered at the figure. "Oh yes. She should be in the window."

The fair-haired mannequin's face was damaged, the plaster flaking away so she only had one eye. If her counterpart in the window hadn't been maimed too, I might have thought Sylvia had retired her on aesthetic grounds. But then Sylvia didn't seem the type to care about appearances.

"I'm just not very organized, I'm afraid. I haven't had any help in the shop for months. No one seems to want to work any more."

And most of the young people in Port Sentinel had more than enough money without having to spend their time in a dark, filthy junk shop, unlike me. According to Tilly, Sylvia was exceptionally wealthy and could easily afford to pay me, so I didn't have to feel guilty about taking her money. But if I was going to take it, I was determined to earn it.

I squared my shoulders and smiled. "Well, I'm here now. Let's see how much I can get done this morning. Is there anything in particular you'd like me to do?"

"Oh, I don't know. Where do you want to start?" Sylvia's hands were fluttering. I'd already noted that was a sign she was stressing out.

"I was thinking I might unpack the bags first—just to make some room—and then I could do a bit of tidying, maybe?" And give the place a good clean while I was at it.

"That sounds perfect." More fluttering. "I could make us a cup of tea."

"Yes please," I said, resolving to find some way to throw mine away. I wasn't going to consume anything in Fine Feathers until I'd made sure to bleach every mug, and I'd be bringing my own milk. Maybe my own tea bags too, I reflected. You couldn't be too careful. I was willing to bet Sylvia's were antiques.

Unaware of what I was thinking, she twittered off to the back room to find the kettle and I picked up the bag nearest me. As I hefted it by the knot, the plastic gave way and the contents fell to the floor.

"Oh, perfect."

I bent down to pick everything up, starting with a shoe that had slid under the nearest rack of clothes. Nude patent leather, slightly scuffed sole, very high heel. It looked as if it had only been worn once. I turned it over to check the label inside, more from habit than anything else, and stopped dead.

Louis Vuitton.

"You're kidding." I scrabbled in the heap of clothes at my feet, looking for the other shoe. It would be too cruel if the one I'd found was a singleton, but it would make more sense than someone voluntarily giving away expensive designer footwear that was practically new.

The other shoe turned up in the middle of a tangle of jumpers that proved to be cashmere and incredibly soft. One had a tiny hole in the sleeve; the rest looked unworn. And there was another pair of heels in red leather—very strappy sandals made by Salvatore Ferragamo.

Sylvia crept back, carrying a tray with two mugs and a plate of biscuits on it. "Is everything all right?"

I was sitting on the floor surrounded by designer clothes.

My mind was officially broken. "It's just the stuff—the stuff people give you—"

"What's wrong with it?" She slid the tray onto the cash desk. "I do worry about it, but beggars can't be choosers."

"No, it's not that. It's amazing. It's all such high quality. And there's nothing wrong with any of it, really."

"Oh. That's good."

"Didn't you realize?" I held up a top. "This is a Marc Jacobs. That dress is from Whistles—which, OK, it *is* a High Street shop but still, expensive. Those trousers are Stella McCartney. Paul McCartney's daughter," I added, not seeing even a hint of name-recognition and trying to come up with a cultural reference old enough for her. "You know. The Beatles."

"I don't pay much attention to fashion, dear. But people are very generous. And it's all in a very good cause, you see." She held up a spoon. "Sugar?"

"No, thanks." I was unpicking the knot on the next bag, half expecting to find it full of unwearable dross. The first one had to be beginner's luck. I took out a crumpled white blazer with a lipstick stain on the lapel—much more like the usual charity-shop thing. Except for the Ralph Lauren label inside it.

Before I could delve any further, the bell above the door jangled and I twisted round to see Darcy standing behind me. Today her hair was in two fat plaits and she was wearing a pale pink dress with stripy leggings. Just to make sure she didn't look too sweet, her eye makeup was pretty close to what the well-dressed panda was wearing this summer and her nails were painted black. She looked thrilled to see me and I found myself smiling back, wanting to like her in spite of Petra's concerns and Will's warning. In fact, given Will's hostility to her I should really have been on her side. Instead of sleeping I'd spent quite a bit of the previous night deciding I didn't trust him—not at all—so arguably I should do the opposite of whatever he suggested. Which meant being nice to Darcy. I pushed the doubt to the back of my mind where it could stay until I'd formed my own opinion.

"Hey." She knelt down beside me. "I bumped into Hugo just now. He told me you were working here."

"Did he, indeed." I was surprised. I hadn't thought Hugo was the gossipy type.

"It's a genius idea. Really. You'll get to see everything first, before it even goes on the racks. You have your pick of everything." Darcy leaned across to root through the bag that was in front of me. "Oh my God. Are these shoes alligator-skin?"

"I don't know. I hope not." I took them out of her hands and slung them back in the bag. Sylvia was safely out of earshot, but I dropped my voice anyway, not wanting to hurt her feelings. "If this is such a great place to work, how come Sylvia couldn't persuade anyone to help her?"

Darcy rolled her eyes. "She's mad. It's too much trouble to keep her happy. Hello, Miss Burman." She waved at her and got a confused stare in return. "Besides, it's more fun to shop here than to actually work."

"You shock me."

"It's not that bad. You'll make it fun. And you really will be able to dress well, you know. You'll get a staff discount and everything."

"I'm not sure high fashion mixes that well with my current style." I looked down at my T-shirt and frayed jeans. "I don't think heels and a Ralph Lauren blazer would work with this."

Darcy wrinkled her nose. "Maybe it's time for an image change."

"Maybe it's time I did some work." Sylvia wasn't what you'd call scary but I didn't want to disappoint Tilly by getting the sack on my first day. I went back to sorting through donations. "I still can't believe how expensive all this stuff was when it was new."

"Welcome to Port Sentinel." She rummaged in the bag again, finding a strapless top. "Do you think this would fit me?"

The truthful answer was no. "Maybe. But do you want it to?"

"Not really."

"Do people in Port Sentinel really care about owls or something?"

"Owls?" Darcy looked bewildered. "Oh. You mean Sylvia's charity?"

"The reason for the shop's existence."

"No need to be sarky. No, owls aren't big around here. But fashion is. And you don't want to be seen to get two years out of your designer clothes. Everyone makes it a mission to get rid of last season's stuff."

"That's so wasteful."

She shrugged. "Get used to it. Anyway, this is the only charity shop in town. The others couldn't afford the rent and closed down. Sylvia is loaded so she was able to afford the overheads and now she gets everything that's going."

"I'd have thought the shop would be packed. You're the only customer we've had all morning."

"Not surprising, is it? Most of the locals wouldn't buy anything here in case someone spotted them wearing out-of-date secondhand clothes. Imagine if the previous owner saw you in the boots she'd thrown away." She waggled a black suede ankle boot at me. The toecap was covered with gold studs. It was sort of luxury punk, and quite hideous.

"Those would be hard to miss," I agreed.

"And out-of-towners don't always risk it. It's not the most appealing shop on the street." Darcy's voice dropped to a whisper. "Sylvia does the window displays herself, you know."

"How do you know all this? About the shop, and the rent, and the customers?"

She bit her lip. "Oh damn. I wasn't supposed to tell you."

"Tell me what?"

I don't think Darcy wanted to go on, but she just couldn't help answering. "Freya worked here the year before last. She did Saturdays—Sylvia didn't bother to open up during the week because it was the low season and there were no customers at all. I used to help out now and then."

"Why am I not surprised?" I had found a box full of hangers and began putting clothes on the racks with a little bit more force than was strictly necessary. "Everyone seems determined to make me into Freya's understudy. If I just kept my mouth shut and learned to paint it would be like she'd never left."

"I'm sure that's not why Tilly recommended you for the job. In fact, I know it's not. Hugo said she came up with the idea after Sylvia told her the shop was getting to be too much to manage on her own. Tilly thought you could help her get organized."

"I can't make things much worse," I whispered.

Darcy snorted a laugh. "You could give things away for free. That wouldn't be ideal."

"Oh crap." I had completely forgotten price tags. Maybe Mum was right; I *did* need experience in retail.

Darcy started to take the clothes off the rail again. "I can see you're going to need me to help out. I'll stick around."

"Are you sure?"

"Nothing better to do." She grinned. "Besides, I like it."

"Will you help with the window display? If I can get Sylvia to let us tackle it, that is?"

"Good luck with that."

"I might not need luck." I held up a skirt, assessing it. "I've got an idea and I think I can persuade Sylvia to give me a chance. But I'm going to need your eye for fashion."

Darcy saluted, almost putting her eye out with the end of the hanger. "I am on it like a bonnet."

I assumed that meant yes.

It took almost an hour to empty the bags and sort the contents. Only one was the usual charity-shop stuff, and therefore disappointing—sagging tracksuit bottoms and ancient novelty T-shirts.

"Bin," Darcy said firmly, holding up a faded yellow top with a cartoon banana on it. "We can't have that sort of thing in here."

"Someone might like it," Sylvia protested.

"No one would want it. Believe me. Even the person who bought it in the first place, who obviously has zero taste."

"Darcy," I said, trying not to laugh. "Don't be rude."

"I'm not being rude. But Fine Feathers is not a rubbish

dump. And that's where this needs to be." She lowered it into the bin. "And good riddance."

I had set aside a pile of clothes for the window display, having coaxed Sylvia into letting me change it. She didn't seem convinced that a fresh look was required but I pointed out that we had all these new clothes and no way to show people they were there unless we changed the window. And since she was so busy . . .

"You're amazing." Darcy was wrestling with the mannequin from the back room, trying to force her into a navy chiffon dress with a plunging front and a full skirt. "Remind me never to let you persuade me to do anything."

"I didn't do anything."

"We never, ever got permission to touch the window display last year. It 'sets the tone,' apparently." Darcy's impersonation of Sylvia's quavery voice was spot on. "It drove Freya mad, but she still couldn't persuade Sylvia to let her have a go."

"Well, she doesn't want me to leave on my first day. And since she's said yes once, she'll probably agree next time." I shrugged. "Simple, really."

"Scary," Darcy declared.

I had found the model's missing hands in the back room. Now the challenge was to make them stay on the poor thing, who was at least sitting properly on her dingy chair. She wasn't getting a new outfit—yet. But I was planning to brush her hair. I wedged one hand on but the other was too difficult, so I arranged her arms to hide the stump. It was a problem for another day.

On closer investigation, the two handbags in the window

were Mulberry and Gucci. Stuffing them with some paper and giving them a good dust made them look more like what they were—very expensive designer accessories. One went on the blonde mannequin's arm. The other dangled from her outstretched hand as she offered it to her unfashionable counterpart. I had found a pair of sunglasses on a shelf beside a tangle of costume jewelry and now I handed them to Darcy.

"Here. Put these on Blondie."

Darcy slid them on. "Perfect. You can't see she's only got one eye now."

"That's what I was hoping." I was far too hot. I pushed back my hair, forgetting that my hands were filthy until after I'd done it. "Do I have a dirty mark on my face?"

Darcy glanced up. "Just a bit."

I rubbed at it.

"That's making it worse."

I sighed. "Look, remind me to wipe it before I leave."

"How are you getting on?" Sylvia peered into the window, looking dubious. "Goodness. What's going on?"

"The idea is that this one gets a makeover." I patted the brunette on the head. "Her name is Brenda, by the way. I'm going to change her outfit gradually, with something new every day so she gets more and more glamorous."

"It's sheer genius," Darcy told me.

"Don't be stupid." I turned away, embarrassed by her open admiration, especially since I didn't truly think the idea was all that amazing.

"Keep up the good work," Sylvia quavered, and she retreated to her chair and a fat romantic novel. Delegating her responsibilities was working out quite well as far as she was concerned.

Without asking for permission, since I didn't think I'd get it, I started to peel the owl posters off the window. Not wanting a row, I decided to compromise and leave the ones at the edges, where they didn't prevent potential customers from seeing what was in the shop. I squinted out at Fore Street as I tried to scrape away ancient sellotape that had baked onto the glass. The sun had come out for the first time since I'd arrived in Port Sentinel, and everything looked a hundred times better because of it. Even the people.

Even Ryan Denton, who had looked pretty good before. He was standing on the other side of the street talking to one of his friends—Alfie? Dan? I couldn't remember—in jeans and a tight gray T-shirt that clung to the muscles of his torso. The short sleeves showed off his tanned arms. As I watched—OK, stared—he slid his sunglasses up to sit on top of his head. His eyes were narrowed against the sun but I could still see that they were a brilliant shade of dark blue.

And then they focused on me.

I whipped round and busied myself with Brenda's wig, feeling the heat rise up from the neckline of my top. Being caught staring was bad. Being caught staring while reorganizing the window display in a frankly weird charity shop was worse. Actually working in the charity shop, even if it was for money, was so beyond acceptable that I should probably start packing to leave town straight away.

I was still hoping he hadn't noticed me when the shop door opened and set the bell going again.

"I wondered when I'd see you again." Ryan smelled of fresh air and clean clothes, and I turned to face him wishing I'd spent more than a couple of minutes on getting dressed. I *thought* I'd brushed my hair, but I couldn't be sure. He grinned. "You don't look all that pleased to see me."

"I am. I mean, I'm not *not* pleased." It was as if I'd set out to make a bad situation worse. I tried desperately to salvage something. Anything. "I just wasn't expecting to see anyone I knew, that's all."

"Maybe you should try not standing in the window, then."

"You might be right." I blinked up at him. He was taller than I had realized, and more handsome now that I had time to look at him, and he was one of those people who seem to bring the sunshine with them; I was dazzled, pretty much. *Say something. It doesn't have to be intelligent.* "Were you looking for anything in particular in here? Men's clothes are over there."

He threw a quick glance over his shoulder. "Yeah. Not my style, if you know what I mean."

"There's amazing stuff over there. Designer labels."

"I'm not into that kind of thing."

"What are you into?" It sounded impossibly flirty when I'd said it and I fought the urge to apologize, or put my hand over my mouth and laugh. "I mean, what sort of clothes are you into?"

"Don't know. Ordinary, I suppose." He looked down at himself. "This, basically."

"If it works, why change it?"

"Do you think it works?" He raised one eyebrow.

In that your stomach is a handy visual reminder of how to count to six, yeah, sure . . .

"Hi, Ryan," Darcy said breathily, saving me from having to answer.

"Hi." He gave her a quick smile, then switched his focus back to me. "So you're working here?"

"Helping out."

"Good for you."

"Good for my bank balance," I said tartly, not wanting to give the impression I was a volunteer. An owl sex–obsessed volunteer.

"What time do you finish work?"

"In about half an hour," Darcy said. She came to stand beside me, almost tripping over Brenda's right foot. She nudged me extremely hard in the ribs as she regained her balance.

"Ow. Watch it."

"Sorry." She made a big play of rearranging her hair, patting her face fussily. I stared at her, not understanding what was going on. If she was competing with me for Ryan's attention, it was sort of working. He was staring too, and he looked as baffled as I felt.

"Anyway," he said slowly, turning back to me, "I was wondering if you'd like to come for a walk. I could show you around town."

It was too good an opportunity for me to say no. *Please don't say you've already given me the tour, Darcy.*

"I've already given her the tour."

"I haven't seen everything," I said quickly. "The harbor, for starters."

"Do you like boats?" Ryan asked.

"I don't mind them," I said carefully. I knew precisely nothing about boats except that I could get seasick while stepping over a large puddle. The one thing I didn't want was to find myself out at sea, impressing Ryan with the volume and velocity of what I was throwing up.

"Well, let's start at the harbor and go on from there."

"Great."

Darcy nudged me again, fanning her face. "It's so hot in here. You should probably give Jess time to go home and shower before you meet up."

He shrugged. "OK."

"Thanks, Darcy." If he hadn't thought it before, Ryan was certainly now convinced that I was a sweaty mess, probably with BO, though the smell of mothballs was masking it nicely.

"My pleasure." She swiped at her forehead a couple of times and then glared at me meaningfully. I frowned, then froze.

Ryan checked his watch. "In ninety minutes, then. At the harbor."

"Great," I managed. "See you there."

He nodded to me and Darcy, waved at Sylvia, and swaggered out of the shop. I sat down on the floor where I couldn't be seen, burying my face in my arms. Darcy crouched beside me and patted my shoulder.

"Are you OK?"

"I forgot about the smudge on my forehead," I said in a tiny voice. "You tried to remind me and I thought you'd gone mad. But it was the smudge."

"Smudge? Yeah, you could call it that." She laughed. "Never mind. It didn't put him off."

I sat up. "No, it didn't. And I find that weird."

"Really?" Darcy looked amused. "From what I know of Ryan, he likes dirty girls."

"Oh, very funny."

She waved a hand dismissively. "Never mind that now. We're wasting valuable time. We've got far more important things to talk about."

"Such as?"

Darcy rolled her eyes. "Such as what you're going to wear."

7

In the end, I was actually glad that I'd had Darcy there to negotiate an extra hour for cleaning up. I had to have an epic shower to get rid of the worst of the charity-shop grime. While I was in the bathroom Darcy occupied herself with searching my wardrobe for a suitable outfit. I came back from the bathroom wrapped in a towel to find her in despair.

"Do you have a grudge against your figure or something?" She was looking at the jeans I had left on the bed. "Seriously, Jess. You can't tell me these are the best you can do."

"They're fine."

"Fine for what? DIY? I suppose it wouldn't matter if you got paint on them. Or set fire to them." She clasped her hands together. "Please let me go and get something for you to wear. I have tons of stuff that would look incredible on you. *Ple-e-e-e-ease.*"

I was shaking my head. "This is what I wear. I wouldn't be comfortable in your clothes."

"Oh my God, you are so stubborn." She sat down on the edge of the bed. "At least let me do your makeup."

"Absolutely not."

"Come on. A little eyeliner and mascara would go a long way."

"I'm already wearing mascara," I pointed out. "Just not so much that I can't open my eyes properly."

"Is that a dig? That's a dig, isn't it." She gasped in outrage. "How dare you."

I was searching for the top I'd planned to wear—a delicate pin-tucked shirt that was almost sheer, with short sleeves and tiny mother-of-pearl buttons down the front.

Darcy brightened when she saw it. "That's better."

"I'm glad you think so. It's all part of the plan."

"What plan?"

"I'm just going to get dressed," I said casually.

"Don't leave me like this! Tell me about the plan first. Jess . . ."

By the time I got back to my room, Darcy was bouncing up and down with frustration.

"What plan?"

"Playing up to Mr. Denton by making him think I'm interested in him."

Darcy pulled a face. "If you're trying to pull Ryan, Natasha will kill you."

"Who said anything about pulling him?" I bent to look in the mirror, which was small and in the darkest corner of the room. I could barely see myself in it. I'd have to take Darcy's word for whether I looked OK or not, and her version of OK probably wasn't the same as mine. "I've met guys like Ryan before. I have to show a certain amount of—let's call it appreciation—or he'll lose interest and I won't get as far as finding out what he thinks about what happened to Freya. But I don't want to go too far either, or that hell-witch will make my life a misery for the rest of the summer."

Darcy nodded. "So nice top and makeup with skanky jeans and—please tell me you're going to dry your hair before you leave the house."

I had pulled it back into a loose knot at the nape of my neck. "I was just going to leave it like this."

"No." Darcy shook her head so violently her plaits flew into her face. "I absolutely refuse to let you do that. You look as if you've just been swimming."

"It'll be fine when it's dried a bit more."

Darcy slid off the bed and went to stand with her back to the door. "Hairdryer. Now."

"I don't want to be late."

"You won't be." She checked her watch. "OK. Maybe just a few minutes late. But that makes it look as if you spent ages trying to decide what to wear and primping. Wet hair means you couldn't care less what he thinks of you."

"Which is pretty much true."

"Don't dismiss him too quickly," she warned. "You're underestimating him if you think he's just about the looks and the girls."

"Does somebody have a little crush?"

"No. Not at all." But she was blushing. "It's just too easy to make assumptions about him because he's cute. He's not stupid."

"I didn't say he was."

"He can't help how people react to him either. He's not in charge of Natasha."

"I didn't get the impression he minded, though."

"Maybe he's flattered by it."

"Oh, probably. You don't wear a T-shirt that tight without having a fairly well-nourished ego." I unravelled my hair and shook it out. "Do I really have to dry this?"

"That hair is a privilege." Darcy sounded stern. "You need to make the most of it."

Thirty minutes later I was hurrying toward the harbor, hoping Ryan had been patient enough to wait for me. It was unfortunate but typical that the harbor was on the other side of a fairly steep hill; making up the time wasn't easy. My arms ached and my cheeks were still red from the heat of the hairdryer, but my hair hung down my back in perfect curls. Even I had to admit Darcy had been right to make me dry it properly.

I slowed down a little when the harbor was in sight, not wanting to look hot and bothered when I arrived. I'd had enough of being at a disadvantage in front of Ryan Denton, if I could possibly avoid it. It didn't seem likely that I could actually impress him, given my previous track record, but I thought I'd get more out of him if he wasn't quietly laughing at me most of the time.

He was there before me, which wasn't a surprise given how late I was. He was leaning against some railings, his hands in his pockets, and his sunglasses were hiding his eyes.

"Sorry. It took me longer than I expected to get changed."

"You're forgiven." A big smile with lots of very white teeth. "I don't mind waiting when it's something worth waiting for."

"Too kind." I glanced at him, trying to work out if he was flirting with me or just practicing for when he really wanted to charm someone. With the shades, I really couldn't tell. "Thanks for showing me around."

"No problem. We can't have you missing out on the best Port Sentinel has to offer."

Like your good self, maybe?

I scanned the small harbor. "Wow. Look at all the boats." It was full of sailboats at anchor, dipping and bobbing as the water moved under them.

"That's why we're here. So you can look at the boats."

"You have to admit, they're quite impressive."

"They're OK."

"You don't sail?"

"I used to. I don't have time for it these days. Too busy playing football at weekends." Ryan shrugged. "I prefer surfing anyway. Less kit. More fun."

"I wouldn't know."

"You don't surf?"

I shook my head, amused at the idea.

"Have you ever been sailing?"

"No. It's not really that easy to find somewhere to go sailing in London."

"I keep forgetting that's where you're from."

"I wish *I* could." I sort of meant it, to my surprise. It was good to be away from my usual world for a while. I took a deep breath of sea air. "It feels as if London's a million miles away. Have you always lived here?"

"No. My family moved here from Bristol about eight years ago. I've only lived here for half my life."

"Long enough to be a local."

Ryan laughed. "No way. Your parents have to be from here before you count as local. And that's at the very least. Grandparents are even better."

"So I practically qualify. On my mother's side, anyway." I wrinkled my nose. "I still think you might know it better than I do."

"That's why I'm the tour guide and you're the tourist."

"OK. Get guiding."

I fell into step beside Ryan and we strolled along the edge of the harbor. There was a slight breeze, enough to ruffle the surface of the water and make music from the ropes on the boats as they tapped against their masts. It sounded like hundreds of tiny bells ringing.

"So. This is the harbor. I think it was once used for proper fishing but now it's mainly leisure craft."

"Right." The harbor wall curved out into the sea and ended in a beacon. "Are we going down there?"

"Only if you want to see the harbor from a different perspective. It's not very exciting."

"Fine."

"Do you see the rock just beyond the harbor wall?"

I shaded my eyes. "It's hard to miss it. What's special about it?"

"That's where the town gets its name. That's Sentinel Rock. Sailors used it to navigate into the harbor. The water's pretty shallow here and the seabed is rocky, so there's basically only one channel that's deep enough for the boats to come in safely. Before there was the beacon—"

"There was the rock. I get it." I grinned at him. "I may be

a nonsailing Londoner but I understand that boats need to float."

"How's the tour so far?"

"Riveting. But I get the feeling your heart isn't in it."

"Ah. You spotted that." Ryan shrugged. "It's a good excuse for a walk on a nice day with a pretty girl."

"I'm flattered."

"OK. We move on." He put a hand in the small of my back for no reason I could see. I moved away a little and he dropped it down by his side. We walked on for a few paces and I felt something touch my hip, then settle there, as Ryan draped his arm around me again. I looked down at his hand, then up at him.

"Ryan, can I ask you a question?"

"Go for it."

"Are you seeing anyone at the moment?" I knew how he would interpret that and the grin on his face told me I was right.

"Nope. You?"

"I just broke up with someone."

"And you're heartbroken? On the rebound? In the mood for a holiday romance?"

"None of the above," I said firmly. "I was just wondering because Natasha seemed kind of possessive of you."

He looked out to sea. "Ignore her."

I persevered. "You were in a relationship, though."

"Not officially."

"I don't think there's any such thing as an unofficial relationship. Either you're involved with someone or you're not."

"Well, we're not involved any more."

"What about last year? Were you seeing Natasha while you were chasing after Freya?"

Ryan stopped walking. "Where did that come from?"

"It's just what I've heard."

"From Darcy? You don't want to listen to her. She's full of it."

I frowned. "I didn't get that impression from her."

"She loves to gossip."

"So you weren't keen on Freya . . ." I said slowly.

"I didn't say that." He took off his sunglasses, squinting a little, but his eyes were steady. Honest, you'd have said. "I really liked her. She was beautiful. But you know that already."

I blushed. "I never met her."

"You know you look exactly like her."

"So I'm told."

"Well, then." Ryan leaned in, staring at me. "It's amazing. You're really identical."

I shook my head. "You've just forgotten the details. If she were here, you'd see we aren't that alike."

"I remember her," he said softly. "I'll never forget her. And you're just the same as her. Even the hair." He picked up a strand of my hair where it had fallen over my shoulder and ran it through his fingers. "Just the same."

"I thought her hair was short."

"Yeah. She cut it." He let go of my hair abruptly. "I liked her more before."

"So you stopped chasing her once she'd cropped her hair?"

"I still liked her. I just preferred her with longer hair." He laughed. "Anyway, I wasn't chasing her. I don't do that."

"So what's your technique?"

"I told her I thought we should get to know each other better. It was up to her whether she went for it or not."

"And she didn't."

He gave a one-shouldered shrug. "It didn't happen."

"Maybe because she didn't like the idea of helping you to cheat on Natasha?" I knew I was on thin ice but Ryan was so laid-back, I thought I'd get away with it.

He grinned. "You're almost right—there was someone else involved. But it wasn't anything to do with me. Freya was in love with someone else."

"What makes you say that?"

"She told me."

"Who was it?"

"I didn't ask," he said, sounding as if it was a stupid idea.

"This is a small town. You can't guess who she meant?" I had a fair idea, and I'd been there less than a week.

"Not really. I thought she was single. That's why I told her how I felt about her."

"And you never saw her with anyone?"

Ryan shook his head. "But she seemed serious about him, whoever he was."

There was no easy way to ask this. "Are you sure he existed?"

"What do you mean?"

"Well, it's one way to turn you down without hurting your feelings, isn't it?"

"I wasn't hurt." His tone contradicted the words—he had been hurt, and annoyed, and it still rankled with him that she hadn't been interested.

"Obviously not," I agreed. "But Freya was a nice person,

from what I know of her. She might have been worried about it—even if there was no danger of you being upset."

"So she invented a boyfriend to put me off." He shook his head. "You've got a heck of an imagination."

"Really not. It's just a possibility. Aren't you curious?"

"Not as much as you are, obviously." Ryan frowned. "If you're hoping I'll tell you what was going on with Freya, you're out of luck. I didn't know her well enough for that."

"You knew her well enough to be sure you wanted to go out with her," I pointed out.

"That wasn't so much to do with her personality." He gave me a cheeky sidelong glance.

"I know you're not that shallow."

He laughed. "OK. It wasn't all based on how she looked. I did like her as a person. She was so different."

"From Natasha? I bet."

"Nats is all right."

"Nats is terrifying, quite frankly. Maybe Freya was too scared to get involved with you."

"I wouldn't know."

"Maybe Natasha told her she had to put you off."

"You'd have to ask her." We had walked up the hill, back toward town, and down the other side, and now we were approaching the beach. "You can ask her now, if you like. She's over there."

Ryan pointed at a café on the seafront. It was surrounded by tables with blue-and-white striped umbrellas. Every table was full. It took me a second to spot Natasha. She was sitting in the sun, slender legs stretched out to add to her even tan, with two of her friends. She was wearing white linen shorts and a fitted top, but her main accessory was a scowl the size of a family car.

"Oh no."

"Don't worry. I'll protect you." Ryan put his hand on my back again and I flinched.

"Don't touch me in front of her, and don't defend me either. She'll never believe you're not interested in me if you act like that."

I had picked up speed to get past Natasha before I burst into flames from the sheer hatred she was directing at me, but Ryan put his hand on my arm and made me stop, then turn to face him. The two bimbos at Natasha's table were murmuring to each other, openly staring. I recognized one as the girl who'd seen me on my first day in town, and the other from the seafront gathering.

"The thing is, I don't want to mislead her. It's not fair to pretend I don't like you." He looked past me to where Natasha was sitting and waved at her.

"Is this a game for you two?" I demanded. "You make her jealous, she defends her territory—is that it?"

"By no means." He sighed. "Look, Natasha and I were together for a couple of years. It wasn't an easy break-up. It's my fault—I'm really bad at walking away. I've told her it's over but I want to stay friendly with her. This is a small town, as you've noticed. I don't want any hassle. It's boring."

"Boring. Right."

"That doesn't mean I can't see other girls. I know Natasha would prefer it if I didn't, but I'm not going to stop myself from going after someone if I like them." Ryan seemed completely sincere and I believed him. It wasn't unfair, I thought, that he should get to move on even if Natasha didn't want to.

And some unworthy part of me was pleased that I was annoying her just by standing beside Ryan. I put my hand on his arm, knowing that she was watching my every move.

"Let's keep going. It would be a shame to stop halfway through your tour when I'm enjoying it so much."

"You are?" He looked genuinely pleased. "OK. Well, this is the beach."

"I noticed," I said, but I softened it with a smile.

We kept walking by the sea as Ryan told me all about surfing and why I should really try it. I enjoyed listening to him even if a lot of it made very little sense to me; I certainly had no intention of actually getting into the water. I liked to stay dry. At the end of the bay, the path snaked up the headland and disappeared among the trees that covered it. Ryan stopped at the foot of the hill. He was looking at it as if he'd forgotten it was there.

"Do you want to turn back?"

"Not particularly," I said, wondering why his enthusiasm levels had taken a dive.

"There's not much to see up here."

"There's the view of the town," I observed. "I haven't really seen it and it would help me to get my bearings. And there's the view out to sea."

"Well, this is definitely the place to go if you want a view." He didn't set off up the path, though.

"Is there something wrong?"

"Nope." But he wasn't looking at me.

"If you've got somewhere else to be—"

"Of course I don't."

"OK then." I looked at him curiously. "Should I go on my own? Meet you later?"

"I'll come with you. If that's where you want to go." Ryan grinned but it was a pale imitation of his usual smile. "Can't have you wandering around on your own. You might trip over a fallen branch or something."

"My hero." I began to walk up the path, feeling the steepness of the hill in my thighs and calves almost immediately. "Ugh. I'm so unfit."

"I wouldn't say that."

I ignored the remark. I'd come to realize that if Ryan was awake and breathing, he was likely to be flirting. Besides, I needed all my breath for the climb. I didn't mind that the going was slow and the ground uneven. The sun was shining through the trees. The leaves were thick overhead but they allowed plenty of light through in narrow beams that made coin-sized spots on the path. Between the trunks, the sea gleamed blue and silver below us. Tiny insects hummed and birds sang in the trees, and I felt happy for the first time since I'd been in Port Sentinel. All the questions that had been bothering me subsided. I was actually enjoying myself. *And* toning my thighs at the same time. Bonus.

The climb was totally worth it, I thought, as the ground started to level out and the trees thinned. The top of the headland was bare, apart from a few gorse bushes. Someone had put a bench there to reward anyone who made it to the top and I collapsed on it, breathing hard. The view was incredible—the town spread out below, the sea dotted with small boats and a large container ship like a toy far out on the horizon. The sky was pure blue, with just a couple of wispy white clouds. I shaded my eyes, picking out the landmarks I knew and the places I'd been. I couldn't see our holiday home but I was able to identify the red brick and ivy of Sandhayes. Will's house was lost in the trees behind.

It took me a couple of minutes to realize that Ryan hadn't joined me on the bench. I twisted round, looking for him. He was a few meters back, leaning against one of the last trees. The sunglasses were back and his face was like a mask, but his face was pale.

"What's wrong?"

"Nothing."

"Really?" I turned and knelt on the seat of the bench, hanging over the back. "Are you feeling OK?"

"I'm fine."

"You don't look fine. Do you want to sit down?"

"No thanks."

If he didn't want to go exploring with me, I wasn't going to force him. He'd seen it all before anyway. I climbed down off the bench and strolled across the headland to see what was on the other side. Another bay, it turned out, but instead of a slope, there was a steep drop to the sea. The waves came in at an angle, churning and swirling around sharp-edged rocks. Even on a calm day the water was white-flecked and choppy.

"What are you doing?" Ryan's tone was sharp.

"Just looking."

"Don't go too close to the edge."

"I'm not." I stopped where I was. "Ryan—"

"It's probably time to head back."

"Oh. OK." Something was upsetting him, that was clear enough. Maybe he didn't like heights. "Thanks for showing me this place. I really enjoyed the tour."

"I'm glad." He peeled himself away from the tree and headed down the path, not waiting to see if I was following. Before I did, I cast one glance over my shoulder at the glorious view. I would come back, I thought. I would come on my own and sit in the sunshine.

And I'd find out what was bothering Ryan. If I ever caught up with him.

He was far too quick for me on the path. I took my time, not wanting to fall, slithering on the dry earth where the ground was particularly steep. Too polite to abandon me altogether, he was waiting for me at the bottom of the hill, and he wasn't alone. Hugo was standing beside him, his arms folded. His expression was at least as disapproving as Natasha's had been earlier.

"Hey."

"Jess." Hugo sounded cold.

"I'd better go," Ryan said. "I'll see you around, Jess."

I was starting to feel like I'd done or said something unforgivable, but I couldn't imagine what. "Thanks again."

He walked off with his hands in his pockets.

"Well, that went well," I said cheerfully.

Hugo frowned. "I wouldn't have thought he was your type."

"Oh, he's totally not. But he seems nice."

Hugo snorted.

"Do you two not get on, or something?" I asked.

"He's OK." He nodded at the headland. "What were you doing up there?"

"Just looking around."

"Was it his idea to take you there?"

I tried to remember. "N-no. Mine, I think. He wasn't that keen."

Hugo nodded, his expression lightening a little. "I thought he'd made you go there. For kicks."

"Far from it. I basically dragged him up there." I put my hands on my hips. "Am I being thick or something? What's going on?"

I could only describe the look on Hugo's face as pitying. "You didn't realize? Up on the headland—the other side of it—that's where Freya was when they found her."

I stared at him, feeling stupid, suddenly chilled to the bone despite the warm sunshine. I couldn't have known but I still should have guessed.

Hugo looked past me, at the shaded path, and I had the feeling he wasn't really seeing it, or me.

"That's where Freya died."

8

I know you're above fashion but please, I'm begging you, try it on."

"Absolutely not."

"Oh, come on." Darcy was literally jumping up and down with frustration. She was wearing a short salmon-pink lace dress with a full skirt and looked like she'd just skated off the ice after a top-scoring short program at the Winter Olympics. "I'd do it but it wouldn't fit me. I know you've got an incredible figure somewhere under all that baggy material."

I glanced at the dress she was holding up, then returned to cleaning the display cabinet.

"Don't look like that," Darcy snapped.

"Like what?"

"Like—" She scrunched up her face.

"The glass cleaner was making my nose itch."

"I'm sure."

"Really." It certainly had nothing to do with the teeny tiny dress with its plunging neckline and bum-freezer skirt, the dress that I called slutty and Darcy, her voice reverent, called Versace. It would take a lot more than the one-two punch of Darcy's bullying and flattery to persuade me out of my jeans and hoodie and into the scrap of black silk and sequins that she was waving around.

"Miss Burman, will you tell Jess to try this dress on?"

Sylvia looked worried. "I don't think I could do that, Darcy. It wouldn't be fair."

"But you're her boss. She'd have to do it if you told her to," Darcy wheedled.

"And why exactly do you care?" I asked.

"Because I really want to try it on but it wasn't made for a girl shaped like me. Seeing it on you is the next best thing."

I snorted. "Put it on Brenda. Or Marilyn. Marilyn would rock it." Marilyn was the one-eyed blonde, named by Sylvia in a rare burst of imagination once I'd introduced her to Brenda.

"Not the same." Darcy pressed the material against her, measuring the waist. "Ugh. I wouldn't get it over my head."

"Too bad."

"You are no fun." Darcy hooked the dress onto a rail. "This job is wasted on someone like you who doesn't care about fashion."

"*My* job, you mean. The job that you're basically sharing for no pay."

Sylvia looked worried. "I could probably manage a little, Darcy. You are being very helpful, dear."

To give her her due, Darcy didn't consider it for a second. "No way, Miss Burman. I'm just hanging out in here because

I really like it and I've got nowhere else to be. I don't mind helping while I'm here."

"But if you're helping in the shop I should make sure you're recompensed."

"Really. I don't need anything." Darcy was looking stricken. I leaned out from behind Sylvia and flapped my arms up and down. It took her a second to catch on to what I meant, and even then she wasn't totally sure she'd got it. "I want to do it for free because . . . I love owls so much?"

"Who doesn't?" Those two words were the first clue we'd had that anyone was watching us. It was my fault. I'd wedged the shop door open to allow some light and air in, so there had been no warning, no tell-tale jangle from the bell to tell us anyone had come in—but there Will stood, smirking. Even though I knew his voice the moment I heard it, I jumped. Darcy whirled round with one hand to her chest, dramatic as ever.

"God, Will, you scared the crap out of me." She looked back over her shoulder. "Sorry for swearing, Sylvia."

Sylvia looked up from her book. "What?"

"Never mind," I said at the same time as Darcy. To Will, I said, "You really do love to make an entrance, don't you?"

"I don't know what you mean."

"It's just that you seem to like surprising people."

He raised an eyebrow. "People?"

"Me."

"It's not intentional."

I was starting to blush under his cool scrutiny. "What can I do for you?"

"Absolutely nothing." He lifted up the toolbox I hadn't noticed he was carrying and rattled it. "It's what I can do for *you*.

Or rather, Miss Burman." The smile he gave her was considerably more pleasant than anything he'd thrown in my direction so far. "Dad said you wanted to get a couple of things fixed."

"Oh yes. You're so good to think of it, Will." Sylvia got up and began to wring her hands. "The changing cubicle—I don't know if it's possible to fix it, but the curtain isn't quite right."

"The rail's broken," I said.

"I'll have a look at it."

"And that shelf." I pointed. "The bracket's come away from the wall. We can't use it at the moment." The whole thing tilted at a drunken angle.

"Should be easy enough to sort out."

"I was going to have a go myself, but I didn't have any tools." *Just because I'm female doesn't mean I need help with any vaguely practical task.*

"OK, then." Will put the toolbox down on the floor in front of him. "Help yourself."

I looked at it, wishing I hadn't said anything.

"Don't be stupid, Jess. Let Will do it." Darcy sounded bored. "He's good at that kind of thing."

"It's not fair if I have all the fun." He was looking amused and I bristled.

"That's fine. I have other things to do. But thanks."

"Any time." Will picked up the toolbox again and went over to the changing room, where he spent a couple of minutes tinkering with the curtain rail. I couldn't help watching, but if he was aware of that, he didn't show it. He looked very much as if he knew what he was doing too.

"Can you do anything with it?" Sylvia asked eventually.

"It'll be good as new." He said it with quiet confidence and it was totally unfair of me to be annoyed by it. I couldn't help hoping, though, that the rail would fall down as soon as he started to work on it, or that he'd hit his thumb with a hammer, or drop a screw and have to go hunting for it in the twilight dimness of the shop. Any mistake would do.

Unaware of what I was thinking, Will started to work. I forced myself to concentrate on what I was doing—arranging jewelry and accessories in the now sparkling display case. No one had ever lined up bracelets with more care. No one had ever spent longer getting a knot out of a chain. Anything to keep my focus on the job in hand and my eyes away from Will, though I was hyper-aware of every sound he made. He was taking his time, working with as much attention to detail as if he had someone really difficult to impress, when Sylvia would have been delighted if he'd nailed the curtain to the plywood wall of the cubicle and called it fixed.

I was so busy not watching Will I completely missed Darcy trying to get me to look at her. The first I knew of it was when a faded felt hat with a bunch of glass cherries on the brim skimmed across the counter.

"Hat frisbee, woo-hoo. Throw it back," Darcy said, clapping her hands.

"No." I brushed some dust off the crown. "You'll ruin it."

"Who's going to buy that? It's hideous."

"Someone will love it. That's the whole point of charity shops. One person's rubbish is another person's treasure." I put the hat on, settling the brim over my eyes. "What do you think?"

"Perfect if you were starring in a 1980s film with John Cusack as your love interest. Here and now?" Darcy looked pitying. "Pensioner chic."

"I like it," Sylvia said.

"There you go." Darcy grinned. "I knew I was right."

"OK. You've made your point." I handed it to Sylvia. "It's yours. Try it on."

She put it on gingerly, much too far back on her head, and I leaned over to adjust it. It actually suited her.

"How does it look?"

"Perfect."

"Come and see, Miss Burman." Will was holding back the curtain so she could see herself in the mirror. She peered at herself shyly.

"Oh, I don't know."

"You look lovely." He smiled at her reflection and I stopped in the middle of what I was doing, genuinely surprised by how nice he was being to her. She blushed and scuttled away, muttering something about putting some money in the till, but she looked delighted as she disappeared into the back room.

"How's the rail?" Darcy asked.

"Fixed." Will let the curtain swing back down. "Now you can try on whatever you like."

"If only." She picked up the dress again and sighed, but she was looking at me over the top of the hanger.

"Forget it," I said.

"You don't have any excuse now. The changing room is fixed."

"That wasn't why I said no before, and I'm saying no again."

"You're a bad person." Darcy wandered over to where Will was testing the broken bracket under the shelf. "Will, you'd like to see Jess in this, wouldn't you? Why don't you ask her to try it on?"

He didn't even glance at it. "No chance."

"Why not?" Darcy asked what I was thinking. I'd have said no, obviously, but it would have been nice to think he'd have liked to see me in the skimpy dress. *Just so he could see what he could never have*, I told myself, slamming the cabinet door so hard that all my carefully arranged necklace stands fell over. I swore under my breath and opened the door to start again.

Will raised his voice over the rattle of costume jewelry. "I mean, you have no chance of persuading her to wear it. You're more likely to see Sylvia parading around in it than Jess."

This time, I was the one who asked the question. "Why do you say that?"

"Because you're incredibly stubborn and once you've made up your mind, no one can persuade you to change it." He said it in a matter-of-fact tone, without turning round. I gave a little gasp of outrage. He was right, but I could still be affronted.

Unmoved, he went on. "Besides, it's not you."

"How would you know?" I wished I could see his face.

"I've got eyes." He was tightening a screw, putting some force behind it. "You would never wear anything like that."

I didn't answer him, which made him look round, eyebrows raised. "Am I wrong?"

I shook my head.

"So give up, Darcy. Not going to happen." He tossed the screwdriver up in the air so that it flipped end over end a couple of times, then caught it.

"You're no help. But I suppose that shouldn't come as a surprise. I'll see you later, Jess. I've got somewhere else to be." Darcy dumped the dress on a chair and stropped out of the shop.

"Maybe I should just have tried the stupid thing on."

"Don't break your heart over her. She'll survive."

I was just about to ask Will what he'd meant about not trusting Darcy when Sylvia emerged from the back room, blinking like a tortoise coming out of a long hibernation.

"Is Darcy gone?"

"Just now," I said, hoping she wouldn't ask why.

"I'm going to make a move too," Will said. "The shelf's fixed. Unless there's anything else?"

"I don't think so. Thank you, Will."

"Any time." He knelt down and started to tidy away his tools, his hands quick and methodical.

"Hands," I said. Will looked up, surprised. "Brenda's hands. The mannequin. In the window." I pointed. "Her hands have fallen off and I can't get them to stay on."

"It's not my speciality but I'll have a go." He stood up. "Show me?"

I was acutely aware of him standing behind me as I retrieved the hands. Brenda was wearing a new skirt that just happened to be floor-length and therefore perfect for hiding things, such as her missing body parts. The hand I'd reattached had fallen off again during the night and acquired a new chip on the wrist. He turned them over, examining them.

"What do you think, Doctor? Is there any hope?"

"Traumatic amputation. That's never pretty." He shook his head. "I'll do my best, but I think her embroidery days are over."

"As long as she can wear bracelets again, I'll be happy."

Will grinned. "Super Glue should do it."

I sat down on the floor beside him to watch him work. "Why are you helping Sylvia?"

He shrugged. "Because I can. She's a nice lady."

"And you really care about owls."

"Of course." He looked at me sideways. "Then there's the fact that my father volunteered me for this."

"Oh, you got volunteered too?"

"Who signed you up?"

"Tilly."

"I'm sure she had her reasons. And I'm sure you had your reasons for saying yes. You're here for the money, I take it."

I put my chin on my knees. "Are you going to make me feel bad about that?"

"Nope. I'd never criticize anyone for earning their own cash instead of just taking their parents' money."

"None to take," I said cheerfully. "At least, Mum doesn't have any."

"What about your dad?"

"He wouldn't share it with me. He needs it for his girl-friend."

Will's eyebrows drew together as he considered that. "So they've split up? Your mum and dad?"

"Last year."

"Is your mum seeing anyone else?"

I frowned, surprised. "Are you interested in her or something?"

"Got it in one." A quick glance at me. "You don't know why I'm asking?"

"Nope."

"You don't know anything about why she left this place, do you?"

I had gone very still. "What do you know?"

"You need to talk to her. Ask her about it."

"I have. Of course I have. She's not very forthcoming."

"I can't say I'm surprised." Will had stuck the fake hands into place and now he tilted Brenda so they were braced against the wall. "Don't move them. The glue needs a few hours to stick properly. She won't be adjustable any more but you should be able to accessorize her outfits from now on."

"Don't change the subject. What do you know about Mum leaving?"

"It's not my place to tell you."

I squeezed my arms around my knees, maddened. "You are being intentionally unhelpful."

"Just ask her." Will was packing up his stuff again, his eyes on what he was doing. "Ask her what happened before she left. Ask her why she couldn't come back."

"Will." The word cut through the shop like a ninja throwing star.

Will flinched. He stood up, shoving his hands into his pockets. For the first time I saw him look awkward and I wasn't mean enough to enjoy it.

"Dad."

I stood up too, craning to see over the rack of hats in front of me, and felt a jolt of shock. The new arrival was Will—a broader, graying version of him with deep lines around his eyes and mouth, but pretty much Will in twenty years. He looked at me and the steely scrutiny was familiar, even though his eyes were a muddier shade of gray than his son's.

"And you are?" He asked it as if he had a right to know the answer.

"Jess Tennant."

"Jess Tennant." His face hadn't changed but he kept looking—staring, really—until I was too embarrassed to stand it any longer. I headed for the relative safety of the cash desk, letting my hair fall forward to screen me from his gaze. There was nowhere to hide, of course. He crossed the shop and stood in front of me, still staring.

"You're a recent arrival in Port Sentinel. That's why we haven't met."

I smiled, still on edge. There was something about his face—something was missing, something I'd seen and responded to in Will's. A hint of sensitivity about the mouth, maybe—a softness to the eyes. Will's father was pure granite. If I had to name one emotion he was experiencing, based on the look in his eyes, I'd have to pick hatred. Which was impossible.

"I've been here for a few days. On holiday," I said.

"Not much of a holiday if you spend it working."

"I don't mind."

"Good for you. I like someone with get up and go. I have to make Will find something useful to do with himself during the holidays. Otherwise he'd spend his time lazing about doing nothing."

It was completely at odds with the opinion I'd formed of his son. Politeness demanded that I laugh, but I glanced over at Will and found that I couldn't, quite. Not at his expense. Not with that guarded look on his face. It was hiding something; something that I thought was hurt.

If I wasn't smiling, Will's dad made up for it, grinning at me. It transformed him and almost wiped away the terrifying first impression he'd made. He stuck out his hand. "Dan Henderson. I'm the local bobby."

"I thought you were more senior than a bobby." His palm was rough against mine, calloused in places, as if he spent a lot of time out of doors.

"I'm the local inspector," he admitted. "Stay out of trouble while you're here, Jess, and we'll get on very well."

"That's certainly my intention." I was aware of Will watching us, of the tension in his posture. I wondered what he was afraid of.

As if he could hear what I was thinking, his father wheeled round abruptly. "What have you done so far?"

"I've finished," Will said quietly.

"Let me see."

Mutely, Will indicated the curtain rail. His father shook it as if he was testing its possibilities as a trapeze. "Not bad. But you made a bit of a mess at this end. You should repaint that wood."

It was on the tip of my tongue to correct him; he was talking about the end of the rail that hadn't needed to be fixed. If it was an untidy job, that was down to whoever had installed it in the first place. But Will was as capable of pointing that out as I was, and he said nothing, nodding when his father looked round at him. And if Dan Henderson was as determined as he seemed to be to find something wrong, letting him settle on something that simple was probably a good idea.

"What else?"

Will pointed out the shelf, which passed muster.

"And what were you doing in the window?"

"Talking to me, mainly," I said cheerfully. I didn't think Dan would approve of the Super Glue solution. Will didn't look at me, but Dan turned.

"I see. Have you two met before?"

"Not properly." Fine, so it was a lie, but Will's eyes met mine for a split second and I saw a gleam of relief.

"I'm sorry I interrupted, then."

"You didn't interrupt anything." And even if we had been having a romantic liaison, I wouldn't sit in a shop window on the main street in town to do it. I didn't even know if that was what he had been implying.

"We should go." They were almost the first words Will had spoken since his father arrived.

Dan clapped him on the shoulder hard enough to knock him off balance a little. "Never outstay your welcome. You're learning."

"You're so kind," Sylvia said. "He's a good boy, Dan. He's just like you were at the same age."

"I don't know which of us would be more disappointed if that were true." Dan smiled at her as if he'd said something pleasant instead of cutting.

Will picked up his toolbox and nodded to Sylvia. I got a glance as he went out of the door, a look that was too quick for me to be able to guess what he was thinking. In contrast, his father took his time to leave, shaking my hand again and holding onto it for a fraction of a second too long as he stared into my eyes. He had got as far as the door, and I had got as far as letting my shoulders slump with relief, when he turned back.

"Jess . . . Do tell your mother I was asking for her."

"Um. OK." *Or I might not mention it.* There was something about Will's dad that made me nervous. He'd walked into the shop and what little light there was seemed to have seeped out. Intimidating wasn't the word for him—and that was when he was trying to be nice. You could say I was overprotective but I didn't want him anywhere near my sweet, gentle mother.

He looked at me as if he knew what I was thinking, and I had to resist the urge to fidget. I just kept staring back, my face as neutral as I could make it, until he got tired of standing there and left. And it was only because of the ache in my lungs that I realized I'd been holding my breath.

9

So far, all I'd had were questions—questions that led to more questions, generally. That afternoon I finally started to get some answers. But it's true what they say: you should be careful what you wish for. Because once you know, that's it. There are no more possibilities. No more explanations. There's just the truth, no matter how much you might wish things were different.

After I finished work I went looking for Darcy. She wasn't at the beach, or in any of the cutesy cafés around town where I expected to find her indulging in some mild posing. I was pretty much at a loss after that; I didn't know her or Port Sentinel well enough to have any ideas about where she went when she was upset. As a last resort I tried her house, which she'd pointed out to me the previous day, and struck gold.

It wouldn't be fair to say she was sulking, but she was lying on her bed, headphones on, sketching unwearable shoes with dramatic platform soles. I sat on the edge of the bed and the movement made her look round and take the head-phones off.

"Hey. What are you doing here?"

"Your mum let me in."

"Not an answer to the question, but OK."

"You left Fine Feathers in a hurry. I wanted to make sure you were all right."

She rolled back onto her front. "That's nice of you. I'm fine."

"You were upset."

"I lost my temper. I shouldn't have."

"I know you were annoyed about the dress," I said, treading carefully. "But I wasn't expecting you to leave. I didn't think you were taking it that seriously. If I'd known—"

"You still wouldn't have tried it on."

"Probably not," I acknowledged. "But I might have handled it differently."

Darcy sighed. "It wasn't really anything to do with the dress. Or you. So don't feel bad."

"Was it something to do with Will?"

"Maybe." She wriggled. "I don't find him easy to get on with."

"That's because he's not," I said, thinking of the prickly conversations we'd been having, the apparently endless potential for giving offense.

"You seem to manage."

"What does that mean?" There had been a definite under-tone to Darcy's remark.

"Just that you seemed to be getting on well when I walked up Fore Street on my way home. You were sitting in the window. Ring any bells?"

"He was fixing Brenda's hands."

"Oh. It looked very cozy."

"We were just talking."

"Right."

"Darcy, do you like Will or something?"

She reacted as if the suggestion was an insult. "Totally the opposite. I would never go near Will Henderson. Not for anything."

From what I had observed, Darcy was never understated about how she felt, but there was something particularly venomous about the way she spoke that shocked me. "Don't hold back, will you?"

She crawled to the top of the bed and curled up against the pillows. "I'm sorry if it upsets you, but it's true. Don't waste your time with him, Jess."

"He said something similar about you. Why don't you like each other?"

Darcy sighed. "It's not a new development. We've never got on. Freya used to say we were like the bad angel and the good angel, sitting on her shoulders, trying to persuade her to do what we said."

"Who was bad and who was good?"

"Depends who you're asking. We always seemed to be pulling in different directions. He's not my kind of person. Too serious."

"Is that it? He's too serious?"

"Sort of." She fiddled with the hem of her skirt. "I don't like being judged. I don't like it when people look down on me just because I like frivolous things like fashion and shoes."

"He's a boy. When it comes to shoes, he's not going to see the point, Darcy."

"Yeah. Well."

"It seems like there's more to it than that, though." Will's warning to me didn't really fit with Darcy liking fashion too much, but I couldn't bring myself to tell her what he'd said.

"Will Henderson has a real problem with being popular. As in, he isn't, and he didn't want Freya to be popular either. He wanted to keep her to himself." She sounded bitter.

"Why isn't he popular?"

"The policeman's son?" Darcy laughed. "This is a small town, Jess. It's hard enough to keep a secret without involving the cops."

"That's stupid. I doubt he runs to his dad with every bit of gossip that comes his way." I was thinking of the look on Will's face when his father was systematically humiliating him in the shop. I was pretty sure their relationship was the opposite of close. "Why would he tell tales on his friends?"

"He's done it in the past."

"What do you mean?"

But that was as far as Darcy was prepared to go. "It's an old story and I don't know what really happened. But he got a reputation for talking out of turn and it means no one trusts him. He's a total outcast. You can't be friends with him and be popular. It's as simple as that. So he's got no mates at all."

"That's so sad. I thought he was just a loner." I was trying to imagine growing up in a small town without friends, without the possibility of making friends. It would be worse because there was nowhere to hide. Suddenly London didn't seem so bad.

"He wouldn't want your pity. He told Freya he didn't care." And Darcy was happy to take that at face value, because it suited her to believe it.

"Freya was his friend. Didn't she care about being popular either?"

"No." Darcy shrugged. "She was always loyal to the people she loved. And being Freya, she kind of got away with it. She didn't really notice that people treated Will like an outsider. She just assumed everyone would like him as she did, and no one really had the heart to tell her to cut him off."

"Except you." There was something in the way Darcy's eyes wouldn't meet mine as she spoke that told me she had been quite OK with stabbing him in the back.

"So what? Freya needed to live in the real world. Ryan really liked her. It was her opportunity to get in with his gang, and she didn't take it, for really stupid reasons."

Which meant that Darcy had missed out, I thought. Being friends with Freya doomed her to social exile too. It was easy to see what had motivated her to try to separate Will and Freya. I had a problem with her reasoning, though.

"Hold on. If she'd liked Ryan, Natasha would have skinned her alive. She'd never have forgiven her. I'd have thought that was the quickest way to become an untouchable."

Darcy shook her head. "Natasha would have had to live with it. Obviously she's crazy about Ryan but it's more important to her to be in the gang than to keep him to herself. She wouldn't have liked it, but she'd have pinned her hopes on Ryan getting bored with Freya. He'd have come back to her eventually."

"You sound very confident of that."

"Ryan and Natasha are meant to be together. They're made for each other."

And Darcy was now a fully paid-up member of Natasha's fan club. They were Natasha's words she was parroting.

"You know, I'm with Freya. If being popular means hanging around with Natasha and her idiot friends, I'd prefer social death, thanks."

"They're not that bad. I like them."

"You're pretty friendly with them now, aren't you? Now that Freya's gone."

She stiffened. "What's that supposed to mean?"

"Nothing." I was genuinely surprised by her reaction. "Just that things have changed for you since Freya died. What did you think I meant?"

"I don't know." She looked confused. "I thought you were trying to say that my life is better now than it was. Because Freya's dead."

"That wasn't it at all." I looked at her curiously. "But is that what you think? Even though you don't want to admit it?"

"Don't be stupid." She had gone red. It was nice to see someone else succumb to the Blushing of Truth that was my speciality, but I was sorry to see it all the same. I liked Darcy—she was fun to be around—but I was starting to see Will's point of view. I didn't trust her either.

I left Darcy's house with a stinking headache and resolved not to think about or talk about Freya for a few hours. Even if I hadn't needed a break from puzzling about what had led to her death, there was something else I wanted to do with my afternoon. The tricky part was persuading Mum she really wanted to go for a walk through town, all the way down memory lane, to run through the little anecdotes she'd never shared with me about growing up in Port Sentinel.

"I don't like not knowing anything about you. People keep assuming I've heard all about them and how you knew them and I don't have a clue."

"You'll pick it up. You don't need me to help." Mum was sitting on the sofa in the holiday cottage, editing pictures on her laptop. She had been out on her own, taking photographs in the countryside around Port Sentinel. Soft-eyed cows featured heavily, as did close-ups of weathered posts, rusting water troughs, and delicate greenery. I sat on the arm of the sofa and looked over her shoulder as she flicked through the images. Cow. Cow. Tree. Water in a ditch. Flowers. Cow. A rogue donkey to keep things interesting. Cow. It was all totally fascinating. I wanted to suggest that maybe later on we could watch the mud dry on her wellies to round off the day's entertainment, but I managed to bite my tongue.

"The thing is, I'd like you to tell me about what it was like growing up here." I kicked the sofa with my heel, making her jump. "What's the point in us coming down here together for the first time if you spend your time hiding here or at Sandhayes and never spend any time with me?"

"I thought you'd be too busy with your job. And you've been getting to know your cousins. You've been making friends. I don't want to get in your way."

"It's not getting in my way to talk to me," I pointed out. "It would even be a help. I can understand you not wanting to go into too much detail, but I'd really like it if you could just tell me why you left Port Sentinel and decided you'd never talk about it again. It's like something really bad happened and you were too traumatized to let yourself confront it until now."

She laughed. "You're so dramatic, Jess. Everything is life or death. It wasn't a big deal."

"So why won't you talk about it?"

"Because there's nothing to say. I met your father when he was down here visiting a friend. He was living in London. We had a long-distance relationship for a while. Then I moved to London. He didn't get on with the family and it was easier to stay away than drag him down here to be disapproved of. He asked me to marry him and I said yes. Then you were born and I was too busy with you to think about anything else. The end." She snapped her laptop closed. "Sorry if it's too boring for you."

"It's not boring. I just think it's incomplete." Will wouldn't have told me to ask her about it if it was that straightforward. And I was very, very worried that the reason he knew what had happened was because it involved his father, Inspector Prince of Darkness himself.

Mum laughed. "You wish it was more complicated than it is because you love secrets."

"That's not true."

"Of course it is. You look for them everywhere."

And find them, Mother dearest.

She leaned over and patted my head. "I'm not hiding here, by the way. I will come for a walk with you through town, in public, in daylight, and I will tell you whatever you want to know. Happy?"

"Ecstatic."

And I *was* pleased. She was acting like herself again, instead of the edgy, withdrawn version of my mother I'd been worrying about since our arrival. We walked down into town, shoulder to shoulder, and for a while it was how I had imagined our holiday would be. She told me a few stories along the way, about Susan Shefflin and how Mum pushed her off a wall—in fun, she insisted—and broke her arm. That led into a story about the first date she ever had, with a boy named Keith who took her to the seafront and bought her an ice cream.

"Did you kiss him?" I wanted to know.

"Ugh. No. He'd been eating chocolate ice cream and it was all over his mouth like lipstick. And there were far too many people watching. It was a Saturday lunchtime in high summer. My dad wouldn't let me go out at night, which I thought was very unfair at the time."

"How old were you?"

She thought for a second. "Fourteen."

"Did Keith try to kiss you?"

"He did. I was so appalled I dropped my ice cream in the sand."

"That doesn't sound very romantic."

"It was a massive disappointment, for him and for me. I was sad about the ice cream. He was mortified about the kiss. But as first dates go, it wasn't what I'd dreamed about, that's for sure."

"Did you go on any other dates with him?"

Mum laughed. "One was enough. I only went because I was so surprised to be asked."

"And you didn't want to hurt his feelings."

"That too. How did you know?"

"You haven't changed much. You like to make people happy."

"It's not always a good thing." Suddenly serious, she said, "You have to be true to yourself, Jess. Don't do what other people want you to do if it's not what you would have done anyway."

"Words to live by," I said lightly.

"They are."

"OK." I nudged her affectionately. "You've done your mothering bit for the day."

"You probably didn't need me to tell you to be yourself. You're far more self-possessed than I ever was."

"So you say. Not always when it counts, though." I was thinking about Ryan, and how unsettling it was to be on the receiving end of his attentions. He had answers for everything and most of them were designed to make me blush. Which they did. I wasn't used to being a target for someone that attractive. I couldn't quite believe he was really interested in me. Two things had occurred to me: he was using me to annoy Natasha, or he was flirting to distract me from asking questions about Freya. And why would he want to distract me unless there was something he didn't want me to know? The only time I'd seen him lose his self-assurance was up on the headland. I didn't like seeing him so rattled; I wasn't comfortable with what that suggested to me. He'd been shivering like a frightened dog. That strong a reaction made me think that Ryan knew what had happened to Freya because someone who'd been there told him. Or, which was infinitely worse, because he'd been there himself.

Either way, I needed to ask him about it again, and I really didn't want to put myself in the path of his steamroller charm, especially if he was hiding something truly dark behind the handsome face, the eyes as blue as the deep sea. Nor did I want any more reasons for Natasha to hate me.

And I was thinking about Freya again, I realized. Almost at random, I asked, "Who else did you date?"

"Oh, a few people," Mum said vaguely. "I can't remember all of them. I must be getting old."

"You must be able to remember some of them. Was there anyone special?" *Like Dan Henderson.* I was afraid for a second I'd said his name out loud.

"There really wasn't anyone in particular. Not until your father turned up."

"Really?"

"You sound disappointed."

Yeah, it's always a disappointment when you think your mother's lying to you.

"Not disappointed. Just surprised."

"I was only eighteen when I met him," she reminded me.

"That leaves plenty of time to have a proper boyfriend. Years."

"Well, I didn't."

"Was there anyone who liked you? Or someone you liked?"

"Probably." Mum stopped and stared at me. "What's up, Jess? Why so interested in my love life?"

"I don't know." I wriggled. "Just . . . I just wondered, that's all."

"Wondered what?" Her voice was sharp.

"Wondered if you left someone behind when you ran away to London."

She gave a tiny gasp, as if I'd hit her. "Where did you—? Who have you been talking to?"

"Am I right?"

Instead of answering, she gave me a long doubtful look that answered my question. And although I was pretty sure she wouldn't tell me anything else, I didn't need her to. I could work out the rest for myself from the expression on her face when someone across the street called her name.

"Molly!"

I didn't need to look round but I did anyway—Dan Henderson, closing fast. He was smiling and the resemblance to his son was jarring. He came a little bit too close before he stopped, and he stared at Mum as if he was trying to memorize every detail of her face. I had to resist the urge to jump in front of her.

"Molly Cole. It's been a while."

"It has." She looked dazed, but she rallied. "Less of the Cole, though. I still go by Tennant."

"I thought you were divorced."

"That's right." She gave him a smile that didn't reach her eyes and didn't say anything else. I felt like cheering.

"Where have you been hiding? You've been here for a few days, I gather."

"I've been around."

"No, you haven't. I've been looking for you." Dan said it gently, though, and Mum blushed.

"It's taken me a little time to get used to being back."

"But now you're at home."

"Not quite. It's still strange, being here."

"It hasn't changed. Nothing changes."

"I don't think that's true. Time makes a difference to everything."

"Not to everything. Some things stay the same." His voice was heavy with meaning and Mum blushed again, obviously knowing exactly what he meant.

Oh, please don't talk about this in front of me. I wanted to know what had happened, but I didn't want to be a spectator at their reunion if I could avoid it. I coughed and the two of them looked at me as if they'd forgotten my existence up to that point. "Hi."

"Oh, sorry. This is Jess, Dan. My daughter."

"I know. I met her this morning." He frowned at me and I could tell what he was thinking. *You didn't tell her.* I was so busted.

"We were just going for a walk," I said. *And so, good-bye.*

Dan was back to staring at Mum. "Why don't you come for a walk with me instead, Molly?"

Mum looked terrified. "I couldn't take you away from your work."

"It's OK. I'm not busy."

I cut across Mum, who was starting to wibble. "Yeah, but this is sort of a mother–daughter thing we've been planning."

Dan glared and I could have sworn the temperature dropped to Siberian levels. "How old are you, Jess?"

"Sixteen."

"Right. Well, you've had sixteen years to do mother–daughter things. I haven't seen Molly for even longer than that. So I think that means I get to decide what happens here, and I'm afraid it doesn't include you. Your mum and I have a lot of catching up to do."

"Dan, stop bullying her." Mum put her arm around my shoulders. "You don't get to decide what happens, actually. *I* do."

Dan looked as if he'd been sucker-punched by a rabbit with a mean left hook, which made it all the sweeter. *You weren't expecting that, were you?*

And then Mum turned to me.

"Jess, is it OK if we have our walk another time?"

"Sorry?" I wasn't being a smartass; I genuinely couldn't believe what I was hearing.

"I'd like to talk to Dan."

"What happened to doing what you want?" I hissed.

"This *is* what I want." Mum was still pink, but she looked determined too. Determined to get rid of me. "I haven't seen him for a long time and we need to get a few things straight."

I knew she was expecting me to kick off and ask what sort of things they needed to get straight, but I didn't. I knew already. It was in the way he looked at her, and the way she was holding herself, her arms wrapped around her body as if that was all that was keeping her in one piece. This was it—this was the serious relationship she'd been refusing to discuss a few minutes earlier. This was what had driven her into my father's arms. This was why I existed, if it came to that. And I didn't want to know any of the details. One of them had broken the other one's heart—that much was clear. I just couldn't tell who had done the damage.

"OK. That's fine," I lied. "We'll do it another time."

"Thank you, Jess."

"Don't thank me. I'm just respecting your choice."

Dan was grinning again, this time in triumph. It made me feel sick. I walked off, not really thinking about where I was going or why. I just wanted to get away from them. I must have walked right through the center of Port Sentinel but later I couldn't remember anything about it. Somehow, I found myself on the path that wound through the woods, panting as the steep hill punished my legs again. I came out into the sunshine on the exposed headland with the distinct feeling that I was in the right place. I stood with my hands on my hips, letting my heart slow down, taking in the glorious view. I hadn't planned it, but I'd ended up exactly where I needed to be.

Which was just about the worst place I could have picked. That whole thing about sensing I was walking into danger? Not a flicker. I didn't realize how stupid I'd been until it was far too late.

10

At first I didn't notice that there was anyone on the headland except me. Weirdly, although it had played a grim role in recent family history, I felt at ease there. It was something about the high ground, the sense of space, and air that no one else had breathed. I stared out to sea and saw nothing but endless distance. There was just peace. If I wanted to kill myself, I mused, I'd choose somewhere like that.

Kill myself?

And . . . breathe. The thought had come from nowhere, jarringly, and I became aware that I was shaking. It was the climb, I told myself. I was unfit and my muscles were complaining. It wasn't the ghostly presence of my dear dead cousin lurking behind me. I wasn't going to throw myself off the cliff either. Suicide was very far from my mind. As it had been from Freya's, I was increasingly sure. I hadn't heard one thing to make me think she was depressed when she died. There was no sign that she felt she couldn't carry on. And there was no note. Freya would have left an elaborate manuscript complete with illustrations and calligraphy if she'd been signing off for good and always. What I *had* discovered was that there were plenty of people who didn't want to talk about how Freya had died. If it was murder, I had a long list of suspects already.

I crossed to the bench and sat down, curling my legs under me. More deep breaths. I was enjoying the peace, I told myself. I was enjoying the solitude. I was glad Mum had ditched me in favor of her creepy old flame. It was easy to see where Will got his talent for upsetting me; it came naturally to both him and his father. It was the one thing they seemed to have in common—apart from their looks, obviously. Mum had pretty shocking taste in men if you were talking personalities, but she knew how to pick a looker.

The gorse bushes smelled sweet in the warm sunshine, their scent mingling with saltwater and pine trees and grass and dusty earth. Bottle it and you'd make a fortune. There was something else though; something sharper threading through the air. It was bittersweet, too faint to identify at first, but it grew stronger and more brackish as I sniffed the air. When I finally realized what it was, it was so banal and familiar a smell that I laughed. Someone was smoking nearby and the smoke had carried to where I sat. I hoped they weren't planning to finish their cigarette on the bench I was occupying. I could do without reeking of secondhand smoke. Mum was bound to think it was my latest gesture toward teen rebellion.

I still had a smile on my face when I turned round to see if I could identify the person who was invading my space, and discovered that yes, I could. The other thing I discovered was that the headland had been a really bad choice. It was a dead end, for starters. I had nowhere to go to get away, and that was all I wanted to do, because Natasha Watkins was striding toward me on pipe-cleaner-thin legs clad in spray-on pink denim, her heels digging divots out of the dusty ground. She was flanked by her two friends, who were dressed in much the same uniform, and all three had huge sunglasses hiding their eyes. What I could see of their faces was not encouraging. The cigarette smoke came from the taller one—Claudia, if I remembered rightly. The smaller one, the one who'd seen me on Fore Street, didn't look happy to be there, but that could have been the difficulty she was having balancing on her narrow heels. She didn't look like a natural stiletto-wearer. She was too athletic for that.

As if they'd rehearsed it, they split up, Claudia going to one end of the bench and her mate to the other. Natasha came and stood in front, between me and the sea. I didn't like being boxed in like that—not one bit—but I wasn't scared. Not yet.

"I've been looking for you." From the tone of Natasha's voice, it wasn't because she wanted us to be besties. "I thought I warned you to stay away from Ryan."

"Yeah, you did warn me."

"So what happened?"

"I decided to ignore your warning and take the consequences." I crossed my legs and folded my arms. *Two can play the body-language game.* "So what's it going to be? A fight? Or are you going to glare me to death?"

Natasha's nostrils flared, which I assumed was a genuine and involuntary reaction to being very annoyed. She would never have done it if she'd seen how it looked. "I could get really tired of your attitude."

"Well, that's one thing we've got in common. Two things, if you count Ryan."

"Don't." It wasn't Natasha who had spoken; it was the smaller girl. I realized I didn't know her name.

"Don't what? Provoke her?" I laughed. "Sorry. I'm not scared of any of you. I've been more frightened on a funfair ghost train."

"You should be trying to make friends here. Not enemies," Claudia said. She was all legs and tumbling brown hair but nature had given her a proper horseface to offset them. She was holding her cigarette away from her body, as if she wasn't quite sure what to do with it.

"I'm sorry?"

"You'll regret it if you piss us off. It's no fun being on the outside."

I raised my eyebrows. "You mean it's better to be in the pack? Regardless of what you have to do to stay in it?"

The other girl flinched. "What do you mean?"

"I mean that I like to makeup my own mind about things. I'm pretty comfortable with being on the outside if it means I can be my own person." I shaded my eyes so I could see Natasha's face more clearly. "You're going to need a new threat, Tash. Tempting though you obviously think it is, I don't want to be your friend. I've got friends."

"Not here, you don't," Claudia said.

It was stupid to mind, but I did, and I couldn't stop myself from replying. "Actually, I do have friends here."

"Friends? Like Darcy?" The other one laughed. "You wait and see. She'll drop you in a second if Nats clicks her fingers."

"Coco," Natasha said. "Shut up."

I sat up at that. "Don't shut up, Coco. Tell me more about Darcy."

Coco looked at Natasha nervously. "Um. Nothing, really. Just that she wants to be in with Nats so you can't count on her backing you up."

"Is that what happened with Freya?"

"It came down to choosing a side. Darcy chose us," Natasha said, very calm although I had seen her react to Freya's name with a tremor that ran through her skinny frame.

"Darcy chose you. What did that mean for Freya?"

"Darcy left her to fight her own battles."

"Like what?"

"Like the bad things that happened to her because she wouldn't leave Ryan alone."

I allowed myself a proper eye-roll. "Oh, for God's sake. He's not all that, Natasha. You need to get out more."

"We're meant to be together," she snapped—and just like that, I lost my temper.

"No, you're not. Let me help you with this one, because I have a feeling your favorite book features romance with the beautiful undead and it's rotted your mind. You're not star-crossed lovers. You're not battling through adversity to seal your immortal pact. You're just really desperate to hang onto a boyfriend who was never that committed to you in the first place, and it's making you behave like a lunatic."

Natasha swore at me and I almost forgot to be annoyed with her, I was so impressed with the vocabulary she had at her disposal. When she paused for breath, I grinned.

"Proving my point."

"You smug bitch. I bet you wouldn't be so smug if you knew—" She broke off.

"Knew what?"

"Knew how your cousin got her haircut. She wasn't so pretty when I was finished with her." She'd recovered enough to smirk. Coco shifted uneasily; I had the impression she'd thought Natasha was going to say something else.

"That was you, was it?" I wasn't actually surprised. It was Natasha's logic all over. *Ryan likes long hair. Ryan likes you. If you have short hair, Ryan won't like you any more.* Basic, stupid, dangerous. She wouldn't change. I was quite happy with my hair as it was, and sweet reason wasn't going to put her off. I stood up, enjoying the fact that I was still taller than her in trainers, despite her high heels. "Well, try it on me and I'll have you done for assault. That's if you can cut my hair. I don't mind a fight and I don't have any problem with hitting to hurt."

"Mm. Freya wasn't keen on having her hair cut either. But the odds are against you if you're on your own."

"Listen, Tash. I gather you're trying to make me feel intimidated. Let me save you the trouble. I'm not interested in Ryan."

"That doesn't matter."

"It doesn't?"

"No, it doesn't. What matters is if he likes you."

"I can't stop him from liking me. Not that he does, I'm sure."

"I *saw* you yesterday. He was *groping* you." She was vibrating with anger. I almost felt sorry for her.

"Don't you think you were supposed to see it? He's messing with your head. It's easy to keep you keen by flirting with me."

"You don't know him. He's not like that."

"Really? Maybe you're too close to see what he's doing." I took a step nearer her. "Let me tell you what I think. You spend your time with your friends talking about him and why he hasn't called you today, or what his last text meant, or why he tweeted that thing about Rihanna's latest video. If he mentions he likes you in pink, you go shopping and buy every shade from bubblegum through to fuchsia. You spend weeks planning for his birthday or Christmas present and he gives you something random or nothing at all. He laughs at the messages you send him and shows them to his mates. He's probably got nude pictures of you on his phone and so do half the male teenagers in the southwest because that kind of thing gets passed on pretty quickly. He knows exactly how to freak you out, and sometimes he'll say something about you putting on weight to see how long it will take before you eat again. He looks at other girls, he flirts with other girls, and he won't commit to a proper relationship, but you'd still die if he went off with someone else because you are thoroughly and completely in his power. So I'm sorry, I don't see why I should be scared of you when you don't even have the sense to see you're being played."

"Shut up. You're wrong."

I glanced at Claudia and Coco. "From the looks on their faces, I'm on the money."

"You don't know anything," Claudia said. "You should be scared."

"Of you?" I pointed at Natasha. "Of *her*?"

"You do know what happened here, don't you?"

Claudia had finished her cigarette and now she was clawing at the packet to take out another, her hands shaking as she put it in her mouth. I looked from her to Coco and then straight at Natasha, trying to read the expressions on their faces. Defiance, mainly, but there was a strange undertone of fear. I needed to tread carefully. Literally, looking at the edge of the cliff, which was all too close.

"I know Freya fell here. Do you know how it happened?"

Instead of answering, Claudia looked at Natasha, who glowered.

"You've said enough, Claude. Don't tell her anything else."

"Yes, trot along, Claude. Time to get back to your stable." It was rude but I was fed up with the three of them.

"You don't get to talk to her like that," Natasha said. She took a step closer to me and her face was white. "You don't get to talk to me like that."

"Nats . . ." Coco was looking terrified.

"I'll show you how scared you should be." Before I could move, Natasha shot out a hand and grabbed a handful of my hair.

"What are you doing?" I'd never felt less like laughing, but I managed it. "Don't tell me you brought your scissors on the off-chance you'd get to use them."

"Come on." She yanked on the hair she was holding and I couldn't help it: I stumbled toward her. It felt as if the whole lot was going to come out. She tugged again. "This way, bitch. Walkies."

"Let go." I was holding onto my hair. With my other hand

I dug my nails into her skin, but it had zero effect. I kept them short—useless for self-defense—but even if they'd been talons she wouldn't have noticed. Her face was white, her lips bloodless. I'd read about mad people being able to perform incredible feats of strength, and Natasha certainly looked insane. "Get off me."

She pulled as hard as she could, leaning back, and I took another two steps. It was like being in a nightmare—nothing I did or said made any difference to her. I was vaguely aware that Coco and Claudia had moved to stand together, a little way off. They weren't joining in but they weren't trying to stop her either, and I wondered if they were as surprised as me at how strong Natasha seemed to be. I also wondered if they knew what she intended to do. The direction she was taking made me think it wasn't going to be something I'd like, because we were moving toward the edge of the cliff, step by miserable step.

"What are you doing?"

"I want you to see what you should be scared of. I want you to see what Freya saw."

"I thought it was nighttime when she died. Shouldn't we wait until after dark?" My smart mouth was going to get me killed, I thought. Really, genuinely dead. I should be begging her to let go, pleading with her, groveling so she could see I was completely in her power, but something in me wouldn't give in. Pride, probably. Which was stupid. She wasn't stopping and the edge of the cliff was getting closer. Apparently Natasha wasn't as scared of heights as I was. Or she was too angry to care. Or she was straightforward crazy. Whatever the reason, she didn't seem to be anything like as worried as I thought she should be. The ground sloped a little, which didn't help. Unless someone came to the rescue in the next five seconds, I was going to be in serious danger. Scared? I'd have been stupid not to be.

Four and a half seconds later, to my eternal relief, the cavalry showed up.

"Let her go."

It was a male voice, deep and authoritative, and I felt Natasha's grip slacken for a second as she turned to see who it was. With one part of my brain I recognized Will, thanked God for his very existence, regretted ever having disliked him, and hoped he had a plan—more or less all at the same time. The rest of my mind was focused on escape, apart from the bit that was wondering whether I'd smash myself to bits on the way down the cliff or just drown when I got to the bottom. I twisted away from Natasha, trying to break free while she was distracted, but I couldn't quite manage it. My feet slipped on the loose earth and I heard pebbles and sand rattling over the edge, falling all the way to the sea. I couldn't hear them splash into the water, but it was a long way down.

"Natasha. Seriously. Give it a rest." Will sounded bored if anything, but he was moving quickly as he came toward us.

She didn't reply, but she waited until he was a few paces away and shoved me, hard, as she let go of my hair. I was completely off balance with no hope of recovering before I fell. There was a horrible, sick moment when I didn't know if I'd land on solid ground or fall into space, and even when I found myself sprawling on the dusty earth at Will's feet I was terrified I might still slide down the slope and over the edge, far beyond help or rescue. I dug my fingers in and pressed my face against the grit. I think I was probably praying.

Will completely ignored me. "What exactly is it that you're trying to achieve?"

"I want her to be scared."

"I'd say you've succeeded."

"I have, haven't I?" From her voice, Natasha was exceedingly pleased with herself.

Somewhere in the distance, I heard the unmistakable sound of throwing up. I was still lying on the ground, trembling, but I risked putting my head up after a few seconds to see Coco wiping her mouth, looking ashamed. I felt very slightly better. I might be lying in the dirt but at least I hadn't vomited. Or peed myself. Or . . . well, things could have been a lot worse.

Will's feet moved past me and I was vaguely irritated that he hadn't stopped to help me up. I was nowhere near ready to stand without assistance, but I was curious enough to lever myself up onto one elbow. He was between me and Natasha, and the sun was behind both of them so I couldn't see much for squinting.

"I think you're finished here. Time to go home."

"You don't tell me where to go, Will. You don't even talk to me. You're nothing," Natasha sneered.

"So I've heard. Go on. Start walking." He was keeping the same conversational tone in his voice, ignoring the jibes, as if he was used to not rising to the bait.

"What are you going to do if I don't? Call your dad and get him to arrest me?"

"I could. If Jess wanted to report you for assault, for instance."

Natasha didn't even glance at me. "She won't."

"Maybe not." He paused. "You should still go."

"Why are you on her side?"

"I'm not taking sides. I don't want to see either of you get hurt."

"Do I look like I'm in any danger?" She bent away from him, her whippy body angled so she was leaning over the edge. "What about now?"

"That looks more risky."

Abruptly, she straightened up. "This is boring. I can't understand why I'm talking to you and I can't understand what you're doing here. You've never seemed bothered about being a knight in shining armor before. What's different now?"

He didn't say anything.

"It's because you like her, isn't it?" She laughed. "Actually, it's perfect. Two losers together. I should have thought of it myself. Of course you'd want to impress the new girl in town. You've got a chance with her. Until she finds out the truth about you."

"That's really not it. Not at all." Will twisted to look at me but he was a shadow against the light, his face hidden. He turned back. "I'd say you won this round. Why don't you quit while you're ahead?"

"Come on, Nats. Let's just go." Claudia had an arm around Coco, who was still looking distinctly ropy.

"Fine." Natasha leaned close to Will, her chest practically touching his. She couldn't help herself. She was made to be a flirt. It still made me want to throw things at her. All I had to hand were bits of gravel, unfortunately, when what I wanted was more like a grenade.

"It's a shame you're such a goody-goody," Natasha purred. "You'll never know what you've been missing all these years."

"Herpes?" I suggested from my position in the dust. My voice was a croak but Natasha heard it. She pushed past Will and paused beside me for a kick that caught me full on the kneecap. I hadn't been expecting it and I grabbed onto my leg, holding it, as if that would help. The pain was too agonizing to scream, or swear. All I could do was bite my lip, turn my face into the dust again, and wish I had the ability to restrain myself from making smartass comments.

By the time I was able to take notice of what was going on, Natasha had disappeared down the path. Claudia and Coco were following, moving more slowly. Coco glanced back as I watched. No smile, no wave, no "Let's be friends." Just a stare that was hostile and—what?—worried, maybe. As if something was bothering her and it was my fault. Was she embarrassed about throwing up? Upset that Natasha had gone so thoroughly loco? Whatever it was, I had the impression she wished I'd just roll off the edge and save them all a lot of trouble.

"Was it worth it?" Will sounded interested. He came and stood with one foot on either side of me, holding out his hand. I took it and he pulled me up. I was nose to nose with him when I got to vertical. There were worse places to be. Like splattered all over a rocky outcrop at the foot of a cliff.

"Not completely worth it, no." I was still holding his hand and I leaned forward, peering over the edge. "Dear God, that's a long drop."

"Do I dare ask why she was trying to push you over the edge?"

"I upset her."

"Evidently."

"I attracted the attention of her on-off boyfriend. He must have a thing for blondes." I was still staring at the sea, hypnotized as it surged in and crept up the rock face, a little further every time, then slid away again.

"Do you mean Ryan?" Will pulled me back, away from the cliff, and gave me a little shove in the direction of the bench. "Sit down before you get into any more trouble. What does Ryan want with you?"

"He wants to do naughty things," I said primly. "At least, he wants Natasha to think that. I get the impression they have a stormy relationship."

"I believe that's true."

I pounced. "You don't know?"

"Neither of them really confides in me."

"I've been hearing you're the cat that walks by himself."

"Have you." It wasn't a question; his voice was flat. He might as well have said *I don't want to talk about it.*

I really have never learned when to say nothing. "Yeah, apparently you've got highly contagious social leprosy. I'm risking my status just sitting here with you."

"It won't kill you," he said dryly. "Falling off the cliff might have done it."

"Might have? I don't think it's a maybe. No one could survive it."

"That's not necessarily the case."

"What do you mean?"

Will shook his head. "Don't change the subject. Go back to my embarrassing social condition. Who's been talking about it? Darcy?"

"Good guess."

"I can also guess she wasn't very nice about me." The gray eyes were fixed on the horizon.

"She said some nice things."

"Like?"

"Like you were a good friend to Freya."

"She doesn't think that. And she'd be wrong if she did."

"You sound bitter." I was staring at the side of his face, trying to read his expression and failing.

"No, that would be guilt."

"Why?"

"Lots of reasons."

"Details, please."

"Some other time," he said.

"There's no time like now."

"Leave it alone. Leave the whole thing alone." Will turned to me and his eyes were dark and narrowed in anger. "You don't know when to stop, do you? You push people too far, Jess, and it's going to get you hurt."

"Is that what happened to Freya?"

"You're nothing like her. I told you that the first time I met you."

"I remember," I said softly.

"Natasha isn't someone you can push around. She's vicious. If she was a dog, you'd never walk her without a muzzle."

"Do you think she was just trying to scare me?" I was aiming for casual but the tremor in my voice was a giveaway.

"Probably. But she's not in control of that temper. Her dad's something big in banking but her parents split up years ago. She's spoiled rotten. She never sees him—just sends him requests for money or clothes or jewelry. Her mum's exactly like her except she doesn't keep to one man. Far from it, in fact."

"You're almost making me feel sorry for her," I said. "But not quite."

"You don't have to like her, but stay away from her. Seriously, Jess. It's too dangerous."

"I'm not scared of Natasha Watkins. She caught me off guard. Next time, I'll be ready for her."

"You're not listening. There can't be a next time. I might not be around next time." Will was actually losing his temper, which was good, because so was I.

"Look, I didn't plan it. She came and found me here."

"And you didn't provoke her into attacking you."

"I'm not going to let her bully me. Anyway, it wouldn't have mattered what I said. She was determined to pick a fight with me."

"Oh, right. None of it was your fault. I see that now."

I sighed. "Look, I really was minding my own business. I like it up here and I came up when—" *When my mum dumped me for a hot date with your dad.* "I came up when I had nowhere else to be. Natasha and her mates turned up unexpectedly. If it had been up to me, I would have picked somewhere less isolated for our little chat. Somewhere less high. But I wasn't expecting her to get so punchy."

"She's more than capable." Will leaned forward, his elbows on his knees, and went back to staring out to sea. "I know there's no reason for you to listen to me, but I think you need to start being more careful. I don't think you should come up here on your own."

"In case Natasha comes back?"

"In case Freya was killed." The last word hung in the silence for a second, a short, brutal syllable. I swallowed, and Will went on. "Hasn't it occurred to you that if she was murdered, the person who did it might want you to stop dragging it all up again?" He looked back at me, his face grave. "Hasn't it occurred to you they might be willing to kill again?"

"*If* she was killed."

"That's what you believe, though, isn't it?"

"And what do you believe?"

"I don't know."

"No one knows anything. But I do know that I've learned a lot just by hanging around up here."

"Stubborn."

"Determined," I countered. "I'm going to find out the truth."

"And you have every confidence in your abilities," Will said sarcastically, and somehow I couldn't lie to him.

"If you really want to know the truth, I don't have a clue."

He raised his eyebrows, looking amused more than angry. "Really?"

"I'm just getting more and more confused." I laughed. "I need to get all my suspects to come up here and explain themselves."

"You've got as far as having suspects? That's a start. Who's on the list?"

"Natasha, with or without her friends." I was thinking about

Coco's pallor, and her fear. "Darcy's not off the hook. Ryan, obviously. Then there's the guy Ryan said she said she liked, if I knew who he was. And—" I broke off.

"Go on."

There was no way out of it. I took a deep breath. "Well, since you ask . . . there's you."

11

As soon as I'd said it I regretted it; I'd have taken the words back if I could. But it was the truth. I risked a look at Suspect Number Six, who didn't look remotely perturbed.

"I thought so."

"Is that it? That's all you've got to say?"

Will shrugged. "What should I say?"

"What about trying to persuade me I'm wrong?" I pulled my feet up onto the bench and turned to face him, my arms wrapped around my knees. "What about asking me why I put you on the list in the first place?"

"Actually, I *would* like to know." He wouldn't meet my eyes, staring at a completely uninteresting bit of ground instead.

"You're obviously feeling guilty about something to do with Freya—you said so yourself. And you were close to her at one time." I was getting into potentially awkward territory but I carried on, focused on finding out what had happened between them. "You could have been jealous of her and Ryan, or her and the mystery boyfriend. If it wasn't you."

"Not me. I suppose it's possible I might have been jealous." From Will's tone of voice the idea amused him and I couldn't tell why.

"You got shut out, didn't you? That's why you stopped coming to the house. You couldn't be around her any more."

He slid down with his back against the bench, his hands in the pockets of his jeans. He looked completely relaxed, and only the rapid rhythm he was tapping with one foot told me he was in any way bothered by the turn our conversation had taken.

"I did stop coming to Sandhayes before Freya died, and it *was* to do with her. But it wasn't that she'd turned me down."

"Let me guess. It was the other way round."

He glanced at me. "You wouldn't believe that?"

"No. I would. I mean—obviously. Of course." Of course he was handsome enough to have anyone fall for him, and from a height. And the emotional damage would be roughly similar to what would happen to your body if you stepped off the cliff, I thought.

"I don't like talking about it because Freya's not here to tell her side of the story and my side sounds—" Will broke off and shook his head.

"I'll give you a pass on being big-headed, if you like. Just tell me what she said and what you said."

"No."

I raised my eyebrows.

"Not in detail, anyway," he said. "I'm not going to betray her trust."

"I get the picture. You're a gentleman. That's fair enough." But it wasn't enough to make me drop the subject. "Paraphrase it."

He took a deep breath. "Right. Well, a few months before she died, Freya made it clear to me that she liked me."

"She told you?"

"Not in so many words. And I'm not going into detail about it."

And if I pushed him, he would leave. "What happened next?"

"I . . . didn't feel the same way."

"Did you tell her that?"

"Of course."

"Was she upset?"

"Yes. Initially. And a bit embarrassed, even though I didn't think she should mind. It didn't really change things between us, as far as I was concerned."

"Come off it. You must know it doesn't work that way. Once something like that is out in the open, you can't ignore it."

Will raised his eyebrows. "Speaking from personal experience?"

"Speaking realistically."

"Well, I disagree. I don't think it would have made a difference. It didn't bother me that she liked me—I was flattered, if anything. I just didn't feel the same way. She was more like a sister than a potential girlfriend."

I winced. "Did you say that to her?"

"Might have."

"Ouch."

"It was true." He sounded defensive for the first time.

"Yeah, but it's not exactly good news if you like someone. A lot, presumably, or she wouldn't have risked the humiliation of being turned down."

"I didn't take it lightly. I just couldn't pretend I felt the same way. And it was kinder to tell her that, I thought, so everyone knew where they stood."

"Sometimes people don't want to know where they stand, though. Living in hope is a lot less brutal than knowing you don't have a chance."

"Again, personal experience?"

"None of your business," I said firmly.

"Yeah, well, being honest didn't work out as I'd planned, so maybe you're right."

"Presumably that's when you stopped going round to the house."

"Nope. Though maybe I should have." Will saw the look of surprise on my face. "It was a bit awkward at first, but Freya was more upset about that than she was about me turning her down. She said her mum would never forgive her if she was responsible for pushing me out."

"Tilly has basically adopted you, hasn't she? Why is that?"

He shook his head. "That's another conversation."

"The man of mystery strikes again. You see why you ended up on the list of suspects? You never give me a straight answer."

"I'm not going to tell you about it now because it's got nothing to do with Freya and I don't want to get sidetracked. As for straight answers, I'm being honest with you, I promise." His eyes were steady and I looked away before he did.

"Get back to Freya, then. You did stay away, so something else must have happened."

"It was a couple of weeks before she died. Freya asked me if I was the one who'd been sending her messages—the mystery man you're trying to track down too. Freya didn't know who it was either. At least, not at first. But she didn't spend too much time thinking about it because she assumed it was me."

"Why did she think that?"

"I don't know. The things he said and the way he said them, according to her. I thought at the time it was just that she read what he sent her as if it had come from me because she still hoped we might get together."

I didn't say anything—too busy considering what he'd said—and he shifted uneasily beside me.

"I knew I was going to end up sounding like an arrogant twat."

"Don't be silly. You're just telling me what happened. If that's the truth of it, that's what you've got to say. She still liked you and the messages made her think you were starting to feel the same way."

"I had to tell her again that I didn't fancy her, which was worse than the first time—weird, that, because you'd have thought it would be easier second time round."

"Oh no," I said seriously. "Much worse. You can't let someone down gently twice in a row. It's kicking her when she's down but you're wearing steel-capped boots. And you stepped in dog dirt just before you started kicking."

"That's more or less how it felt."

"Why wouldn't you just have told her you'd changed your mind? Why would you bother with anonymous messages?"

"No idea. Maybe she thought I was shy."

"Yeah, but you're not."

"I don't know . . ." Will said slowly. "It's difficult, sometimes—getting up the nerve to tell someone how you feel about them. Especially if you're not sure what they'll say."

"But you knew she liked you."

"I wouldn't have been worried about telling Freya, if I'd liked her. It would be different with . . . someone else."

I blushed, aware that he was looking at me. It was very quiet up there on the headland, apart from the birds singing in the trees behind us and the waves rushing against the rocks below. Quiet enough that I could hear my heart thumping. Had he almost said "you" before he broke off? *Wishful thinking*, I told myself firmly, and struggled to find something intelligent to say.

"So you're saying it definitely wasn't you because you wouldn't have made a production out of telling her you liked her."

"Got it in one."

"And the reason you couldn't go to Sandhayes any more was because you were too embarrassed."

"No, the reason I couldn't go to Sandhayes any more was because I wasn't welcome."

"After turning her down again?"

"After I put my foot in it."

"What did you say?"

"I told her not to waste her time with someone who wasn't willing to tell her who they were."

"Sensible," I observed.

"You might think that. Freya didn't." Will looked grim. "She thought I was being condescending. *Patronizing* was the word she used, actually."

"I can sort of see where she was coming from. I wouldn't

have enjoyed being warned I was in danger of making a fool of myself."

"Yes, but she wasn't like you. She didn't have a cynical bone in her body."

"Whereas I'm a registered card-carrying skeptic."

"Exactly. She needed to be told. You'd have had more sense. You'd have been entitled to be peeved about getting a warning from me."

"Move on," I ordered. "Less about me. More about Freya. What did she tell you about the mystery boy?"

"Just that she'd had messages from him."

"Messages? As in e-mails or texts or what?"

"I don't know. I didn't see them."

"What did he say in them?"

"I don't know exactly. It was someone who knew her, she said. Someone who saw her regularly, because he mentioned things that had happened that he wouldn't have known about otherwise. She said he said he was in love with her and he was just waiting for the right moment to tell her. She said he was articulate and intelligent."

"And like you."

"Supposedly."

"So she wasn't impressed with your warning and . . . what? You had a fight?"

"She told me to stay away from her and the house so the guy, whoever he was, wouldn't be put off."

"In spite of Tilly."

"She was too cross with me to care about what her mum thought."

"And you just did what she asked?"

"I didn't know what else to do." Will looked troubled. "The thing is, I had the feeling something was off with this person who was sending her messages. It was too perfect. The only reason he had for not talking to her face to face was that it was complicated, apparently, and that made me think something weird was going on."

"Did you try to work out who it was who was contacting her? There can't have been that many possible candidates, and everyone seems to know everyone else in this place so you could have narrowed it down quite easily."

"No." He was looking uneasy again. "It was none of my business, as Freya made very clear. Besides, I know this is going to sound mean, but I couldn't shake the idea that she was making it all up as a way of making me jealous."

I sat back, surprised. "Was she like that?"

"I don't know. Maybe not. Don't say anything about it to Tilly. Or Hugo. They'd hate to think she'd have done anything like that. Especially given how it turned out."

"So what makes you say that she might have?"

"Because whoever he was, the guy never made an appearance. Not before she died, and not after. If he existed, he kept his grief to himself."

"Didn't Freya meet him?"

"I wouldn't know. You could ask Darcy, I suppose." Will sounded deeply unenthusiastic.

"I might do that. If she knows, she'll tell me."

"You sound very confident about that."

"She's incapable of keeping a secret. The girl talks and talks."

"Doesn't mean she's telling you the truth."

"Honestly, you should really get to know her better. She's not as bad as you seem to think she is."

"She's a herd animal. Everything she does is motivated by the desire to fit in. Even if she was willing to get to know me, I wouldn't bother." Will got up and walked a few paces away, suddenly restless. Over his shoulder he said, "You know she wouldn't talk to me anyway. Not in public, like this."

"Because there are so many people to see us sitting here."

"You wait. You'll be surprised. Everyone down there will know about it by sunset."

"Know about what? We're just talking."

"Yeah. That'll do."

"God. Not enough happens around here if that counts as news."

Will turned round to face me, his hands buried in his pockets. "Well, first of all, you're involved and you're interesting on two counts: your mum is a local but you're new in town. Then there's the fact that you're talking to me. No one talks to me." He said it without self-pity but the sadness of it cut me to the bone.

"Because of your dad's job."

"Who told you that? Darcy?"

I nodded.

"It's a bit because of that. And a bit because of other things."

"Darcy was vague on the details too."

"You were asking for the details and you're being rude about what passes for news around here?"

"I was interested," I said, willing myself not to look embarrassed. "And I still am. What did you do?"

"Originally?" He sighed. "It was a long time ago."

"But no one's willing to forget about it so it must have been a big deal."

"Yeah. You're going to be disappointed." Will stretched, then came back to sit down again. This time he sat on the back of the bench with his feet on the seat. I turned round and tucked my legs under me, looking up at him. Yes, he was incredibly handsome from that angle too. What a surprise. I made myself focus on what he was saying. "It's one of those things that's been turned into a big scandal but it wasn't, really. And now it's just a rule. *Don't talk to Will Henderson because he can't be trusted.* I bet no one remembers the details, not just Darcy."

"You obviously do."

"You're not going to give up until I tell you, are you?" I didn't have to answer; the look on my face was enough. "Right. Well, it goes back a while, like I said. I was ten. Just a little kid."

I tried and failed to imagine Will as a skinny ten-year-old.

"I had plenty of mates, but my best friend had moved away at the end of the school year and I missed him. There was a new boy in my class in September and we got on straight away. He was good at sport too and we started hanging around together, messing about. Kid stuff. The only thing he took seriously was tennis—he was properly good, a lot better than me. He spent hours practicing. I'd get bored but he'd keep going, hitting against the back wall of his house."

"That's how the top players get to be the best."

"He was shaping up that way, definitely." Will stared into the distance for a few moments. "Then this gang of older boys started to pick on us. Small things at first—pushing us off the pavement, or taking over the football pitch at the recreation ground even if we were there first. Something we did had pissed them off. Or we hadn't done anything, but they were bored and we made life more interesting."

"How much older were they?"

"Two years, maybe three. There was this one lad, Stevie, and he was obsessed with dogging us. He hated my dad with a passion. And he hated us too. He used to hang around smoking dope, making a nuisance of himself, trying to pick a fight. Petty things, mostly. Nothing we couldn't manage. Until Ryan lost his temper with him and shoved him off the harbor wall."

"Ryan? That's who your friend was?"

"Didn't I say?" Will looked amused. "Hard to believe, isn't it? Mr. Popular and me, hanging around together. Anyway, Stevie was on the large side and fat floats so he wasn't in any danger, but it was November and the sea was cold. Besides, it was a hell of a loss of face. Everyone in his gang saw it and they didn't rush to throw him a lifebelt—they were too busy laughing. The only way he was going to get his rep back was if he paid us back. He told Ryan he had to meet him after school one day so he could fight him. If Stevie won, he was going to break his arm."

"That's horrible."

"The worst thing was, Ryan was prepared to go through with it. He thought he had a chance at winning, which was laughable because Stevie was twice his weight and height. He knew he'd have to have the fight sooner or later because there was no way he'd keep out of Stevie's way long enough for the dust to settle. And he definitely didn't want to tell any grown-ups about it."

"But you did."

"I was having nightmares about it—waking up screaming. It was going to be the end of Ryan playing tennis, apart from anything else. And just the thought of Stevie breaking his bones deliberately." Will pulled a face. "It was the middle of the night before the fight was supposed to happen and I was crying in my sleep. My dad came to see what was wrong. He woke me and I told him. I was half asleep—I didn't even know what I was saying—but no one cares about that. I told on Stevie and his parents got told about what he was planning and he got excluded from school, permanently. In the end they sent him to boarding school to keep him away from the other kids who were a bad influence on him. Actually, he was the bad influence on them, but you couldn't expect his own parents to see that."

"Wasn't Ryan grateful to you?"

"For what? Two weeks later, Stevie's mates caught up with Ryan. He didn't put up a fight but they broke his arm any-way."

"Oh no."

Will nodded. "It wasn't nice. But Ryan wouldn't tell my dad who did it. He kept his mouth shut and got a lot of re-spect for it. He gave up playing tennis and he never spoke to me again."

"It wasn't your fault," I said hotly. "You didn't do anything wrong."

"I told. You don't tell." He shrugged. "It's not worth worrying about."

But I could imagine years of loneliness—years of having to pretend he didn't mind that no one talked to him or sat with him at lunchtime or picked him for their team—and the bleakness of it took my breath away.

"Don't you hate them?"

"Who?"

"Everyone else. It's a stupid reason to pick on you."

"You're telling me." Will glanced in my direction. "Don't get too worked up about it. I realized early on that I had a choice. I could mind a lot and run the risk of going a bit mental thinking about it, or I could make the most of people like the Leonards who didn't care about that sort of thing and forget about the idiots. I went for Option B."

"Easier said than done."

"Not really. I keep my head down at school and work instead of messing around, which is probably what I'd choose to do anyway. The only thing I missed out on was playing football and rugby. So I did cross-country and climbing instead."

The don't-care attitude was like armor plating and I wasn't going to be able to put a dent in it even if I didn't believe he was as laid-back about it as he pretended. The whole story made it a lot easier to understand Will's self-contained quality, and his loyalty to the Leonards. "I suppose I get why you're not too bothered about Darcy. But she's not a bad person."

"She's the definition of a bad friend."

"I thought that was you." I said it to tease him but he looked grim.

"Yeah. You could say that."

"Come off it, Will. It doesn't sound to me as if you have anything to be guilty about. Not about Ryan or Freya."

He didn't look at me and I had to lean forward to hear him. "What if she killed herself because I kept turning her down and making her jealous didn't work?"

"Unlikely."

"You didn't know her. She was emotional. Impulsive. She loved the idea of love and she read too many stories about it that ended badly."

I shook my head. "It wasn't dramatic enough for that. It wasn't a beautiful event. She pitched over the cliff on a summer night without leaving any kind of note, without showing any sign of being anything other than happy in the run-up to her death. There are only three possibilities: suicide, accident, or murder. I'm inclined to rule out the first one, so you're off the hook."

"Not necessarily."

"What do you mean?"

"You said accident. It might have been."

"Well, that wouldn't be your fault either." I was genuinely puzzled.

Will stood up and jumped off the bench, then held out his hand to me. "Do you trust me?"

"What?"

"Do you trust me enough to come to the edge with me? There's something I want to show you."

I put my hand in his, though strictly speaking I didn't need to hold it for the ten or so paces that took me to the edge of the cliff. His hand was warm and he held onto mine firmly but not too tightly. I could have wished the cliff were a lot further away. Not least because being back at the edge was an unwelcome reminder of what had happened with Natasha. I couldn't suppress a shudder as the ground sloped away and I caught a glimpse of the sea spray far below.

"Don't panic. I've got you." Will had been peering over the edge, moving along slowly. Now he braced his foot against a knot of rock hardly bigger than my fist, kicking at it first to make sure it was firmly bedded in the ground.

"Is that safe?"

"I wouldn't be here if it wasn't." He leaned out much as Natasha had done, but looking for something, not showing off. "There. See that ledge?"

Don't think about how high up you are. Look at the cliff, not the water. I copied him, craning over to see what he was looking at.

"Bit further. Here, let me help." His arm went around my waist and I nerved myself to inch a little bit further toward the edge. "See the little patch of green? About four meters down."

All at once I saw what he was talking about—a narrow step in the rock where grass and tiny pink flowers had seeded themselves. It was about a meter wide and rather more than double that in length.

"Lovely. Can I step back now?"

"If you like."

I scuttled backward, feeling my heart rate drop with every step I took away from danger. Wild horses wouldn't drag me back to look again. "What's so exciting about the ledge?"

"It's somewhere to stand. You can drop down off the edge and be perfectly safe."

"How on earth did you find that out?"

Will shrugged. "I've climbed up and down most of these cliffs. I used to like sitting there for a rest. You get the view and there's no chance of anyone turning up to spoil the peace and quiet."

"So what?"

His forehead creased. "So I told Freya about it. I played a trick on her and Hugo once—pretended I'd fallen over the edge."

"Funny."

"I thought so at the time. I told them how to find it. Ten paces from the bench, then eight to the left. You just have to jump straight. And overbalance toward the cliff if you don't get the landing right, or you're screwed."

I looked at him doubtfully. "You think Freya might have been aiming for the ledge?"

"I've wondered about it."

"It was her choice, if she did. I still don't see where the guilt comes in."

"Don't you? She'd never have thought of it if it weren't for me." Will's eyes had gone very dark—the sky before a storm. "She wouldn't have died if I hadn't taught her how to fall."

We argued it out for another half-hour, going round in circles. Will was determined to believe he was responsible for Freya's actions, and I was equally determined to convince him he was wrong, that it belittled Freya to suggest he was in control of what she did. Neither of us was willing to back down.

"We'll have to agree to disagree," Will said at last. "Unless you find proof of why she did it."

"That sounds like a challenge."

"You were planning to do it anyway."

"You're right. And you don't have to take any responsibility for me. What I do is my choice, and I choose to keep poking around."

"You really don't give up, do you?"

"Not often."

We started down the path, walking side by side. I slid a little on the steep slope. "They really need to put in a cable car."

"Why did you decide to come up here?"

"I told you, I had nowhere else to be."

"You could have gone to the beach. Stay on the level. Much less effort all round."

"I like it up here. Besides . . ." I hesitated and Will stopped, eyebrows raised. "I wanted to get away."

"From what?"

"My mum." To say it or not to say it. Before I'd decided, I heard my own voice: "And your dad."

"Dad?" He frowned. "What about him?"

"Mum and I were going for a walk. Then he turned up and she decided she'd rather spend the rest of the day with him."

Will's face was grim. "She needs to stay away from him."

"That would be my preference too."

"I mean it. You have to tell her."

"I'm not sure she'll listen to me." I looked at him curiously. "What's the history between them? Do you know?"

"I know my mother would be gutted if she knew they were together." He was angry, I realized. "Mum's not in a position to compete with yours. She shouldn't take advantage of that."

"Compete? I don't think my mother is that sort of person."

"Don't you? It sounds as if you've got a lot to learn about her."

I folded my arms, annoyed. "I know her a lot better than you do. If you're so worried about it, why don't you tell your dad to stop flirting with her?"

"He was flirting?"

"Definitely."

"That bastard," he said, more to himself than to me. Then, abruptly, "I have to go."

Without waiting for me to reply, he turned and began to stride off, far too quickly for me to be able to follow with my knee still aching from Natasha's kick. It was as if the past hour had never happened; he was as withdrawn and remote as ever, and it sharpened my irritation into anger.

"It's nice that you care about your mum," I called after him. "But don't you think it's their problem, not ours? I mean, your mum is old enough to stand up for herself."

Will stopped and half turned. "That's the one thing she can't do, actually. She's in a wheelchair."

Oh, shit. I was never going to take anyone's side against Mum, but it changed things to hear that. It was hardly a fair fight, if it was a fight at all. I was remembering what Tilly had said about her, or *not* said, and the look in my mother's eyes when Dan Henderson spoke to her, and I didn't want to know anything more about it all but I couldn't stop myself from asking: "What's wrong with her?"

Will's face was as bleak as I'd ever seen it. Quite suddenly I knew what he was going to say even though I hoped I was wrong.

"She's dying."

12

There was no sign of Mum at the cottage, which was both a relief and a worry. I didn't want to talk to her if I was going to have to break the news about Mrs. Henderson and exactly how much of a disloyal dirtbag Will's dad was. On the other hand, it would have been nice if she'd been back already, bored to tears by him, so I could reassure Will that she wasn't a threat to his mother's peace of mind. As it was, I didn't know what to think. *Please, Mum, just don't make another bad decision because you've fallen for the wrong man.*

I got a drink from the fridge and lay down on the ratty old couch, propping my feet up on the back of it without being too concerned about how dusty my shoes were. I was more tired than I could remember being, and even lifting my drink was an effort. I was glad to be on my own for a bit. It gave me time to think. I needed to organize what I'd been told about Freya, and the people around her, and work out where to go next.

Which made it all the more annoying that the only thing on my mind was Will, and the look on his face when he'd told me about his mother, and the motor neurone disease she'd been enduring for years that meant she was unable to walk. Oh, and the stupid, clichéd things I'd stammered before he took pity on me and strode off, leaving me to walk home alone. I hadn't known what to say—and it wasn't as if there was anything I could do to make him feel better, not when his mother was dying—but I still burned at the memory. I needed to apologize. I picked up my phone and put it down again.

I didn't have his number.

Tilly would have it. Or Hugo.

I picked up my phone again, hesitated, then put it back on the table. It wasn't as if I was going to ring him up anyway, and sending him a text was a bad idea. I would end up saying something even more crass than I had already.

Although I wasn't sure how you could get more crass than, "How long has she got left?"

I turned over and put my face into the cushion beside me, burrowing into it as if I could escape my thoughts by running away. It smelled musty and a little bit damp, like everything else in the cottage. That was the smell I would remember, I thought, when I looked back on this holiday. Not the sea air or the fresh green scent of the trees on the way up to the headland, or the warm smell of Will as he held me against him, his body totally relaxed even as he was daring gravity to pull the two of us off the cliff and spin us into oblivion far below . . .

I woke up properly when I snored so loudly I disturbed myself. After a quick, panicky check—still alone, thank God—I rubbed my eyes, then tied my hair up. The air on the back of my neck was cool. It would keep me awake while I definitely didn't think about Will any more and considered what I knew about Freya instead.

Talk about having a one-track mind. All I ended up thinking was how glad I was that Will was off my list of suspects, and how pleased I was that he wasn't the mystery boyfriend. The thought of him falling for Freya and wooing her with anonymous messages and gifts . . . but it hadn't been him.

My phone vibrated against the table, making me jump. I snatched it up to read the message on the screen.

> Sorry bout leaving u w/out proper gdbye.
> Meet on beach @ 10? Full moon 2nite. Ull luv it.

"You're not wrong," I said out loud, sending back a brief message before I ran upstairs to get changed. I was singing as I went. I'd been thinking about Will and he'd been thinking about me, and he'd gone to the trouble of getting my number, and the full moon was rising over the sea on a clear, warm night, and I couldn't help feeling totally, utterly happy.

Experience should have told me that the happy feeling wasn't likely to last. I made it to within a hundred meters of the beach before I realized the mistake I'd made. Unfortunately, the reason I realized was because I'd been spotted, and there was nowhere to hide.

"Jess, over here." Ryan was heading in my direction, waving. There was enough light from the moon to pick him out from the group that had gathered on the beach anyway. It gleamed on his hair and the white shirt he was wearing—and that hadn't been an accidental choice, I thought, raising one hand in a sketchy attempt at waving back. He'd known the impact it would have.

"I wasn't sure you were coming," he said when I was almost close enough to talk at a normal level. But not quite. His voice was loud enough to carry quite a distance. I was aware of faces turning toward me, peering to see who Ryan was talking to. And not turning away again, either. Whatever he did was news, I recalled, passionately not wanting to be part of the headline myself.

"Am I late?" I was, by ten minutes. I would have been even later if I'd known the message was from Ryan. Like, not bothering to turn up at all. The feeling of tiredness was dragging at me again as the disappointment really started to kick in.

"You're not very late. But I was watching for you." Ryan grinned down at me, not having a clue how unenthusiastic I was about seeing him. "I didn't want you to miss out on this."

I wasn't sure if he was talking about the moon, which was round and pure white and made a perfect path across the waves, or the party that was in full swing behind him. There were twenty or thirty people there, all around my age, lounging on the sand like something out of an ad. A gangly boy with untidy hair and a dreamer's face was strumming gently on a guitar, the music floating over the murmured conversations around us.

"How did you get my number?"

"Darcy." He raised his can in a salute and I spotted her sitting cross-legged in front of the guitar player, along with a couple of other girls I didn't know. It made sense that she was there, paying rapt attention to the music. Darcy was born to be a fan. A word that was short for fanatic, I reminded myself. She was completely dedicated to pursuing her goals, to the extent of getting up at six to do her full beauty ritual before she faced the day, or persuading her best friend to make Ryan feel he had a chance with her, just to be in with the in-crowd. I wondered, looking at her upturned face, if she had been frustrated enough with Freya to give in to her temper, on a dark night when no one was watching. One shove would have done it. It needn't have been premeditated. And I'd seen Darcy's temper when I wouldn't try on the stupid dress at the shop. It hadn't taken much to make her angry.

I must have been looking grim, because Ryan looked at me doubtfully. "I hope you don't mind about getting your number."

"Of course not." I smiled at him. I was managing my disappointment well, I thought. It helped a tiny bit to discover that Ryan was responsible for the textspeak in the message, and not Will. It had surprised me that he would text at all. He probably didn't even have a mobile phone; I'd never seen him use one. And there was no point in looking for him on the beach, I knew. He wouldn't be at a party.

"Want a drink?"

"What have you got?"

"One of these?"

I looked at the can in his hand and was surprised to see it was an energy drink. I had caught a hint of alcohol on Ryan's breath and his eyes weren't totally focused. "Is that really what you're drinking?"

"Not exactly. It's mainly vodka."

"Nice." I looked around, noticing that everyone was carrying innocent-looking bottles and cans. Even the girl who was throwing up in a rock pool had a bottle of lemonade beside her. "Let me guess—everyone's drink is spiked."

"If they want it to be. Not if they don't. What's your preference?"

"Without."

He raised his eyebrows. "Being good?"

The girl who'd been throwing up wiped her mouth with the back of her hand, giving herself a sand beard in the process, and not exactly selling it to me.

"I'll build up to something stronger."

Ryan handed me a can. "Just let me know if you want some of this instead."

"Sure. Why do you have to pretend you're not drinking? Some of you must be over eighteen."

"Town rules. No alcohol on the beach. No dogs on the beach. No fires on the beach." He shrugged. "It would be nice to light a fire but it's not worth the hassle. Inspector Henderson would be down on us straight away."

"Inspector Henderson? Will's dad?"

"None other. He runs this place, you know."

"That doesn't surprise me. He acts as if he does."

"So you've met him."

"And Will."

"Will." Ryan sounded very casual.

"A couple of times. We were over there today." I pointed at the headland and he half turned to look, but swung back quickly once he realized what I meant. I'd noticed that before—he didn't even like to look at the wall of rock that formed one side of the bay. "I'm surprised you didn't know about it already."

"Why do you say that?"

"Your girlfriend was there too."

"Natasha's not my girlfriend," he said automatically. "What were you doing up on the cliff?"

"Not falling off it." I sipped my drink then smiled at his expression. "Never mind."

"I'd stay away from there if I were you."

"Is that a warning?"

"Sort of. It's dangerous. You should know that. You know what happened there." Ryan looked past me and acknowledged a guy I didn't know who was calling to him, a quick flick of the fingers that said, *Not now, I'm busy . . .*

"I know what the outcome was. And I know that you didn't like being up there."

"Ah. I wanted to apologize for that." He looked sheepish. "Don't tell anyone but I am shit-scared of heights."

"You are?"

"They make me feel sick. I get dizzy. I know, it's pathetic. It doesn't fit in with my image."

"No, it doesn't." I was remembering him somersaulting off the railing the first time I'd met him. Scared of heights? Well, maybe. "How high are we talking?"

"Anything. A foot off the ground." He shook his head. "Can't deal with it."

He was so convincing I almost doubted what I had seen him do. Almost.

I was wondering what to say next when someone knocked into me from behind, gasping a sort of apology that didn't sound very convincing at all, especially when it trailed off into a giggle. I recognized the girl without remembering her name. She staggered off toward a little group of hair-tossing, chain-smoking girls and I wasn't remotely shocked to see Natasha among them, glowering at me.

"Come for a walk with me?"

I looked up at Ryan, heartbreakingly handsome in the moonlight, and I knew I should find some way of putting him off without making it into a big deal. There were so many reasons to say no, starting with the fact that he had just lied to me. Why did he want me to think he didn't like heights? Because he knew I'd seen him panicking on the cliff? Or to make me think he'd never go up to the headland if he had a choice? Either way, it was a fib, and a stupid one at that, but I should take it as a warning. Ryan was by no means as straightforward as he wanted me to think. Then there was the little matter that going for a walk with him was the equivalent of painting a target between my shoulder blades and handing Natasha a bow and arrow.

So of course I nodded and let him put his arm around me, guiding me away from the music and the people and the hostile stares. Instead of heading down to the sea, he struck back up the beach, toward the promenade. I'd have preferred the firmer sand near the surf, but when I moved that way his arm tightened around me, and he was a lot stronger than I was. It wasn't worth a fight, I thought, following his lead. We walked in silence, not quite matching our strides so I kept knocking into him and having to apologize.

"I'm not usually this clumsy."

"I'm probably not walking in a straight line. What can I say? Any excuse to be close to you."

"Very charming."

"You can't blame me for trying." Ryan drained his can and tossed it toward a bin on the promenade, over-arm like a basketball player. It went in with a noise like a rifle shot.

"That was impressive."

"Good. I only did it to impress you."

"How much have you had to drink?"

"Too much." He pushed his hand through his hair. "I'll start talking rubbish in a minute."

"I'll look out for that."

"You can be quite mean, can't you?"

"Yes, but you like that in a girl."

His eyes widened. "I was just going to say that."

"What an amazing coincidence," I murmured. Chapter Three in *The Big Book of Chatting Up Girls*: "The Put Down That's Really a Compliment." I'd been on the receiving end of that kind of thing before. And it had worked, once or twice.

"So Will said you used to be friends."

Ryan's arm jerked on my shoulders: surprise, I gathered. "Will was talking about me?"

"About what happened. Years ago. Your broken arm."

"Oh. That."

"It sounded awful. Hurting you deliberately—in cold blood."

"It wasn't fun. Bye-bye tennis, though." He laughed. "I should have been grateful."

"Grateful that you couldn't pursue your dream?"

"That sounds more fun than spending a million hours running around a court hitting little yellow balls so I could be not quite good enough to turn pro." There was a cynical undertone to Ryan's voice that I hadn't heard before, a hardness that I didn't associate with his usual laid-back style. If telling himself he'd have failed anyway was how he'd come to terms with what had happened to him, I wasn't going to try to persuade him otherwise. I didn't know any better, anyway. But I was more inclined to believe Will's version of it than Ryan's.

"Anyway, it was all a long time ago," Ryan said, offhand.

"But you're both still living with the fallout. I can't believe you're still punishing Will for something that happened so long ago."

"We don't get on. If it hadn't been him snitching on us to his dad, it would have been something else."

"From what Will said, he was trying to help. And he didn't mean to snitch in the first place."

Ryan pulled a face. "You know you don't have to spend time with him, don't you? Just because he's friends with your cousins, you don't have to feel sorry for him."

"I don't, exactly. But I don't like people being treated unfairly."

"Why are we talking about him again?" Ryan was definitely sounding edgy.

"I don't know. I'm just interested in finding out about what I missed. A lot happened last year before Freya died. I missed out on a lot of key moments."

"Like what?"

"Like what happened with you and Freya."

"We talked about her already."

"No, we talked about how you went off her after she cut her hair. What we didn't discuss was who cut her hair and why.

I just found out it was your not-girlfriend who did the Vidal Sassoon impersonation."

"It was nothing to do with me."

"It was everything to do with you! It was supposed to make her less fanciable as far as you were concerned and it worked."

"I didn't know anything about it until it was too late," Ryan said weakly. "I'd have stopped her if I'd known what she was planning."

"Don't you feel guilty about it?"

"No."

"Seriously?"

"I can't take responsibility for what someone does, even if it's to impress me or whatever." He sighed. "Look, I'm sorry Freya's not around anymore. I don't know what happened to her and I think you should just drop it."

"I can't," I said softly. "I need to know."

He shook his head, baffled. "She's gone. You're not going to bring her back. Leave it alone and just enjoy being here."

"It's easy to say that."

"It's easy to do." Ryan stopped walking and held onto my hand until I stopped too. "It's a beautiful night. And you're beautiful."

I could feel my heart thumping. He was looking at me like I was the only girl on the beach, or maybe the world. And I wasn't sure how I felt about him. Tick for good sense of humor. Double tick for good looks. Gold star for athletic ability.

But it didn't add up to being what I wanted. What I wanted was—

Before I could complete the thought, he pushed me so I

had to walk backward—and trust him not to let me fall—until I collided, quite hard, with the wall of a building that proved to be a deckchair-hire kiosk.

"Hey. Watch it."

"Sorry. Did I misjudge it?" Ryan leaned in, and I took a tiny breath, which was all I could manage. The old familiar jolt of fear kicked my heart into a canter. *Oh, here we are. Danger again.* I felt trapped and I was more worried about Ryan and his intentions than I had been before he'd lied to me. Or rather, before he'd lied to me so I'd noticed it. What else had he been faking? But I didn't want to let him know how I was feeling.

"I just wasn't expecting to get a building in the small of my back."

I barely got the words out before he bent his head and kissed me, and even though I had known it was coming, it still took me by surprise. If he'd asked permission I might have said no, but I hadn't been given a choice. I only had two options: kick him in the nuts or try to enjoy it. Option B wasn't really that much of a hardship, I told myself. He was really quite a catch.

Or possibly a cold-blooded killer.

And it didn't honestly matter if Ryan was totally innocent, or if he was by far the best-looking guy I'd ever kissed. He was still the wrong person—quite completely not the one I wanted to be kissing. I felt absolutely nothing beyond a fervent wish that he would stop.

After approximately a trillion years he broke away and leaned back to see how I was enjoying myself.

I cleared my throat. "This is what you had in mind all along, isn't it? You were aiming for this precise place. I bet you've done this before."

"Yeah, but not with you. So that makes it special."

I looked over his shoulder at the party that was going on in the distance, far enough away that the people were anonymous shadows to me. He turned my face back to his and before I could stop him he kissed me again.

It was not a Prince-Charming kind of kiss, second time round. He pressed his body against mine, and with the kiosk behind me I had nowhere to go, but I didn't have enough air to complain. I became aware of the hand that was sliding up under my top at about the same time as I heard a muffled gasp. I grabbed hold of Ryan's wrist and opened my eyes to see Claudia standing a few paces away, stooping slightly to try to make herself look shorter because the boy holding her hand was well below average height. He made up for it by being heavily muscled. His neck was pretty much wider than his head. They looked more lovely than I can put into words since their presence was an excuse to put a stop to Ryan's exploration. Still, there was no point in putting out a welcome mat.

"Where I come from, this isn't a spectator sport."

"Yeah, and the sooner you go back there, the better." Claudia yanked on the boy's hand. "Come on, Henry. Let's go."

"We've only just got here," Henry pointed out. "Here" was obviously the place for a bit of quiet snogging and he wasn't all that pleased about missing out. "Go where?"

"Back to the party," she snapped.

"Yes, hurry back to the party," I said acidly. "You don't want anyone else to get there first. But if you think Natasha is going to be pleased to hear your news, you're mistaken. And you never know—she might decide to shoot the messenger. I'd be very careful if I were you."

"You're the one who needs to be careful."

"Claude." There was a warning in Ryan's voice and she subsided with an evil stare at me. Henry had already begun to walk away and after a second she did likewise, breaking into a knock-kneed run that made her look as if she might collapse into the sand at any moment.

"Not a natural athlete, our Claude," I observed. "But she'll get the message across."

"She should know better. She should keep her mouth shut," Ryan said, and I was surprised by how grim he sounded. Still, when he turned back to me it was with a crooked grin. "Still, no reason to stop now."

"Every reason." I peeled myself off the kiosk. "Time to get back to reality. Or in my case, go home."

"Don't go. Stay for a bit."

"You know, I meant what I said. I'm not looking for a holiday romance." I said it gently but his eyebrows drew together.

"What's that supposed to mean?"

"I mean that this has been nice, but I don't think I should stay any longer. People might get the wrong idea." God, this was difficult. How to put it so he couldn't misunderstand? "*You* might get the wrong idea."

"It's just a bit of fun, Jess. I'm not proposing marriage." There it was again, that little flick of sarcasm I didn't expect from him. I was beginning to realize I'd misjudged him. I'd thought he was cute but harmless. He was a lot cleverer than I'd thought, and he went to great lengths to hide it. The warning bells were ringing so loudly I was halfway to being deaf.

"Fun is fine, in its place." I stuck my hands in the pockets of my jeans. "Look, you're a lovely guy. Really. I just think we should be—"

"Friends?" Ryan laughed bitterly. "That's my line, usually."

"It's not a line. I mean it."

"This is like last year all over again."

"What do you mean?"

"It's pretty much what your cousin said."

"Except she said there was someone else."

"Yeah. She did." He frowned. "What about you?"

"Me?"

"Is there someone else for you?"

"Does there have to be? Oh, that's right. Because there's no way I wouldn't be interested in you otherwise, is there?" I shook my head. "You know, it's a real shame you're scared of heights, because otherwise you could borrow a stepladder and get over yourself."

He took a step toward me and I backed away, right up against the kiosk.

"Why were you asking me about Will Henderson?"

"No reason."

"Is he the one?" His hands were clenched into fists. "I've been waiting for a reason to punch him, so just say the word."

"It's not him. There isn't anyone."

"Are you sure?"

"Positive. I do not fancy Will Henderson." My voice was sharp with irritation and tension, and it came out louder than I would have wanted.

Ryan had opened his mouth to reply when a torch flicked on, right beside us, and caught him full in the face. He screwed up his eyes, struggling to see the person who was standing on the promenade, a couple of meters away from us.

"Turn it off."

"Is everything OK here? Jess, are you all right?" The torch flicked over me, assessing me. I knew my hair was a mess, I suspected my makeup had smudged badly, and I was fairly sure my top was not as it should have been after Ryan had tried to burrow under it. Nevertheless, I tried to look as if I was in complete control of the situation.

"I'm fine, Mr. Henderson." I corrected myself. "Sorry, Inspector Henderson."

"Just call me Dan."

Never. "OK. Well. I'm fine. I was just going to go home."

"That sounds like a good idea." The torch moved back to Ryan. "You should go too, young man, by whatever route takes you in a different direction. I'll make sure Jess gets home."

Ryan shook his head. "I'm not going anywhere."

"Don't come looking for trouble, Ryan. I'll make sure that's what you'll get if you do." The policeman was maintaining a pleasant manner but there was something chilling about his words.

Ryan opened his mouth to argue, then closed it again. He looked at me, then back at Dan Henderson.

"It's fine," I said. "Go home. Or not. Whatever you want. I'm going, though."

"I—I'm sorry, Jess. I—"

I cut him off. "Don't be stupid. I'll see you tomorrow."

"Off you go." Dan's tone didn't encourage any more discussion, and after a few seconds Ryan walked away, his shoulders hunched as if he suddenly felt the cold. I was shivering myself. The night air lacked warmth, but that was the price you paid if you traded cozy clouds for a spectacular display of stars. I leaned back to look up at them so I didn't have to watch Ryan leave, or talk to Dan. Maybe he would forget about me and just go.

"Right. Now to get you back." Dan clicked his torch off. "I'll give you a lift. My car is parked nearby."

I really didn't want to get into a car with him. "You don't need to take me home," I said quickly. "I'll be fine."

"I'd like to make sure you get there safely."

"I can look after myself."

"Is that right?"

"Despite appearances to the contrary."

He laughed, which I hadn't expected. "I'm sure you had a plan."

"I didn't need one. Everything was fine." If I said it enough, I might even believe it myself.

"You and I know that's not true." He tossed the torch up in the air and caught it and I had a strong feeling of déjà vu. It was unsettling until I made sense of it: Will had done the same with his screwdriver in the charity shop. They were so alike. And poles apart, obviously.

"Ryan's not a bad kid but he goes too far sometimes."

"He wouldn't have got much further with me," I said tartly.

"You'd have stopped him, would you? Maybe I shouldn't have got involved, then."

I swallowed the six rude things I wanted to say. "I was grateful. But I wasn't in any difficulties and I am capable of making my own way home."

"You say that, but I can't let you." Dan smiled ruefully.

"It's stupid, I know, but I want to know you're OK. It would keep me from sleeping tonight if I didn't see you home. And anyway, you're cold. You're shivering. I'll put the heat on in the car to warm you up."

He was a police officer. There couldn't be anyone safer to trust, even if I wanted to run in the opposite direction. Maybe it was time to start letting other people help me out now and then. Besides, he had a point. It *was* cold, and a breeze had picked up, ruffling the waves. *Be sensible, Jess.*

"If you don't mind giving me a lift, I'd be grateful."

He held out his hand and helped me to climb onto the promenade. "Knock the sand off your shoes before you get into the car and we have a deal."

"Jess!" Darcy was panting across the beach, making heavy weather of it. She sank to mid-calf in the soft, dry sand with every step. "Wait! I wanted to talk to you."

"Come with me, then," I called. A little too late, I turned to Dan. "I mean, is it OK for her to come with us? Just to my house?"

He was going there anyway; he'd have to be a piece of work to say no. But he had a good old think about it anyway before he made up his mind. "Fine. Why not. The more the merrier."

"Oh, thank you." Darcy clambered up onto the promenade and leaned on a post for a minute, her chest heaving. "God, that was horrible."

"The party or the run?"

"Running, of course." She shook her head. "Anyone who would do that voluntarily would have to be insane. Coco Golding trains on the beach four times a week. I don't know how she does it."

"Coco? As in Natasha's friend Coco?"

"She's an amazing runner—her distance is the four hundred meters. She's trying to get into the national squad."

"Coco. As in, fair hair. Pretty face. Little short legs."

"They may be short but they move quickly."

I was reconsidering my opinion of Coco. "Well, I'd never have guessed."

Dan had been listening with an amused expression. "You don't need a lot of height to be fast, Jess. It's just more bulk to move when you're running short distances."

"I stand corrected." It sounded too wholesome a pastime for one of Natasha's friends, and I wondered about Coco, about whether she was really committed to Natasha's world, and whether she might think about telling me what had made her sick to her stomach on the clifftop. I might ask, if I ever saw her without Natasha or one of her coven in tow.

Though I was finding it hard to like Darcy given what I knew about how she'd behaved toward Freya, I loved her in the car. She prattled away about everything and nothing, keeping the conversation going so I didn't have to deal with Dan. Every so often he aimed a question at me but Darcy got there first. It wasn't a long drive to the cottage and Darcy had plenty to give. By the time we pulled up outside the house, Dan's face was a scowl. He managed to get Darcy to shut up for long enough to offer us a bit of fatherly advice.

"I don't want to see you hanging around on the beach late at night again, either of you. The only thing you'll get out of it is trouble."

"Oh, I completely agree," Darcy said earnestly. "Don't you, Jess?"

"Completely," I echoed. I meant it too. I was planning on staying away from the social scene Port Sentinel had to offer for the remainder of my stay. There were too many potential ways to offend. This was not my world and I didn't want to cause trouble that would resonate after I'd packed up my things and gone back to London. I couldn't flirt with Ryan any more either. Fun though it was to bait Natasha, I didn't want to be in the middle of their games. He'd unsettled me enough that I wanted to stay out of his way, something that Natasha would wholeheartedly support.

I had just started to open the door when Dan's hand shot across and held onto my arm.

"Wait a second, Jess. I want a word with you."

Darcy was already out of the car, standing by the door, shifting from foot to foot. "I need to let Darcy into the house."

He didn't even look round. "It's not raining. She'll survive."

"But—"

"Listen to me." He leaned across, his face inches away from mine. "I know you've been asking questions about Freya's death."

"Who told you that?"

"I hear about everything that happens in Port Sentinel."

I couldn't help thinking of Will, and his reputation, but I forced his face out of my mind. "If you hear everything, do you know who killed her?"

His jaw tightened. "It was an accident. She fell."

"How do you know?"

"Because Freya was a silly little girl with a head full of romantic notions, and she didn't have the sense to stay away from high places."

I leaned back against the seat, wishing I could move further away. "You sound like you knew her well."

"Well enough."

It was a mad idea—completely insane—but I looked at Dan Henderson and found myself wondering if Freya's substitute for Will had been someone who looked a lot like him. Someone well respected, who was confident and controlling and in love with his power. In love with himself enough to encourage a teenage girl's crush? To take advantage? What if something had happened between them? The idea was enough to make me gag, but he wasn't actually that old. Mum was thirty-six. He'd be about the same.

I very much wanted to shower for about fifteen years just for having the thought, but I couldn't ignore it. Dan was watching me. I hoped he couldn't read my mind. Considering what he said next, I was glad I couldn't read his.

"You know, I'm not surprised Ryan was all over you. He's got good taste."

Oh. My. God. I stared at Dan wordlessly. He grinned. "You remind me of her."

"Freya?" I managed.

"I was thinking of Molly."

I cleared my throat. "Well. Not surprising really. Genes will do that."

His grip on my arm loosened, but he didn't let go. Slowly, deliberately, he stroked my wrist with his thumb, trailing it across the veins where the blood ran close to the surface. "Stop talking about Freya. Stop asking questions. You're getting mixed up in things you don't understand."

I pulled my arm away from him and scrabbled for the door

handle, completely freaked out. He reached round and took hold of my chin, turning my face toward him with too much force for me to be able to resist.

"Wait."

"I don't—"

"Your lipstick is smeared." Before I could stop him he drew his thumb along my lower lip, staring into my eyes the whole time. "There. That's better."

I'm not sure how I got out of the car, but I know I did it quickly, before anything else could happen. I know I didn't say thank you, or good-bye. I know I ran to the front door on wobbly legs, and that Darcy's face was all startled speculation.

And I know Dan watched as I fumbled for my keys, unlocked the front door, and let Darcy in.

Somehow I gathered myself together before Darcy could ask what we'd been talking about—she would be the world's worst person to confide in, anyway.

I turned round. "Well? What did you want to talk about?"

Her face was grave; there was no hint of the airhead who had sat behind me in Dan Henderson's car and talked-talked-talked all the way home. She looked different somehow—older and more serious. She had opted for elaborate eyeliner and a fifties-with-a-twist pompadour hairdo that night, and her general look seemed more like a costume than ever.

"I wanted to apologize."

"What do you have to apologize for?"

"I didn't tell you the truth about me and Freya. I want to tell you what happened. And I wanted to give you this."

She reached into her bag and pulled out a sketchbook, and I couldn't quite believe it until I was actually holding it in my hand—a hardback book only a little bigger than a notebook, with an elaborate hand-drawn monogram on the cover, an F and an L intertwined.

"Is this—?"

"Freya's." Darcy couldn't look me in the eye, I realized. "Her last one."

"You had it all along."

"I hid it."

"Why?"

"Because I didn't want anyone to know what was in it."

"So why are you giving it to me now?"

She looked straight at me and her eyes were swimming in unshed tears. "Because I don't want to lie any more."

13

Before I heard any more from Darcy I made us both some really strong tea. I had my priorities in order. Freya was dead, I was in shock, and Darcy was cold. Our need was greater than my poor cousin's. So, tea first. Then talk.

"Sorry, no biscuits." I handed Darcy her mug and curled up at the other end of the sofa. She was sitting on the very edge, shredding a tissue all over the floor and sniffing every ten seconds or so, but she had pretty much stopped crying.

"Why are you being so nice to me?" she asked.

"Because you obviously feel terrible about whatever happened last year and I want to know why. If you don't calm down I won't be able to understand what you're telling me. It's self-interest, really."

"That's not true. You're just a good person."

"It's at least half true." I extended one leg and poked her in the thigh with my toe. "Come on. Drink up, sit back and tell me all about it. But not too loudly. I don't want to wake Mum."

Mum who was upstairs, safely tucked up in bed, and fast asleep when I'd checked on her. There was no way to tell when she'd got back or what she'd been doing, but I would find out. I would tell her, I thought, that Dan had given me a lift home, but I wouldn't say what had happened afterward. It was the sort of thing he could laugh off, if I made a fuss. I wasn't even sure what had happened myself, and I couldn't allow myself to dwell on it when Darcy was sitting in front of me, ready to tell all.

"Where do you want me to start?"

"The beginning, obviously." I laughed at the look on Darcy's face: pure disgust. "Right. You and Freya were really close until something happened, a few weeks before she died. Petra said you had a row. Was it about Ryan?"

"It was about Freya wanting him to leave her alone. She wasn't interested and I couldn't persuade her to fake it." Darcy peeked at me through the wreckage of her eye makeup—falsies were not made for crying fits and hers were peeling off. "I tried to explain to her that it was a golden opportunity. I've spent years watching Ryan and his friends have fun. It was our turn to join in and she just couldn't see it."

"You blamed Will for that the last time we spoke."

"Well, it was his fault really. Freya was obsessed with him. She wouldn't even consider seeing Ryan because he didn't measure up to Will." Darcy snorted. "I don't know what planet she was on. Will is so boring compared to Ryan. He doesn't go out. He barely talks. He works obsessively—even in the holidays he's always busy doing jobs. He's like a machine or something."

"He's not your type. We know that."

"We sure do. But he was Freya's type even if he wasn't interested in her." Darcy cupped her mug in both hands, shivering. "That was a help—knowing what she liked. I'd heard about him often enough."

"A help with what? What did you do?"

Darcy stared into her tea as if she were trying to read fortunes, mainly so she didn't have to look at me.

"It wasn't my idea in the first place. It was Natasha who came up with the plan." She swirled the mug so the liquid in it spun around, threatening to slop over the side. "You know she thinks Ryan is irresistible. She was panicking in case Freya suddenly realized she'd been wrong about him, because obviously Freya had to be crazy if she was turning him down. Natasha wanted to distract Freya—find someone else for her to fall in love with. There just wasn't anyone obvious around."

"So?"

"So she invented someone."

"The mystery boyfriend? The one no one knew about?"

"He never existed. Except in Freya's head." Darcy blew her nose again. "She was completely taken in."

"Because you were helping to make him into her perfect man," I said, suddenly getting why Darcy was finding it hard to confess. "They couldn't have done it without you, could they? They didn't know Freya well enough to create someone she would find appealing. But you did. And that was how you got into the gang."

"I betrayed her trust. You didn't put it like that, but it's true." Darcy's voice was hollow, a world away from the high-velocity chatter that was her usual way of talking. I was starting to realize that it was all an act. She was fake to the ends of

213

her fingernails and I wasn't even sure the woebegone figure on the end of the sofa was the real her.

"How did you do it? Invent him, I mean?"

"It was easy. It was just an e-mail at first. He told her she was looking beautiful and sent her a picture that reminded him of her—*The Lady of Shalott* by John William Waterhouse."

"I don't know it."

"You'd recognize it," Darcy said. "It's a Pre-Raphaelite painting of the Lady of Shalott floating down the river to Camelot—very atmospheric, very beautiful, and a little bit fey, so it was perfect for Freya. There's a print of it in the art room at school so it wasn't a massive stretch to think that one of the boys might have seen it and thought of her. They call it 'the bird in the boat.'"

"That was clever," I commented. "To choose an image anyone might have known, I mean."

"Don't. I feel terrible about it." Darcy *did* look uncomfortable. "Anyway, she wrote back and asked who he was."

"And you said?"

"That he just wanted to be known as 'Pale Knight.'"

I snorted. "That sounds like a kind of beer."

"It's a reference to a Keats poem, actually. 'La Belle Dame Sans Merci.' He said that Freya was the Belle Dame and he was enchanted by her." Darcy sounded defensive and I guessed that had been her idea too.

"I know the poem and it's not very nice about the Belle Dame, if I remember it correctly. She turns out to be a vicious life-sucking hag."

"At the end. Before that she's a beautiful girl with wild, wild eyes," Darcy said dreamily, back to her old self for a second. Then she snapped out of it. "We wanted Freya to think that he was too shy to tell her how he felt, to explain why he was hiding behind his secret identity. Otherwise there was nothing to stop him from telling her who he was. Port Sentinel's a small place. There weren't too many guys who the mystery man could be, so we needed to keep her guessing."

"I see. So the boy was supposed to be interested in Romantic poetry and Pre-Raphaelite art." It sounded like the kind of thing that would make me roll my eyes until I fell over from chronic dizziness, but it had been said before and would probably be said again: I looked like Freya but I wasn't anything like her really. "Presumably this was exactly what Freya liked."

"Exactly. And the messages we wrote were the same—very romantic, very poetic. They had a lot in common."

"Is Will interested in that kind of thing?"

"No, but he would have known that Freya was. And we put in some references to things that he *does* like."

"As in?"

"Fixing up old cars. Photography . . ." Darcy hesitated. "Did you know he took pictures of her for a series of nudes she did?"

"I saw the paintings in the studio at Sandhayes." Though Will hadn't mentioned that he'd taken the photographs, I was pretty sure. Just imagining it made me feel as if I'd been kicked in the chest. I hoped my face didn't show it.

"He took them with her camera," Darcy continued. "In one of the e-mails I asked her to send me those pictures. That really convinced her that it was Will who was writing the messages because hardly anyone knew about the paintings or that there were photographs to go with them."

"Please tell me Freya wasn't stupid enough to send the

pictures." Darcy's expression told me the answer. "Oh my God. That's basic. It's rule one. Never send nude pictures to anyone, ever, no matter who they are. Even if you trust them completely. And Freya didn't even know who she was e-mailing."

"She believed in him. She *wanted* to believe in him."

"You knew that and you totally took advantage of her. There were only a few people who knew about the photographs, so it was your idea to get her to send them. You must have thought it would really impress Natasha."

Darcy reddened. "I know you think this is awful. It *is* awful. But I didn't think it would do any harm. It was cute, you know—we thought of little presents he could send her. Gifts that showed he'd been thinking of her. They were small things, mostly. Jewelry, flowers—that sort of thing. I thought it would make Freya happy for a bit to have someone in love with her, and then, when he disappeared, she'd find someone in real life who would do the same. You have to believe me, I didn't know what Natasha was going to do."

Uh-oh. "What was that, exactly?"

"She let it go too far," Darcy said softly. "She couldn't believe how easy it was to convince Freya that this boy existed and was in love with her. She wanted to find out more about Freya—'know your enemy' was what she said—so she started sending messages asking Freya personal questions."

"How personal?"

"Very. Like who she fancied—Natasha wanted to get her to admit she was mad about Ryan. Like her fantasies. Like whether she was a virgin or not."

And poor innocent Freya, who seemed completely deficient in commonsense, had answered them all in detail.

"What a bitch," I said softly. "And you helped her?"

"I told you—I didn't know what was going to happen."

"You mean it got worse?"

Darcy stood up and started to pace back and forth, but since the sitting room was tiny and full of furniture she only managed a couple of steps in each direction. "She started telling people about what Freya had written—gossiping about her. She sent the pictures around to everyone she knew. She made it seem like Freya was being a huge slut by e-mailing the pictures in the first place. Everyone was talking about her."

"Did Freya know that?" I asked.

"I don't think she knew the extent of it but she knew people were talking behind her back and she knew Natasha hated her."

"She probably got a clue that might be the case when Natasha cut her hair."

Darcy looked sick. "That was horrible. It was in the locker room after school one day. A whole group of girls cornered Freya and held her down so Natasha could cut off her ponytail. Up here." She indicated the nape of her neck. "I didn't know about it beforehand and I didn't join in—I mean, I wouldn't have. I couldn't do something like that."

"Didn't Freya tell anyone? A teacher? Didn't anyone notice that she'd lost about a meter of hair?"

"She decided not to complain. She thought it would make them worse." Darcy managed a lukewarm smile. "She told me it was a relief not to have so much hair to wash and she was glad they'd done it because she wouldn't have had the nerve."

"What was she, Pollyanna? There's looking for the silver lining and then there's being completely out of touch with reality." I was almost getting angry with Freya for not helping herself. "Freya had a chance to get rid of Natasha and she didn't take it. No school would have kept a student who did something like that."

"She would have been expelled," Darcy agreed. "But she would still have been around. As I said, this is a small place. You can't get away from people easily. Even in the holidays, Freya kept bumping into Natasha and her friends. Nothing stopped, just because they weren't in school, and it would have been the same if Natasha had been permanently excluded."

"So what was Freya thinking? If she waited long enough Natasha would get tired of tormenting her and move on to someone else?"

"Basically."

"But that was never going to happen. Natasha's like one of those yappy miniature dogs. She's got a gift for bearing grudges."

"I know." Darcy hugged herself. "She took it too far and she wouldn't listen to anyone who tried to tell her to stop."

"Did you?"

She looked exceedingly uncomfortable. "I don't know her well enough for that."

"So what did you do?"

"Nothing, and I know that makes me a failure as a human being." She brightened. "Except that I stopped helping her with the e-mails. I told her I wasn't going to do it any more and she'd have to come up with her own ideas. I backed out of it completely. I don't know what she was planning and I don't know what she did. I don't even know if she was there the night Freya died. I wasn't. I'd walked away."

"At a pretty late stage. And even then you didn't do anything useful, like telling Freya what had been going on."

"No. I didn't." Darcy sighed. "I don't expect you to understand, but I hope you can forgive me."

"It's not really about whether I forgive you, though, is it? I didn't even know Freya. You should be apologizing to her family and her friends. You should be apologizing to her."

"She shouldn't be dead," Darcy said with a sob that seemed to take her by surprise. *Genuine emotion at last,* I thought. "She should have realized what was happening. She shouldn't have fallen for Natasha's schemes."

"That's right. Blame her. It's all Freya's fault." I was rubbing my eyes. I wanted to go to bed. I wanted to stop thinking about this horrible situation, and stop talking to Darcy, who was spending way too much time blaming other people instead of owning up to what she'd done. I wanted to stop imagining how Freya must have felt, but I couldn't. It was taking me to a very dark and scary place. "You know, this whole thing makes me wonder if she did kill herself after all. That kind of bullying can make you insane. There's something so sick about it. Natasha set Freya up, and the more she did to her, the more Freya depended on this person who didn't even exist. Once she found out the truth, don't you think Freya would have fallen apart on the spot?"

"I suppose."

"And she might have found out the truth the night she died."

"I'm fairly sure she did."

"What do you mean?"

Darcy picked up the sketchbook from the coffee table. "You know Freya used these books as her diary . . ." She was flicking through it, looking for something. I leaned over, seeing page after page of doodles, lists, reminders and heavily shaded drawings flash by. A wide border of birds, lilies, hearts, and briars surrounded one page, very stylized and effective, and I put my hand out to stop Darcy from skipping past it.

"What's that?"

"A bit from 'La Belle Dame Sans Merci.'" She turned it round so I could read the elaborate calligraphy that Freya had used for the central panel.

"*And there I shut her wild wild eyes with kisses four.* How long do you think it took her to do that?"

"Ages. Days." Darcy took it back to look at it. "That was how she was. Obsessive about things. The Pale Knight took over her mind, basically. She was preoccupied with him, with finding out about him and imagining what he might be like in real life. This whole book is all about him."

"She was happy, wasn't she, in spite of the bullying. That's why you couldn't let anyone see the sketchbook. She wasn't suicidal. Then they might have started looking for the Pale Knight and found you."

"I said I'm not proud of what I did," Darcy snapped. "At least I'm telling you now."

"Yeah, it's a real help a year later."

She slammed the book down on the table and pointed. "There. That date is the day she died. *PK, ten p.m., Angel Bridge.* She was going to meet him." Freya had drawn clouds of hearts on the page, and little cherubs holding up a banner with the words written in the center. They had round cheeks and mischievous expressions; she had managed to give them personality with a couple of pencil strokes.

"Where's Angel Bridge?"

"In the woods. It's just a small wooden bridge over a stream that comes down off the headland, but it's very pretty there. People call it Angel Bridge because there's a hollow tree trunk near it that looks like a woman with soaring wings, if you stand in the right place."

"And if you don't stand in the right place it's just a rotting tree."

"Freya loved it there," Darcy said and there was a hint of a reproof in her tone.

"I'm sure she did. So how did she end up falling off the cliff if she was supposed to be on the bridge?"

"I don't know."

I leafed through the sketchbook, recognizing bits and pieces I'd seen on the wall of her room, like the bushes from the Dartmoor painting crammed in at the bottom of a page, under a shopping list. The next page was a bit of verse that I recognized—the lyrics to a song that had been everywhere the previous year. The band had sunk without trace since then and I struggled to remember their name. The lead singer had sky-high cheekbones and a tortured expression. Through excessive cynicism I had not been able to take them seriously. Conrad—and I'm not joking—had a T-shirt with their logo on it that he'd barely taken off. It was a shame he'd never met Freya. He'd have loved a chance to be her Pale Knight.

Love you forever
Forever's too long
Too long to be lonely
Lonely for you . . .

The tune kept playing in my head as I went through the rest of the pages. *Lonely for you.* Freya had been lonely. She had wanted to be loved. She would have done a lot for someone who understood her and wanted her because she was a genius artist who wasn't bothered about conforming. She hadn't worried about being different, until being different made her a threat to someone who was far below her on the evolutionary ladder.

"One step above a slug," I said out loud without meaning to. I snapped out of my reverie and looked up to see Darcy putting on her coat, poised for flight. "Where are you going?"

"It's late. I should go."

"It *is* late." I yawned. "Sorry."

"Don't stay up too long looking at that."

"It's fascinating. It's the contents of Freya's head."

"Which explains why it's mainly about him." Darcy gave me a sad smile. "Don't hate me for what I did. Or what I didn't do, maybe."

"You can't change the past. You can only do better in the future."

She buttoned up her jacket. "With that in mind, can I give you some advice? Don't get involved with Ryan. He's not worth it."

"What makes you think I might get involved with him?"

"The fact that you were snogging him on the beach?"

"Oh. Technically, *he* was snogging *me*."

"Well, technically, Natasha is going to go completely mental when she finds out about it. And I like you. I don't want anything bad to happen to you."

"I can take care of myself."

"Maybe. And maybe she'll leave you alone." Darcy didn't look convinced. "If it was me, I wouldn't take the risk."

"You've done your bit. Whatever happens this time, you needn't feel guilty about it."

"I will anyway."

With that doleful remark she left, and I closed the door after her as softly as I could. I couldn't help shivering as I turned off the lights and started up the stairs, even though I wasn't cold any more. *It was someone walking over my grave*, I thought, and really wished I hadn't.

I got into bed and found myself replaying the evening in my head, over and over.

I don't want anything bad to happen to you . . . Forever's too long . . . I wouldn't take the risk . . . She let it go too far . . . You're beautiful . . . Stay away from there . . . Whatever happens . . . Whatever happens . . .

Not surprisingly, it was a long time before I slept.

14

It was a quiet morning in Fine Feathers, by which I mean Sylvia and I made it to eleven o'clock without seeing a single customer. The sun was shining and it was actually warm for a change. The people of Port Sentinel and the holidaymakers had better things to do than rummage in a charity shop when there was a beach to sit on and ice cream to eat. I stuck a bucket and spade in Marilyn's hand and put a floppy straw hat on Brenda, backward because the front of it was badly frayed, but it was a lost cause. We were never going to pack in the punters on a sunny day.

Sylvia was totally unconcerned. "Don't worry, dear. I like it when it's not too busy. Gives you time to get things organized."

Organization didn't seem to be in Sylvia's skill set but I wasn't about to disagree. A job was a job. Now that the place had been sorted out a bit, it was much easier to keep it ticking over. Sylvia might decide she didn't need me after all, but I very definitely needed her—or rather, I needed the money I could earn by working for her. What I also needed was something to do because standing around waiting for customers was incredibly boring. I couldn't clean the glass of the display cabinet again; it was pristine.

"What should I do next, Sylvia?"

She looked vague. "Aren't there clothes to sort out?"

"We unpacked the last bag when I was here on Tuesday. Unless there have been some more donations."

"I don't think so." Sylvia started to twist the long necklace she was wearing. "Although . . . There's the back stairs. I don't think we've tackled that."

I was puzzled. "Tackled it? I didn't know about it. I thought the shop was just on the ground floor and upstairs there's a flat."

"That's right. But there's a flight of stairs that goes up from the back room—you might not have noticed the door in the corner. I keep it bolted shut."

"I thought it was a cupboard."

"It is really. The door at the top is sealed off and plastered over. So I just use the back stairs as extra storage. Or I did. Until it got too full."

"That explains how there was so much stuff piled up in the shop on my first morning."

"Yes, but there's an awful lot more on the stairs." Sylvia looked worried. "I hope you don't mind going through the bags. They're quite old, some of them. Just things I didn't get around to dealing with at the time, when they came in."

"And then you forgot about them."

"No, I didn't forget. But there were other bags. Other donations . . ." She trailed off. The necklace-twisting was reaching the stage where it would break or she'd garrotte herself, so I smiled reassuringly.

"Don't worry. I like a challenge. I'll just take it one bag at a time." I headed for the back room.

Sylvia called after me, "Be careful when you open the door, won't you, in case anything falls down on top of you."

I thought she was being far too cautious, but since my life plans didn't include being totalled by a rogue platform shoe or a shower of Jeffrey Archer hardbacks, I slid back the bolt and inched the door open with great care.

"Dear Lord above."

It was like something from a TV program about chronic hoarding. The space was rammed with plastic bags of every size and color, many of them split so that their contents were bulging out, and because they were stacked on the (invisible) stairs, it looked like a vast tower of junk, seconds away from cascading down on top of me. I couldn't tell how long Sylvia had been using this space as a dump but it smelled musty and had to have been the work of many months, if not years. It was no wonder she had been reluctant to mention it.

Opening the door—even by a few centimeters—had made the entire pile unstable, as the bags near the bottom pressed forward and the ones above them began to shift. Containing the potential avalanche was the first order of business. I yanked a few of the nearest bags out through the gap, then forced the door closed again.

"Are you managing, dear?"

"Everything's fine," I said firmly, shooting the bolt across and hoping it would hold. Something fell against the door with a loud thud and I winced. One to remember the next time I was getting anything out of Sylvia's secret stash.

I hauled the bags through to the shop, where the light was better, to assess what I'd managed to retrieve. I was dusty and hot and not best pleased to discover that one customer had arrived since I'd left my post, given that the customer in question was Coco Golding. She was wearing cut-off jeans that showed off tanned, lean legs, the muscles super-defined without being bulky. She still seemed on the slight side to be a runner but she certainly had an athlete's body-fat percentage. She was flicking through a rack of dresses, shadowed by Sylvia, who looked distinctly relieved to see me.

"Here's Jess now. She knows where everything is." To me, she said, "I'm making tea."

"Not for me, thanks." I dragged the bags behind the counter and straightened up. "What can I do for you? Were you looking for something in particular?"

"Yes. No. I don't know." Coco abandoned the dresses abruptly. "I wanted to talk to you."

"Why's that?"

She bit her lip. "I don't want to be disloyal."

"To Natasha? Feel free. I won't tell."

"I just thought she went too far. On the headland." The words tumbled out in a rush.

"I noticed you throwing up."

She shuddered. "Don't. That was so embarrassing. I must have eaten something that disagreed with me."

"So it wasn't because you were upset."

"No."

"Because it reminded you of what happened to Freya."

"It was Claudia's smoke. I don't like cigarettes. It made me feel queasy."

I raised my eyebrows. "I suppose hanging around with her is one way to keep your weight down."

"The smoking is a recent thing," she said dismissively. "I'm not used to it yet."

"Right." I lifted a bag onto the counter. "Was that it?"

"There's one other thing." Coco came forward another couple of steps. "This is going to sound really weird, but I was wondering if you'd like me to have a word with Nats about being nicer to you. I feel as if she didn't give you a fair chance. She can be a bit of a bitch."

I frowned. "Why do you care?"

"Because you seem like you'd be fun to have around." She laughed. "I mean, Ryan likes you, so I'm sure you're OK really."

"I thought that was the problem."

"Part of it. But you can handle the Ryan thing. You can persuade him to leave you alone. Natasha will get over it." She hesitated, then said, "The other part of the problem is Freya."

"What do you mean?"

"Nats doesn't like you asking questions about her."

"I bet," I said softly.

"If you could just . . . not. That would be ideal."

"So you want me to drop the whole Freya thing, and tell Ryan once and for all I'm not interested in him. In return, you give Natasha a personality transplant that means she's actually pleasant for a change. And then we could all start again. Get to know one another. Make friends."

Coco nodded, but her eyes were wary.

"That's just not going to happen."

"Which bit?"

"Any of it."

Coco's shoulders slumped.

"You must have known it was a long shot," I said.

"Worth a try." She gave me a tight little smile and turned to go.

"If you don't like bitchy behavior, why on earth are you friends with Natasha?" I said, and Coco stopped, one toe drawing patterns on the floor as she thought about how to answer me.

"She's not so bad."

"I beg to differ." I frowned. "I just don't understand why you hang around with her."

"I don't know. Habit." Another smile, this one more genuine. "I know it's hard for you to imagine, but she can be really funny. It's a good distraction for me. I get too wound-up about training if I'm on my own too much."

"Darcy told me you run."

"A bit."

"Seriously, though."

"You could say that." Her eyes danced. Just talking about it was enough to make her forget everything else that worried her. "It looks as if I might get to compete at the next Olympics."

"That's brilliant." I meant it.

"Yeah." Coco's good mood evaporated as quickly as it had bubbled up. "Well, I did my best. If you change your mind, let me know."

"I will." I watched her go, striding off down the street in a hurry, and wished she had been friends with just about anyone other than Natasha.

Sylvia creaked out of the back room with a steaming mug of pale, watery tea. "Did she find what she was looking for, dear?"

"Not this time," I said, and started to untie one of the bags, concentrating on the job in hand. There were five of them—mainly clothes, although there were also some CDs and bits of bric-a-brac. Pulling on some rubber gloves, I sorted through the first one, untangling a smudged brass candlestick from a pair of fluff-covered opaque tights that were destined for the bin.

"Why should anyone think a charity shop would want their old tights?"

"People don't think. They just want to get rid of things they don't want any more." Sylvia leaned across and took out the candlestick's twin, this one still with bits of wax on it. "Dented. What a shame."

"I'll polish them up and they'll look much better. They might appeal to a Goth." I could already see them in a special Halloween window display, if they didn't sell before that—Marilyn as a vampire and Brenda as her unwilling victim. There was a flowing white nightie that would be ideal for her. It was deflating to realize that by October I would have been back in London for months. Life in Port Sentinel would be going on without me, without anyone much noticing or caring that I wasn't there any more. I would miss them more than they missed me, I thought with a pang.

The bell at the door jangled and Petra bounded in, the perfect antidote to gloom in canary-yellow jeans and a sky-blue T-shirt. "Hi, Jess! Hello, Miss Burman." She craned her neck to see over the counter. "What are you doing?"

"Working," I said repressively. "I'll be finished at one."

"Oh. Can't I help? I'll be excellent at . . ."

"Sorting through donations."

"Yes. That." She turned to Sylvia. "Please, Miss Burman. I won't distract Jess. I'll help."

"Of course you will." Sylvia smiled. "If you want to spend this lovely sunny morning in here, I don't mind at all."

"Wouldn't you rather be on the beach?" I asked Petra when Sylvia had gone into the back room.

"Yes. But I wanted to spend some time with you." It was typical Petra: honest to the point of brutality.

"That's sweet of you."

"There are always too many people around. We never get a chance to talk." She pulled a jumper out of the bag I had given her and held it up. It was a lurid shade of green, with a V-neck. "Who would buy something like that?"

"A golfer, maybe? Someone who came to their senses, anyway, since they gave it away."

"It's been nibbled by moths."

"Badly?"

She turned it round so I could see that it was riddled with tiny holes.

"Throw it out. No one will want that. Hideous is one thing. Manky is another."

"Someone might like it. You don't know for sure." Petra started to fold it. I picked up the bin and held it in front of her.

"Drop it in there. Believe me, we're not lacking in stock for the shop. We don't need anything that will just take up space."

"What are you looking for?"

"This kind of thing." I had found some jeans in the second

bag I was emptying, and I was scanning them like a crime-scene investigator, trying to work out why they'd been donated. "These look perfect. Designer denim. Skinny cut and size six, so they're not going to appeal to everybody, but these were expensive jeans when they were new, and they're not ancient. We'll sell them for a tenner."

"Bargain. I might try them on."

"Feel free." Out of habit I checked the pockets. "Wait a minute. Someone's left something in here."

I held the jeans upside down and shook a silver chain out of the small coin pocket. It slithered onto the counter. There was a pendant on it and I flipped it over to look at it: two lovebirds with a tiny red enamel heart held between their beaks. "That's so pretty. Oh, but the chain's broken. Well, that explains why she forgot about it, whoever she was. Or maybe she wanted to donate it. But I'd have kept the pendant and got a new chain, myself."

Petra hadn't said anything. She reached out and lifted up the pendant, staring at it.

"What's the matter?"

"This." Her face was completely white. "This was Freya's."

"What?"

"This was Freya's," she repeated. "She got it a few weeks before she died. She wore it all the time—I mean, *all* the time. I never saw her without it."

"She must have had one like it. It's pretty, but it can't be unique."

Petra turned it over. "No, it *is* hers. I'm positive. Look, the bird on the left has a wonky tail."

It was true: the tail was set at a slightly odd angle, as if it had been bent and pushed back into shape.

"And Freya's was the same?"

"Definitely. Hugo teased her about it. He said it must have been on special offer because it was broken and whoever had got it for her was a cheapskate."

"Didn't she say who had bought it?"

"It was posted through the letterbox one night. Freya said she didn't know who it was from."

I had a feeling I knew. It fitted all too well with the imaginary boyfriend. "All right. It could be Freya's. Are these her jeans?"

"No. Definitely not. She didn't wear that sort of thing. She couldn't have afforded them in the first place."

"So what's Freya's necklace doing in someone else's pocket?"

"Maybe it fell off without her noticing and they picked it up," Petra suggested.

"Maybe." I was looking at the broken chain, at the links that were pulled out of shape at either end. "Something snapped this chain. Someone pulled on it, hard, or it got caught in something. It didn't just fall off. Did she say anything about losing it?"

Petra shook her head. "As far as I remember, she was wearing it the last time I saw her."

"Which was when?"

"A few hours before she died." The significance of that was starting to sink in. Petra stared at me with wide, haunted eyes. "Oh God."

"Exactly." I sounded as grim as I felt. "So the next question is—"

The shop bell interrupted me and I stopped dead as the door opened cautiously. It was Darcy, today with her hair in ringlets, wearing a lot of peacock-blue makeup around her eyes.

"Can I come in?"

"There's nothing to stop you." Smoothly, and without drawing attention to what I was doing, I slid the necklace off the counter and into the pocket of my own jeans. I was on the wrong side of the counter to kick Petra if she started to talk about it and I hoped like hell she had the sense to stay quiet.

What I had forgotten, of course, was that Petra had no love for Darcy. She straightened up and said to me, "I'm going to have a look around."

"Fine."

"I hope I'm not interrupting." Darcy had turned the cheerfulness up to eleven, obviously hoping to breeze through our first encounter since her confession. "You don't have to stop talking because I'm here."

"Don't be silly." I forced a smile. "What's up?"

She leaned on the counter, her head close to mine, and dropped her voice so Petra wouldn't be able to hear what she said. "I was just wondering how you were today. After what we talked about last night, I mean. Did you read through the sketchbook?"

I had lost an hour flicking through it when I'd given up on sleep, reading the notes Freya had left for herself. It was as close as I could get to hearing her voice. At times, it was almost like having a conversation with her, as I'd laughed at the funny remark she'd overheard in a café and scribbled down.

"I had a look."

"What did you think?"

"I thought what you did was evil," I said levelly.

"*Evil* is a strong word." There was more than a suggestion of a pout on her face. Darcy couldn't or wouldn't see that her behavior wasn't the kind of thing you could brush aside, but I steeled myself to be stern.

"I know. And I also know you came in here to see if I'd forgiven you for the part you played in making a fool out of Freya."

She flinched. "If you want to put it like that."

"I told you, it's not my place to forgive you. I didn't even know her." I looked over at Petra, who appeared to be immersed in a scurrilous biography of Marilyn Monroe. "You should be apologizing to her sister."

Darcy shot out a hand to grip my wrist. "You can't tell her. Don't tell the Leonards. Don't tell anyone. I'd have to leave Port Sentinel if everyone knew. I told you the truth but it was private. Off the record." She was beginning to sound hysterical.

I freed my arm with some difficulty. "Calm down. I'm not going to spread it around. But I think you should explain what you did to them. It's the only way you're ever going to be at peace with yourself."

"I'm not ready for that," she whispered. "It's too hard."

"Now, maybe. But one day, you'll do it." At least, I hoped she would. Fundamentally, Darcy wasn't a bad person, even if she was as changeable as the weather, but she was weak. I still wasn't sure I'd seen the real her. I wasn't actually sure that Darcy herself knew what the real her was like.

In the meantime, reformed character or not, she could make herself useful.

"Let's talk about something else." I held up the jeans. "Look at these. Aren't they lovely?"

"Oh my God. Seven for All Mankind." She reached out and rubbed the material between her finger and thumb. "Feel the quality."

"Someone donated them to us. You wouldn't have any idea who, would you?"

Darcy narrowed her eyes, considering. "They're from last year. A couple of people had them."

"Like who?"

"Stephanie Cardew. She's on holiday in Hawaii at the moment, lucky her. But I think hers were a different wash. They were darker." She frowned. "Natasha had a pair just like these and I haven't seen her wear them for a while. I think they belonged to her."

I dropped them as if they were red-hot. "Suddenly I don't like them so much."

"Don't blame the clothes because someone mean owned them." Darcy stroked the denim lovingly. "I'd buy them but they would never, ever fit me. Natasha's tiny."

"Isn't she, though." I caught Petra's eye; she was looking wild, as if she were about to rush out and confront Natasha. I held her gaze for a couple of seconds while Darcy was drooling over the jeans. *Leave this one to me. I'll sort it out.* "Are you sure they were Natasha's?"

"As sure as I can be." Darcy was sounding more certain of herself. She peered at a small bleach spot on the left thigh, a mark that I hadn't noticed. "Yes. Natasha's, definitely. She wore them loads. She was gutted when she dropped bleach on them. Maybe that's why she gave them away."

I wasn't actually shocked to learn that the jeans were Natasha's, but having Darcy confirm it made my heart race so fast that I was surprised she couldn't hear it. I made conversation for a few minutes, chatting as if nothing of consequence had happened. I didn't trust Darcy enough to tell her what we had found, and Petra evidently felt the same way. She had gone back to the Monroe biography, reading it from the end. Darcy talked. I smiled. The clock on the wall ticked. Nothing had changed; there was no urgency about what I had found out. There was no reason why my hands should slip on the counter top, slick with sweat. Stupid adrenalin, kicking in when it definitely wasn't required.

I could have kissed Sylvia when she poked her head out of the back room. "How are you getting on? Making progress?"

"I'm doing too much talking," I said ruefully. "I haven't finished these bags yet." To Darcy, I said, "I'd better get on with it."

"I could help," she offered.

"I can manage." I walked over to the door with her, holding it open. I had to stop myself from pushing her out. "Thanks for dropping in."

She stopped on the threshold. "Are you sure you're all right? With me, I mean?"

"It might take a while, Darcy." She looked properly crestfallen and I felt sorry for her, despite the fact that she had chosen to betray her friend. *What would Freya do?* "Be nice" was the answer that suggested itself to me. "I'll give you a call later on. We can go for an ice cream."

"Frozen yogurt instead?" Darcy suggested. "I'm inspired by those jeans. I've got to lose some weight."

"It's the best day of the summer so far. You can have yogurt. I'm having ice cream."

"Ice cream is like frozen lard."

"Ice cream is delicious," I said firmly. "I'll see you later."

When I turned back after closing the door, Petra was standing right behind me. "What are we going to do?"

"I'm going to finish my shift." I had another hour to go; I already knew it would feel like a hundred years. "Then you and I are going to go to the police and show them Freya's pendant."

"And say what? That it was stolen?"

"And say that she was murdered." I gave her a grim smile. "Maybe this time they'll take it seriously."

"So that's how you've been keeping yourself busy." I felt my face flame as Dan Henderson smirked at me. The jeans were folded on his desk; the pendant with its broken chain lay across his blotter. "You must have a very vivid imagination, Jess. You've made up quite a story."

"I haven't made up anything." My heart had plummeted into my boots when the desk sergeant told me I had to speak to Dan. So far he was living up to my expectations, refusing to believe a word I said and being faintly insulting at the same time. Knowing I would probably fail, I tried again. "I heard about Freya's death when I got here and it bothered me. Something wasn't right. Then I found her sketchbook, which proves she was happy, and that she was going to meet her boyfriend the night she died—although, as I said, someone tipped me off that he didn't even exist—he was just invented to distract Freya from Ryan, by Natasha Watkins and her friends. And then I found the pendant."

"In a pair of jeans you say Natasha Watkins used to own."

"I'm sure it would be possible to prove they belonged to

her if you looked into it. The pendant was Freya's favorite piece of jewelry. She never took it off. And it's broken, look. Someone took it away from her with force."

"Or she caught it on a branch when she was running through the woods."

"And Natasha Watkins happened to find it? That doesn't seem likely. What would Natasha have been doing there, anyway, unless she was pretending to be the secret boyfriend?"

"This is the boyfriend who gave Freya the necklace, but didn't exist." The sarcasm in Dan's voice was off the scale.

"You're making it sound as if none of this makes sense, but it does." I changed tack. "There was an autopsy, wasn't there? Did she have any injuries to her neck?"

"She had injuries to her neck. She had injuries everywhere. She fell off a cliff and landed on some rocks. She wasn't a pretty sight by the time her body was recovered. There was hardly an inch of her that wasn't damaged in some way."

I winced. "OK. But specifically her neck?"

"I don't remember." Dan leaned forward, lacing his hands in the approved listening-parent manner. "Look, I appreciate that you're trying to help. I can understand how you might be fascinated by Freya, since you look so alike. I can even understand why you would fixate on Natasha Watkins. She's a pretty girl. I remember from my schooldays—the other girls would gang up on the pretty ones."

"That's not why I mentioned her," I ground out through clenched teeth. "And I don't dislike her because she's pretty and I'm jealous. I dislike her because she killed my cousin."

"You've no proof of that."

"The jeans belonged to her. The necklace belonged to Freya,

who was wearing it the last time anyone saw her, as far as I can tell, or as far as anyone will admit. Natasha must have encountered her before she died. She pulled the necklace off Freya's neck by yanking on it so the chain snapped. Then she put the whole thing in her pocket and forgot about it. She donated the jeans to the charity shop to get rid of them in case there was any forensic evidence on them linking her to Freya's death, but Sylvia forgot about the bag of donations and hid them, and it was only today that I found them and the pendant. Natasha probably thinks they were sold months ago. She probably thinks there isn't anything to connect her with Freya."

"The jeans weren't in her possession when you found them. Anyone could have put that in the pocket. You could have done it yourself."

"I wouldn't," I said, shocked. "It was there when I unfolded them. Petra saw me find it."

"There's nothing to prove these are Natasha's jeans, though."

"Darcy said—"

"Darcy says a lot." Dan shook his head. "Not proof."

"If Natasha admitted they were her jeans . . ."

"It still wouldn't prove that she put the pendant in the pocket. Or that it was ripped off Freya's neck in malicious circumstances. Or that Freya was murdered." He stood up. "You've got a bee in your bonnet about this and I can understand why. It would be much more exciting if she'd been killed. But there was an inquest. The coroner was quite clear. It was an accident. Death by misadventure. And I told you to stay out of it, didn't I?"

"If I'd stayed out of it you'd never have known Natasha Watkins was involved. If you could just look into it—"

"Not going to happen. I have enough real crimes to deal with. I don't need to invent more work for myself."

I looked at his in-tray, which was almost empty. "Yeah. You look as if you're run off your feet."

"Was there anything else I could help you with?"

"No. Just Freya's unsolved murder." Frustration made my voice waver and I dug my nails into my palms. I would not cry.

"That's enough." Dan said it quietly. "Leave it now. We've talked about it, and about Freya. It's time to leave her in peace. Enjoy your holiday. Stop trying to rake up trouble."

I was shaking, I discovered. "What happened to justice? What about the Leonards? Don't they deserve the truth?"

"This is the real world, Jess. There's no such thing as justice."

"Do you really believe that?" I was taken aback.

He shrugged. "I've seen a lot of court cases but I've never seen anyone get the sentence they deserve."

"At least ask Natasha to explain how she got the necklace. *I* can't take this any further. *You* can."

Dan shook his head. "I'm not going to harass the girl on your say-so. Charles Watkins is an important benefactor in this area. He would not be pleased if I started upsetting his daughter."

"His daughter the murderer."

His eyebrows snapped together. "You're getting into dangerous territory, accusing people of murder."

Anger gave me the courage to go on. "What if I don't forget about it?"

"If I hear you've been talking about Freya's death being murder—and I will hear, believe me—I will be very unhappy."

Dan's eyes were the dark gray of dirty snow. "There was no murder. She died in an accident. That's all there is to it."

"Are you angry because you didn't realize she'd been killed until now and it makes you look bad, or because a murder would make the town look bad?" I held up a finger. "Or—wait—is it because you don't want anyone to look into Freya's 'romantic notions?'"

"I don't know what you mean."

"That's good," I said. "Very convincing."

"Don't push me, Jess. You won't like it if I lose my temper." Dan sat down again and scribbled something in a notebook. Without looking up he said, "This conversation is over. You know where the door is."

"Thanks for your help." I didn't even try to sound as if I meant it.

"I know you're disappointed, Jess. You'll just have to trust me."

I couldn't imagine a future when I ever trusted Dan Henderson. I stuffed the jeans and the pendant into my bag and swung out of the room without another word to him. In the reception area, Petra was waiting, her face pinched with tension. I had practiced explaining what I knew on her, and her reaction had been very different from the inspector's. She had believed me and she had been devastated that her big sister had been treated so cruelly. In that version of the story I downplayed Darcy's role. It was for her to explain what she'd done, or not. Besides, Petra had been upset enough without sharing the full extent of her betrayal.

Petra jumped up and followed me through the revolving

door onto the street. I was moving fast and she had to run to catch up.

"What happened?"

"Nothing at all. He didn't believe me."

"Why not?"

"He wants it to have been an accident because he made a mess of investigating it in the first place." That was the PG version, anyway.

"Can't you talk to someone else? He must have a boss."

"Not in Port Sentinel. And anyway, he was right about one thing." I could admit it to Petra, even if I had been prepared to argue it out with Dan Henderson. "There isn't enough proof."

"So she's going to get away with it? That's not right." Petra was halfway to distraught, which I totally understood. I'd have felt the same way if I hadn't got through the anger stage and started thinking again.

"We're going to come up with a plan. A plan that will get us the evidence we need, once and for all."

"What kind of plan?"

"Something very sneaky." I hugged the bag to myself. "Don't worry. I have an idea. But I'm going to need your help."

The smile that lit up her face was brighter than the sun.

15

Recruiting Petra as an assistant was a stroke of genius. Getting an invitation to dinner at the Leonards' house wasn't difficult; I could have managed that part myself. And in spite of the circumstances, I found myself enjoying the meal—the way the conversation flowed, following no particular logic, and the simple food that included strawberries Tom had picked in the garden just before dinner (along with a scattering of greenflies, but that just added to the general chaos). It was being part of a family that made me particularly happy. I felt as if I had slotted into a place that was waiting for me—not Freya's empty spot, and not Will's seat at the table, but somewhere that was just for me, where I had been destined to fit in. Hugo had added me to his list of targets for gentle mockery, and somewhere during an argument about female tennis players earning as much as their male counterparts I completely forgot why I was there in the first place.

It was Petra who brought me back to myself, Petra who cut

into the flow of conversation with a brisk, "If you've finished, Jess, we should go upstairs."

Tilly looked interested. "What are you two up to? Where are you going?"

"Freya's room. Jess wanted to borrow a couple of her books." I was deeply impressed by Petra's ability to lie; there wasn't a hint of hesitation or uncertainty in her answer. After a couple of seconds, I realized it was my turn. I tried to remember what I'd seen on Freya's bookshelves.

"Last time I was here I noticed she had a copy of *I Capture the Castle*. I've always wanted to read it." I had read it about twenty times, in fact, but there was no one at the table to contradict me.

"That's a gorgeous book," Tilly said with a sigh. "One of my favorites. I remember the day I gave it to Freya."

Oh wonderful, I'd picked the one with major sentimental value. "If you'd prefer me to get a copy of my own . . ." I began uncertainly.

"No! Of course not. If she were here, she'd give it to you herself." My aunt smiled at me warmly. "It's just a book, Jess. And you don't have to worry about upsetting me. I want you to get to know Freya, and the best way is by getting to know the things she loved."

Hugo raised one dark eyebrow at me. "That's a good point. How are you and Will getting on?"

I couldn't stop the blush that swept into my cheeks, but I could and did glare at him as an answer.

Tilly laughed. "Like that, is it?"

"No. It's not like anything. He's been very pleasant and—and welcoming." And much though I'd like to pretend I was hiding a more intimate relationship, I was actually telling the truth. He'd been nothing more than friendly. When he wasn't being hostile. Or saving my life.

It was something else I had in common with Freya, I thought, tramping up the stairs behind Petra—Will wasn't interested in either of us. And Ryan unfortunately was. My phone buzzed in my pocket with a message and I glanced at it: right on cue, another text from Ryan. He had sent six since the previous night. Why was it inevitably the wrong boy who got in touch? I felt intensely irritated at the thought of the hurt expression in his blue eyes as his phone stubbornly failed to register a reply to any of the messages he'd sent. He wasn't used to being treated mean. I strongly suspected it would make him all the more determined to win me over, which was absolutely not what I wanted, but I couldn't reply without encouraging him. There was no way to win.

"Find someone else," I muttered, shoving the phone back into my jeans as I rounded the corner to the last flight of stairs. "You can't throw a stone in Port Sentinel without hitting a girl who'd love you to like her."

"What was that?" Petra turned round in the act of opening Freya's door.

"Oh, nothing. It wasn't aimed at you." She looked hurt and I hurried to add, "Boys are very annoying."

"Is there someone waiting for you back in London?"

"Not really." I told her about Conrad two-timing me while I wandered around Freya's room, looking at all the things I'd seen the last time and noticing a lot more on this visit. The bookcase had a postcard propped on top of it, but someone had stuck a pile of books in front of it so I hadn't noticed it before. The picture was of a knight kissing a medieval lady's hand in a stairwell. I unpinned it and read the scrawl on the back:

For you with love PK x

Petra saw me looking at it. "That came with the pendant."

"They went to a lot of trouble, didn't they? No detail too minor." I read the painting's title off the back of the card. "*The Meeting on the Turret Stairs.* Very romantic."

Petra laughed. "You don't sound like you really think that."

"I'm a bit off romance at the moment."

"Can I ask you a personal question?" She opened Freya's wardrobe door and began to rummage in it, facing away from me. "Do you like Will?"

"He's a nice person."

"You know what I mean." I could only see her ear but it was bright red. "Do you *like* him?"

In a flash I remembered Hugo teasing her about her feelings for Will and I knew I had to tread carefully. "I think he's lovely but I'm not here to find a boyfriend. I'll be gone in a few weeks. And I have just had my heart broken. I'm a bit too damaged to want to try again."

I could see her shoulders sagging as she relaxed. "OK. Well. I was just wondering."

"Your secret's safe with me." I wandered over and reached past her to pull out a hanger with a long floaty dress on it—purple chiffon with trumpet sleeves and a low neckline. "What about this one? This looks pretty good. I bet it was the tip of the fashion in nineteen seventy-three."

Petra looked at it and shook her head. "It's a winter dress. The color is all wrong too, and the length. The dress she was wearing the night she died was a fifties one with a wide skirt to just below the knee. It was white and yellow with daisies embroidered on it."

"She would have to have something unique, wouldn't she?" I sighed. "How am I going to find anything like that? I don't have time to scour eBay for it."

"There's this one." She hauled out a dress that was officially my worst nightmare. It was pale yellow, a halterneck dress in broderie anglaise with a nipped-in waist. The skirt was the right length, but bell-shaped.

"Where did she get that? Ava Gardner's attic?"

"Try it on." Petra handed it to me. "You wanted a dress that was typical Freya. You wanted something like what she wore the night she died. That's as good as you're going to get."

"Then let's hope it fits."

It was a close-run thing, involving Petra doing a great deal of tugging on the zip, and I wasn't able to breathe or sit down once I'd got it on, but it did just about do up. I turned side-ways to see myself in the mirror, marveling at the dress's tiny waist.

"Freya must have been a lot thinner than me."

"She wasn't." Petra grinned. "She never wore this. She bought it without trying it on at a jumble sale. She kept saying she needed a proper corset to wear with it."

"I think a corset is the only thing that could make me more miserable."

"You need shoes to go with it." Petra knelt on the floor, peering under the bed. Freya's feet had been a full size smaller than mine, so finding the right footwear was even more of a challenge than getting the dress. My ancient trainers were just not going to cut it.

"I'll have to wear flat shoes. No way am I walking up that hill in heels. Especially if they don't fit properly."

"What hill?"

"The one that leads up to the headland." I clicked my tongue, annoyed with myself. "Oh, I haven't told you what my plan is. Sorry, Petra."

She sat back and stared up at me. "If it involves the headland, I don't think it's a good idea."

"You haven't heard it yet." I really wanted to sit down but it was impossible; I couldn't bend. I leaned against the wall awkwardly. "It's going to happen tomorrow night. I'll come over during the evening to do some more reading. Then I'll get changed into this, do my makeup so I look like Freya did, and sneak out, obviously without being seen by your parents."

"Yeah, you said you want to look like Freya. I still don't understand why."

"Because I haven't explained it yet." I looked sideways at myself in the mirror, assessing the overall effect. "Freya is going to make a reappearance where she died. I'm going to persuade Natasha to meet me at the top of the cliffs. The shock of seeing me will scare her into telling me what she did. She confesses, I go back to the police with proper evidence, justice is done."

"That's the plan?"

"Yep. Shakespeare had it first, but I think my version is better than his." Petra was frowning. "Have you read *Hamlet*? The play within a play? *The play's the thing/Wherein I'll catch the conscience of the king*," I quoted.

"Oh, I know all that. We used to act it out. Hugo would be Hamlet. Freya was Ophelia. I was everyone else."

"OK. So why the frown?"

"Because if something happens to you on the cliffs, you'll be dead too." She looked very young all of a sudden. "I'm worried for you."

"That's so sweet. There's really no need. I know what I'm doing." I said it with a confidence I didn't totally feel. Natasha had really scared me on the cliffs. My only hope was that she'd be so rattled to see Freya standing in front of her in the moonlight, she'd confess straight away. "I'll be in complete control of what happens."

"Including making Natasha turn up? She hates you. Why would she meet you?"

"Ah, she won't know that I know she's coming. But she won't be able to stay away. When I met Darcy earlier I set the whole thing in motion." We had sat on the beach and talked about nothing for an hour—long enough to remind me why I had liked her in the first place, and long enough for her to feel reassured that I didn't hate her. It was true: I didn't. But I still didn't trust her. "I told her I thought I knew what had happened to Freya. I told her I'd be able to find out for sure tomorrow night. I said I just needed to check something on the headland to make sure I was right, but I was sure I knew the person responsible for her death."

Petra looked appalled. "What did she say?"

"She wanted to know what I needed to find out and who I was talking about. I told her to wait and see."

"Do you think it was *Darcy*?" Her name came out as a squeak.

"Of course not. It was Natasha. But I know I can count on Darcy to tell Natasha what I told her. She can't help herself. She has to spread gossip and it's best if she knows something no one else does."

"You're using her."

"Exploiting her weakness. Besides, she owes it to Freya."

Petra was on to it straight away. "What do you mean?"

"Ask me another time." I put one hand on my ribcage. "My chest is seriously constricted. I'm seeing stars. I need to get out of this dress, like, five minutes ago."

"I don't think it's the ideal outfit for fighting crime, I have to say."

I laughed. "If Freya had worn Lycra all-in-one body-suits and a mask, we'd be in business. But I'm stuck with Grace Kelly's cast-offs as my superhero costume."

"You're going sort of blue." Petra regarded me with interest. "You really can't breathe at all, can you?"

"Not much, no." I winced. "Just don't break the zip. You'd have to cut me out and then we'd be back to square one."

"That might not be such a bad thing." She began to work the zip down, a couple of millimeters at a time. "Your idea is mad. And dangerous."

"You're probably right." I took a proper breath as the dress loosened and felt the oxygen rush to my head. "But I really think it's going to work. If Natasha thinks I can prove she killed Freya, she'll be desperate to stop me. She'll be on edge before Freya makes her appearance. I'll never get a better chance to make her tell the truth. As soon as she knows it's me, she'll go back to being the hard-faced bitch we know and love."

"I'll come with you."

I shook my head. "I have to be alone or it won't work. She'd never think Freya's ghost had materialized in front of her accompanied by her sister."

"I could hide." Petra's eyes were like saucers. "I'm good at that."

"I can't take the risk."

"It's still just your word against hers, though, if it's just the two of you there."

"Well, duh. I'm planning to record what she says." I waved my mobile phone at her.

"Oh, and where are you going to put that? You don't have any pockets."

I looked down blankly. She was right. "I'll have to put it down my front."

"Will it fit?

"Just about," I said, experimenting. "Getting it out might be tricky."

"I really don't like this plan." Petra's voice was high and sounded as if she was on the verge of tears. "There must be another way."

"I can't think of one if there is. We need more evidence, Petra. And it's now or never. I told Darcy where I was going and when. I can't back out now."

I said it as if I meant it, and I think it convinced Petra. It almost convinced me.

The closer it got to the witching hour the following night, the more tense I felt. I went round to Sandhayes after not eating dinner, because I couldn't. I had barely eaten anything all day.

My throat closed up every time I attempted to eat, and food tasted of nothing much. It was lucky that Mum was avoiding me so there was no one to ask me why I was off my food. Even if she had insisted, I wouldn't have been able to eat anything. I had tried, and basically failed. It was one more reason to hope nothing was going to go wrong. A last meal of half a piece of toast would be a truly depressing one. Little did Mum know that I was quite happy to stay out of her way, so she wouldn't notice that I was up to something, and so we wouldn't have to talk about Dan Henderson and what a nice person he really was and how much time had or hadn't changed him. He was a creep, I thought, and a bad policeman. But even he couldn't ignore solid evidence that linked Natasha to Freya's death.

Tilly answered the door and looked unsurprised to see me even though I hadn't said I was coming round. There were definite advantages to her being arty and vague.

"I just wanted to return this." I held up the book I had borrowed the night before.

"Have you read it already?"

"Couldn't put it down." I *had* read it again, in fact. It had passed the time between two and five in the morning when I had been unable to sleep.

"Well, take something else. In fact"—she reached behind the door—"take a key. You can come and go as you please."

I stared at the key she was holding out to me, complete with a wooden key ring shaped like a hippo. "Really?"

"You're family."

I took the key and hurried up the stairs, running my hand along the banister, feeling as if I had come home. I opened the door to Freya's room and, as I had expected, Petra was lying on the bed, waiting for me. What I had not expected was that Will would be sitting in the chair by the desk.

"What are you doing here?" I was out of breath, which put me at a disadvantage.

"I wanted to talk to you."

"About what?" I took off my jacket and put it on the bed with my bag.

"Petra and I had a chat earlier."

I looked at her. She cut her eyes away from mine, her face advertising the fact that she felt guilty. "Did you? That must have been nice."

Will was fiddling with a pen, tapping it on the desk. Not as calm as he looked, I thought. "She told me what you were planning to do this evening."

"Oh."

"Petra was worried. Understandably."

"There's no need. And there's no need for you to be here."

"Come off it, Jess." He slammed the pen down on the desk. "Are you out of your mind? You're going to act as bait in a trap to catch a murderer and you think that's a good idea?"

"It sounds sensible to me."

"Why didn't you tell me what you were planning?"

"Because I knew you'd react like this." I took the dress off the wardrobe door, where it had been hanging. "It's getting late. I've got to get ready."

"I can't let you do this."

"I don't need your permission."

Will stood up and crossed the room, stopping very close to me, so close that we were almost touching. His voice was as soft as velvet. "What if I asked you? What if I told you I couldn't stand to see you hurt?"

"I'd say it was emotional blackmail and I wasn't going to fall for it." I glared at him, holding onto my anger to stop myself slipping into the depths of his gray eyes for fear I would never resurface. "I'm going to do this, whether you like it or not. Did Petra tell you about the necklace in Natasha's pocket?"

From the look on his face, she had.

"She's guilty, Will. She's got away with it for too long, and I'm not going to stand back and watch her mince around this town as if she has a perfect right to be free when Freya's not here any more. If I could think of an alternative, I'd take it, but I tried getting your dad to investigate Freya's death again and he wasn't having it. This is the only way to find out what happened."

I knew I'd won when he turned away. "For the record, I think it's a terrible idea."

"Thank you very much." I hesitated. "I still need to get changed."

"Oh, right." He went to the door.

"Are you leaving?" Petra's voice was a squeak.

Will stopped with his hand on the doorknob. "Do you want me to stay?" He said it to her, but then he looked at me.

"Stick around," I said. "You can be the first to see me as Freya."

He nodded. "I'll wait out here. Let me know when it's safe to come back."

The only good thing about not eating was that it helped take a millimeter or two off my waistline so the dress wasn't as uncomfortable as it had been. Freya's shoes were another issue. They pinched my toes and heels from the moment I forced my feet into them, and although they looked like pretty, dainty ballet shoes, they felt like torture devices. The important thing was how they looked, which was perfect. Wearing Freya's clothes and shoes, I didn't feel like myself any more. I looked in the mirror and saw her, and as the light ebbed from the sky I had the strangest feeling that she was there, watching us. I hoped she approved.

"Almost done." I leaned in to the mirror to add a flick to the ends of my eyeliner, aiming for the retro style that Darcy did so well. "You can let Will in."

Petra opened the door, and I turned round in time to see his face when he saw me. He stopped dead.

"Well?" I put my hands on my hips.

"It's uncanny." Will was staring, taking in every detail. "Freya wouldn't stand like that, though. Too confrontational."

I folded my hands in front of me and he grinned.

"Too demure. She wasn't Jane Eyre."

"I'll aim for somewhere in the middle, then." I had put the pendant on a new chain and now I picked it up to put it on, struggling slightly with the fiddly clasp. It was Petra who came to help me, not Will, and I couldn't help being disappointed. Will had returned to his seat at Freya's desk and was staring at her wall of pictures, including the photograph of his hands. I wondered if he was thinking about Freya and how much she had liked him. I wondered if he was even thinking about me a little bit.

"Are you going to wear your hair down?" Petra asked. I had it tied up in a ponytail and she tweaked it, making my hair swish.

This was the moment I'd been dreading, which was why I'd left it until the end. I made myself sound very cheerful indeed. "In a way."

"What do you mean?"

"It's the last thing I need to do to look like Freya did when she died."

"You're not going to cut your hair." Petra took two steps away from me. "Absolutely not."

"It will make all the difference to whether Natasha believes I'm her or not." I went over to my bag and took out a pair of kitchen scissors. I held them out to her. "I brought these."

"I'm not doing it." She shook her head. "No way."

"You have to. I can't do it myself. It won't look right." And I wasn't sure I could bring myself to do it. "You know how long Freya's hair was when she died. I don't."

"I can't." Petra's eyes glittered as tears filled them. She was shaking. "I'm sorry. I don't want to."

I could tell she meant it too. There was nothing I could say to persuade her to help. I turned and looked at Will.

"No."

"Please."

He didn't move.

"OK, then." I turned to the mirror and looked at myself as me for the last time. "It's only hair, people. It'll grow again."

I turned sideways so I could see what I was doing. With a deep breath, I lifted my arms. Cutting my own hair was going to be incredibly awkward. My main concern was chopping off a chunk of ear by mistake as I tried to decide where to make the first cut.

"Stop." Will stood up. "Give me the scissors."

I held onto them. "I've got to do this."

"If you say so." He pushed the chair toward me. "Sit down and hand them over."

I did as I was told. He turned the seat round so I was facing away from the mirror and crouched in front of me, looking up into my face. "One last time, before I do this. Are you sure?"

I nodded, not trusting myself to speak. He ran his hand down the length of my hair, once, for no particular reason, then took a firm hold of it near the top. "Hold still."

It was the sound that was the worst of it as he cut through the thick ponytail, a sound like a hundred locusts devouring dry leaves. I closed my eyes and tried not to think about it as the scissors bit down. I could feel Will's breath on my skin, and the cold steel of the blades when they touched my neck now and then, and the sudden warmth when his hands brushed against me. I was aware of every movement he made and how close he was to me, and how much he was concentrating on what he was doing. It hadn't been fair, really. I knew he couldn't stand to see something done badly when it might be done well. I'd known as soon as I saw him sitting in Freya's room that he would end up cutting my hair. I just couldn't decide if that made it better or worse.

The whole time none of us said anything, including Petra. It really wasn't a what-are-you-doing-for-your-holidays sort of haircut so I could understand the silence, but I'd have welcomed some distraction. It took a surprisingly long time to cut it all, and I only knew Will was finished when I heard him step away and put the scissors down on top of the chest of drawers.

I opened my eyes. "How is it?"

Petra had her hands up to shield her eyes and now she peeked through her fingers. "Oh my God. It's exactly right. That's exactly how she looked. Will, you're amazing. Have a look, Jess."

I turned to see myself in the mirror and couldn't quite believe the change it had made. The shorter hair fell around my face in a ragged sort of bob. My eyes looked huge. My head felt light and somehow untethered, as if it was going to float away. I had never realized how heavy my hair was until it was gone. I reached up a hand to explore the back of it, feeling the unfamiliar ends sticking out at all angles. It felt . . . short.

I hadn't thought I would mind as much as I did.

I had been staring at myself but now I raised my eyes to Will's reflection. His expression was hard. He held what had once been my hair in both hands, twisted into a bright rope that he pulled taut. I glanced at it once and then back at him, keeping my eyes trained on his face.

"Thank you. You did a good job." I smiled, my face feeling stiff and my throat aching from the effort of not crying. "And it's really going to cut down on the number of times I get dragged around by the hair in an average week. It happened more often than you'd expect when it was long."

Will didn't reply. His grim expression didn't waver as he laid my hair down on the bed, then walked out of the room without another word.

"I don't know what he has to be angry about," I said to Petra, who looked sad and wise and pitying, all at the same time.

"Don't you?"

"It's *my* bloody hair," I snapped. "And I'm not flouncing around like tragedy in a frock."

"Yeah . . ." she said slowly. "I don't think it's that, actually."

"Then what is it?"

She smiled and didn't say anything. On reflection, I was sort of glad she didn't.

16

There was something unreal about walking through Port Sentinel in Freya's footsteps. It had been a Friday night when she fell and it was Saturday now, but the feeling of weekend frivolity was probably the same. The pubs were busy, drinkers spilling out across the pavements, and I kept to the other side of the street as much as I could, staying in the shadows. I felt highly self-conscious with my ragged hair stuffed under a beanie hat, and my pale, pretty dress, and I pulled my jacket tightly around me although it was a mild evening.

Freya's mood would have been very different. Freya was going to meet her dream lover—her Pale Knight. Freya would have run to the Angel Bridge with a light heart, full of excited anticipation, not dread. Freya had gone to her death happily, and I went to avenge her with a ball of fear like a stone in my stomach. I dragged my feet and it was only a little bit because of how much they hurt. (It was a little bit because of that, though. Those shoes were just not getting any more comfortable the longer I wore them.)

I had decided to start at the bridge and go from there, since that was what Freya had apparently done. It was easy to follow Petra's directions—to take the upper road out of town and cut down to the woods via a narrow path that ran between a school and a housing estate. I wouldn't have known where it led if it hadn't been for Petra's local knowledge. The sign indicating it was a public footpath didn't mention the bridge, or the woods, or the view that could be yours if you were prepared to hike a mile uphill from it over rough ground. In stupid shoes. In the dark.

I had to be out of my mind.

I had been lucky enough to get a clear night again, the moon rising like a fat golden ball behind the trees. There was enough light to see the bridge from quite a long way off and I hurried toward it, feeling my heart knock in my chest as it registered that this was really happening, now. To stop the tension from spiraling into panic I concentrated on where I was, not why. It was a pretty little bridge, a small but elegant arch over a stream that didn't really need a bridge, at least in summer. It was just a trickle, though I could see there was a wider track it had cut for itself in the soft forest floor. The wood was rough with age, and when I got close enough to run my hand over the railing I saw that it was carved with thousands of initials—big or small, fine or crudely done, but all in pairs. This was where you went to tell the world you were in love. What better place to meet the man of your dreams?

Or your worst nightmare, maybe?

I stopped in the middle of the bridge and listened. The

water sang over the pebbles in the bed of the stream. A breath of wind stirred the trees to a sigh. Somewhere, a late bird twittered. Being a city girl I couldn't pretend I knew what kind of bird it was. I was pretty much lost if it wasn't a pigeon.

"I am so far out of my comfort zone," I murmured, wanting to make my own contribution to the noises around me, just to be a part of it. "Give me Trafalgar Square any day."

I took off the hat and stuffed it in my jacket pocket, running my fingers through my hair to try to make it look a bit less disheveled. It felt strange, unfamiliar. Wrong.

"But it *looks* right and that's the main thing." It didn't get sadder than trying to jolly yourself along after a traumatic haircut. As long as it worked, I didn't care. If it didn't work, I was totally getting extensions.

I peered through the trees, trying to see if there was anything moving. No one behind me. No one in front of me. But there on the left was the Angel Tree. I recognized it in spite of my sniping. I could pick out the curve of the hip, the line of a shoulder, and the head was remarkably formed, looking like a longhaired woman. The tree was entirely rotten, hollowed out, and the other side of the trunk formed the wings in two towering spurs of wood.

"It does remind me of an angel. I'll give them that." I strode over to it and found a hole halfway up the trunk. It seemed to be mostly wildlife-free and I took off my jacket and rolled it and my hat into a tight ball. I slotted the bundle into the hole. At least I'd remember where I left my stuff.

The night air was cold on my skin where the halter-neck dress didn't cover me, which was altogether too many places. It was cut low at the front and across the back, and I missed my hair more than ever because I had nowhere to hide any more. Winter would be tough, I thought, setting off along the side of the stream. I was used to having long hair for insulation. There were a lot of hats in my future, even if I was planning to go to a real hairdresser some time and make it look like I'd meant to have it cut that way.

. . . and concentrate . . .

I was distracting myself from what I was doing because I was nervous about it, but I needed to start paying attention or I was going to miss something. Or fall over; that was the other possibility. While I was thinking that, at the same exact moment the thought crossed my mind, my foot skidded on some dry, dead leaves and I almost face-planted in the dirt. *Almost* being the key word, thankfully, because my dress would not have been the better for a roll on the ground. I had just managed to save myself by putting out a hand in time, catching hold of a useful tree trunk. The skin of my palm burned where I had rubbed it on the bark, but it wasn't a serious injury.

Never mind. Forget about it. Forget the ache in your legs too. Forget the stitch that's starting to pinch in your side. Forget the pain in your heels where Freya's evil shoes are rubbing the skin away. Forget the shallow breaths that are all you can manage with your tight dress and the steep hill you're climbing. Forget the fear that's making your knees tremble. Forget the look on Will's face when he saw you with short hair. Don't even think about what your mother will say when she sees you. Now's not the time to think about why she's been avoiding you, either. Just keep going.

I made it to the top of the hill in one piece, my breath ragged and loud in my ears. I stopped near the edge of the trees to get it under control and to check behind me again. Nothing. No one moved. Nothing stirred. I was feeling nervous again, but now for two reasons. Maybe it hadn't worked, and maybe this had all been for nothing.

Strangely, it hadn't occurred to me that she'd be there already, waiting. As I turned back to face the headland, a movement caught my attention, over to the right. Someone was standing under the trees, a slight figure with long hair. She was doing what I wanted her to do. My plan was working. She had come. I dug out my phone and set it to record, hoping it would pick up something over my heart pounding, and stuck it back into the bodice of the dress with hands that trembled very slightly.

Now for the hard part.

I stepped out from behind my tree and walked forward, into the open. The moon made my dress look white and bleached my skin to a ghostly pallor, exactly as I had wanted. I hadn't really thought about how I was going to attract her attention, but a twig snapped under my foot and she whipped round. She felt as edgy as I did, I realized.

And she was completely the wrong person.

"Coco?" It came out quietly, almost not a sound at all. My throat was tight with tension so my voice was hoarse.

"Oh my God. Freya?" She backed away a couple of paces, her face clearly showing that she was terrified.

I wanted to ask what Coco was doing on the clifftop, but silence seemed to be a better response. I didn't want to give myself away. I peered into the shadows, trying to see if she was alone. I couldn't believe Natasha wasn't there. I could just about believe that she wouldn't come alone, so I shouldn't have been that surprised to see Coco. I *was* surprised there was no sign of her demonic best friend.

Unless she was behind me.

With difficulty, I hid the shiver of fear that ghosted over me. With even more difficulty, I restrained myself from turning round and concentrated instead on the girl in front of me.

"I'm so sorry about what happened. You have to believe me." Coco's arms were wrapped around her body and as she spoke she was digging her nails into her skin, leaving marks I could see even in the moonlight. "I didn't know what was going to happen at the bridge."

I made myself look sorrowful, remembering what Will had said about Freya's demeanor and how it differed from mine. Not confrontational. Not too exaggerated. I settled on turning my head away from Coco, as if I couldn't bear to look at her any more.

"It was an accident," she said.

"Was it?"

"Of course." She gave a sob, her face working as she tried not to cry. "You know I never meant for you to fall."

"What?" I dropped the Freya act for a second, my voice sharp. I couldn't have stayed silent for a million pounds. "You were here?"

"They weren't expecting you to run. You were too quick. The others followed but I was faster than everyone else." She laughed, a brittle, horrible sound. "As usual. I don't know why you're even surprised. That's what I'm famous for."

"I don't remember," I whispered. "Why did I run?"

"Because you were scared." She frowned. "You really don't remember? Everyone was waiting for you."

"Why?"

"To see your reaction when you found out you'd been fooled by the guy we invented."

"You wanted to laugh at me?"

Coco nodded miserably. "And you and Natasha had a fight. A proper one. She wanted to hurt you. You know what a bad temper she has." Her hand went to her throat. "She pulled your necklace off."

My neck burned where the chain lay against it, as if it had actually happened to me. Poor Freya.

Coco continued, "You ran. Natasha said we weren't to let you get away. She wanted to teach you a lesson." She shrugged. "I didn't think about it. I just followed you. If I'd known what was going to happen I would never, ever have done it. But I thought it was going to be all right."

"How did I fall?"

"It wasn't my fault. I tried to stop you." I didn't quite believe her; the self-justification struck a false note. "You'd run into a dead end. As soon as I realized you'd come this way I knew you were trapped, and you knew it too. You were standing on the edge of the cliff when I got here. I didn't want to scare you, so I just said your name. You didn't seem to hear. I tried to grab hold of you to pull you back, but I couldn't get there in time. You went over the edge. There was nothing I could do."

"Did anyone see? Does anyone else know what you did?"

She shook her head. "I was too upset to tell anyone what happened."

"Poor you." It was a me thing to say with that sarcastic inflection, and it irritated Coco.

"I couldn't sleep properly for months. I've failed exams I should have passed and I haven't won races that should have been easy. My training was all over the place—my parents thought I was on drugs. So yeah, poor me." Her eyes narrowed and she came forward a few paces. "Wait a second . . . Jess?"

"The penny drops." I smiled at her, not pleasantly, and moved round to keep the bench between us. "I wanted to know the truth. Did you leave anything out?"

"No." She sounded sulky. "You tricked me."

"You tricked Freya. And you hunted her to her death."

"It was an accident."

"If it was an accident, why didn't you tell her mum how she died? Why didn't you tell the police? Why did you let her friends and family think she killed herself deliberately?"

"I was scared." Coco looked the opposite of scared as she sauntered around the bench, one hand trailing along the back of it.

I moved away a little. "Scared of what? Scared you'd get into trouble?" I shook my head. "That's pathetic. You've got to take responsibility for what you did."

"I didn't do anything."

"You were an active participant in a mob. You bullied Freya, along with your evil pal. You forced her to the edge of the cliff and you helped her over the edge by scaring her that little bit more. She had nowhere else to go. Because of you."

"I knew that was what everyone would say." Coco had moved toward me as I stepped back, keeping the distance between us the same.

"So that's why you said nothing." I took another couple of steps away from her, feeling crowded. The surf boomed on the rocks below us, louder now than I had heard it before.

"Did you come alone?"

I was about to say yes without thinking about it, but something stopped me. I looked at her, at the intent expression in her eyes, and I started to reassess the previous few minutes.

"Are you here on your own?" she asked, more insistent this time. Then she smiled. "You are, aren't you? You'd want to do this by yourself. You wouldn't want to share the glory of solving the crime of the century."

"That wasn't why."

"Oh, I see. Turning up with an entourage would have spoiled the effect." She tilted her head to one side and moved a step closer. "As a matter of interest, did you think I was going to be taken in by your little Freya act?"

"You were," I said simply.

"For about two seconds, and that was only because I couldn't believe you would cut your hair just for this." Another step. I glanced behind me to the edge of the cliff, then back at her. She smirked. "I hate to break it to you, but no one believes in ghosts."

"So was it true, what you just said? Was it an accident?"

Coco shrugged. "As far as anyone can tell. But it doesn't matter."

"Why not?"

"The subject is closed. Freya died a year ago. No one cared about her any more until you came and started asking questions again. No one will care after you're gone."

I folded my arms, trying to look tough. "But I'm not leaving here for a month. And I can do a lot of talking in a month."

"Your plans have changed," Coco said sweetly. "You're going a lot sooner than that."

"What do you mean?" I didn't like how calm she was. I didn't like how close she was, either.

"You're the only one who knows I was there when Freya died. I told everyone else that I was too late to stop her. I said I didn't even see her fall. I can't change my story now."

"But if it was an accident—"

"I didn't change anything by being here," she said quickly. "She was going to jump anyway. I just gave her a helping hand."

I was all too aware that Freya had been looking for Will's ledge so she could escape the hunt behind her. Coco had killed her, but she didn't realize it. And I wasn't about to tell her that while we were alone in exactly the same spot. Not when she had a very strange look on her face, as if she had made a decision about something I wouldn't like.

"You've explained that it was an accident," I said. "I believed you—I'm sure everyone else will too. They'll understand why you didn't want anyone to know what really happened."

"You don't understand. I can't afford to be tainted by association with something like this. It could blow my whole future."

"I hardly think so."

"I can't have rumors about me being involved in what happened here last year. All the work I put in—all the training—it will only be worthwhile if I get some sponsors to pay me to run. I should get some advertising deals if I make the GB team and that's where the money is. Then, after I retire from running, I could move into commentating. And then mainstream television presenting." Her eyes had gone unfocused as she laid out her vision of the future. Now she came back to herself and glared at me. "But that will only happen if I look like a good girl. Getting caught up in someone else's drama is so not in my life plan."

"You have to make the team in the first place. None of it will matter if you're just not good enough." I was trying to distract her, looking for a weak spot. I had to get away from the edge of the cliff.

"I'm good enough." Coco's confidence was unshakeable. "I only have one problem."

"Me."

"You." She sighed. "I could have liked you, you know. You have more character than most of the girls around here. You don't give up. That's why I know you won't agree to keep your mouth shut about Freya's death."

She was right—there was no point in denying it. I was trying to remember how many steps I had taken, and in what direction. I edged to my right a little and she copied me. I couldn't help shivering.

"What happened to Freya—you could call that an accident. If anything happens to me, no one is going to believe it was another one. They'll investigate properly this time."

"Do you think so?" She laughed. "You're not in London now, you know. It's in everyone's interests to hide the bad things about Port Sentinel. Anything that affects the tourist numbers could be catastrophic for the town. I think you'll find there are plenty of people who'd be willing to swear you were obsessed with Freya to the point where you dressed like her, behaved like her and reenacted her suicide down to her last moment, when you got carried away. Whether you meant to fall or not, tragically, you did."

"That's not going to happen." I stepped sideways again. I should really have paid more attention to the size of step Will had meant. He was taller than me. Did that mean I should take nine steps instead of eight? I hadn't asked nearly enough questions, given that it might save my life. Another step. Coco matched it neatly, getting ever closer. She was still completely calm and it was this that made me most scared. She was in control, not me. She had done it before—because I didn't believe she had tried to save Freya, judging by how she was behaving. She might not have meant for her to die, but she hadn't minded too much that that was the outcome. She knew what she was doing. She knew how easy it was to kill. And she was the sort of person who would never give in.

"Don't do this," I said quietly.

"I have to." Completely matter-of-fact, no apology about it. And she was far too close. I was opening my mouth to try a different approach when three things happened, more or less simultaneously and without any warning.

One: A man shouted, very loudly, "Police! Step away from the cliff."

Two: The beams of several powerful torches suddenly stabbed through the dark night, swinging as the people carrying them approached us at speed, effectively blinding me when they passed across my face.

Three: Coco shoved me as hard as she could.

And after that, one other thing happened.

I fell.

17

Falling off the cliff was easy. I don't really have to explain why landing was the difficult bit—landing in one piece and alive, specifically, which was a million-to-one shot. I was almost more shocked to find myself sprawling on the grassy ledge than I was to have fallen in the first place. For one thing, it was so quick. I had only just registered that I was falling when I collided with solid ground, with such force that it felt as if my lungs had exploded from the impact. There was no air left in my body and I struggled for an agonizing few seconds to breathe in again. It was sheer instinct that made me cling onto the grass—instinct and an absolute refusal to let Coco win. As a defining characteristic, never giving up isn't bad, especially when it's all that stands between you and a twenty-meter drop to some very scary rocks.

So I survived.

I still had absolutely no idea how I was going to get back to solid ground.

I kept my face pressed against the ledge, too terrified to think about trying to get my bearings, or even looking round. I had only just made it. One leg was hanging off the edge, and when I could move, I inched away from danger toward the cliff, pulling my knees up onto the ledge until all of me was on solid ground. It took all my concentration and I paid no attention to anything else that was going on around me, lost in my own struggle to stay alive. So it was a surprise when a voice spoke in my ear a couple of minutes later.

"Well done."

"For what?" I turned my head so I could see Will, who was crouching beside me, looking as relaxed as if he was in the middle of a vast field rather than high in the air on a tiny shelf above a sheer drop.

"Getting the proof you needed. Not dying. Take your pick."

"I'm not sure about the second part. I've still got to get off this ledge."

"You'll be fine." He leaned back and gave the thumbs-up to someone I couldn't see on top of the cliffs.

"How did you get here?"

"I came with Dad. Or do you mean the ledge?"

"I *did* mean the ledge, actually." My world had shrunk to a crescent of rock and earth and greenery that was, at a generous estimate, the size of a bed. A single bed at that.

"I climbed down," he said. "We wanted to make sure you were OK. You didn't answer us when we shouted."

"I didn't hear you. I was a bit busy not dying."

"Don't worry about it."

"Don't worry about dying?" I glared at him. "Again, still

stuck on the ledge in case you'd forgotten. I think I'm entitled to be a bit anxious."

"I mean you shouldn't worry about not answering us. I was glad of the excuse to come down and make sure you were all right." Will put his hand on my shoulder. "You'll feel better if you sit up, you know."

"Nope. Not moving."

"Don't worry. I won't let you fall."

"How exactly are you going to stop me?" I demanded.

"By not letting you do anything risky. Come on. You can trust me."

It was easier to do as he said than to argue with him. Very reluctantly I inched forward and turned, pressing myself against the lovely solid wall of rock that was the alternative to the bone-shattering drop on the other side. The view had suddenly lost its appeal for me; I vastly preferred a close-up of the cliff. As I curled up in a tiny ball at the very back of the shelf I noticed I was still pretty close to the edge. It wasn't any wider than it had looked from the top of the cliff. How I had managed to land more or less on it was a mystery to me, but I was fairly sure I owed my guardian angel a drink.

Will sat next to me and leaned his elbows on his knees. "How's that?"

"Better," I admitted.

"Told you so." He grinned at me with that sudden, irresistible charm. "As I was saying, well done. I'm impressed. You did exactly what you set out to do."

"Sort of. I didn't actually set out to end up down here with you." But there were worse places to be. I felt my mood begin to lift, the terror fading to be replaced with an uncontrollable desire to giggle. It was shock, I told myself sternly. Hysterical laughter was not what was needed. Sober discussion about how to get off the ledge would be far more useful. "I didn't actually have a plan for this situation and I have no idea what to do next."

"You don't need to worry about it. Dad's getting in touch with the coast guard but I'd say we've got a while to wait before the rescue guys turn up, so you might as well tell me what you found out."

"Now?" I shivered. "You'd better hear it in case I fall, I suppose. You can give evidence for me."

"I'm not really sure that's how it works." Then, quietly, almost reluctantly, he asked the question everyone would want to ask. "Did she kill Freya?"

"Sort of." I told him what Coco had told me, and the conclusions I had drawn. "I don't know if that makes her officially guilty or not, but as far as I'm concerned she should take responsibility for Freya dying. She changed things by being on the headland—if she hadn't run as fast as she did, Freya would probably have lived. And honestly, I'm not sure Coco didn't give her a helping hand to jump, because she was pretty confident about pushing me over the edge."

"She did *what*?"

I raised my eyebrows. "You were there. Didn't you see her?"

"I thought you slipped."

"You thought wrong. She got me where she wanted me, and then she shoved me. You of all people should know I wouldn't have taken the risk of being that close to the edge voluntarily."

Will's face was grave. "I didn't see her push you. That's all I can say."

"She told me she had to get rid of me. Didn't you hear her?"

"Don't look so surprised—we were running at the time."

"I don't even know why you were here."

"I couldn't leave you to get into trouble." Will stared at me. "Did you really think I was going to sit on my hands and wait to see what happened?"

"How did you persuade your dad to get involved? He wouldn't listen to me."

"I told him what you were planning to do." Will grinned. "One dead teenage girl is a shame. Two is a national news story. And not the feel-good, heartwarming kind. He didn't take a lot of convincing."

"So what kept you?"

"We'd been waiting at the bottom of the main path. No one expected you to go through the woods instead. We'd been there a while when I rang Petra to check whether you'd left and she told us you'd started at the bridge." Will shook his head. "When we realized you were on the headland already . . . I've never seen Dad move so fast. He almost caught up with me on the last bit."

"But you had the edge."

"I had different motivation. I couldn't care less about Port Sentinel and its reputation." He was looking at me and I found I couldn't quite speak, or breathe properly, or form a coherent thought. After a moment, Will went on. "Anyway, I don't know about him but I know I couldn't hear a word she said to you. I just saw you fall."

"So it's my word against hers." I was remembering what Coco had said about how my death would be covered up, how

Port Sentinel would want to preserve its reputation above all else. And I hadn't forgotten how completely uninterested Will's dad had been in hearing about Freya's murder. "It's not going to go away this time, I promise you. I'm not going to give up until there's justice for Freya, and her family. People miss her, a lot. They were entitled to have more time with her. The fact that she's gone is horrible, but the way she died makes it even worse."

"I agree with you but I still don't like your chances of getting Coco to court." Will sounded incredibly reasonable, which was maddening. "You'll need some actual evidence. And she didn't admit anything, from what you said."

"I was paraphrasing." But I couldn't remember her saying she had pushed Freya, probably because she didn't say it. She'd been careful with what she gave away.

"You can't remember her actual words?"

"It was a long conversation," I said, knowing that it sounded a bit pathetic. I shifted and something dug into my skin; I had completely forgotten the phone. "Oh, but there's this."

I ferreted about in the bodice of Freya's ridiculous dress, trying to retrieve the phone. It wasn't as easy as it might have been to get it out. For starters, it came out in bits.

"Oh no. Don't tell me it's had it."

Will picked up the front half of the phone, which was more or less in one piece, and turned it over. The electronic entrails didn't look all that healthy to me, or him.

"I don't think the playback quality is going to be great."

"I must have landed on it when I fell." I swore very quietly under my breath. I was bitterly disappointed. All that and I had come away with nothing.

"They might be able to get something off it." Will glanced

at me, then looked away again, his face softening as he saw the tears I couldn't quite blink away. "It'll be all right, Jess."

"I just feel like I let everybody down. She's going to get away with it, isn't she?" His silence answered me. I rubbed my eyes. "I shouldn't have bothered interfering. I should have minded my own business like you told me to."

"Did I say that?" Will put his arm around my shoulders and pulled me against him, leaning his cheek on the top of my head. "I think I was probably trying to get you to be a bit more careful. And you didn't listen."

"No. I'm not good at taking advice."

"That's why I didn't bother to try to talk you out of it."

"You told your dad instead." I spoke without thinking, and it wasn't until I felt him move away a little that I realized what I had said. "It's nothing like what happened with Ryan. I didn't mean that."

"It's what everyone will say."

"Then I'll tell them they're wrong." I turned so I could see him properly. "Will, you did the right thing. You probably saved my life by distracting her at the right moment. What would I have done if I'd been here on my own? Even if I'd landed on this stupid bit of rock I'd have been stuck here until someone came looking for me. No phone, remember?"

"Yeah. Well, I'm glad I was able to help." He took his arm away from my shoulders and made a big deal out of checking his watch, and I was sure he wanted to know what time it was but I was equally sure it was an excuse. As I'd expected, he didn't put his arm back where it had been. I shivered and rubbed my arms, missing my jacket. Missing him too, though I wouldn't risk asking him to hug me again. I had my pride.

Pride was no help when I needed to get warm. I felt as if the cold had seeped into my bones.

"Are you OK?"

"Just a bit chilly." My teeth were chattering. I couldn't exactly deny that I was freezing.

"We need to get off these cliffs." Will took out his phone and I closed my eyes, leaning my head back against the rock while he spoke to his father. I was completely exhausted, physically and emotionally, and it had left me numb. I couldn't even worry about Will and whether he was angry with me, if that was the reason he was on the phone trying to negotiate an escape route for himself instead of being stuck with me indefinitely.

OK, I had enough energy to worry a little bit about that.

Will's side of the conversation was terse and I wasn't able to work out what was going on, but when he rang off I opened my eyes again. His expression was grim.

"What's up?"

"The rescue guys are on another job. There's been a bad accident on the coast road at Leemouth and they've got victims to recover. We've been classed as not being in any immediate danger."

"So?"

"So it's going to be a while."

"Define a while."

"Hours."

"Great." I squeezed my arms around my knees, holding myself tightly. "Then I suppose we'll have to wait. Or I do. You don't have to stay."

"Don't be stupid." Will settled back beside me. "I'm not leaving here without you."

His words gave me a warm glow that was almost enough to ward off the chill in the night air. Almost.

"Have my jacket." He started to take it off.

"I don't need it." A total lie. "I'm used to the cold." That bit was true. I couldn't actually remember what it was like to be warm.

"Take it." He slung the jacket around me and I held onto it with fingers that were too frozen to feel it. I didn't have it in me to give it back to him, but I felt bad about taking it.

"I'm sorry. I didn't come dressed for scrambling around on the cliffs. If only Freya had liked practical clothes."

Will gave me a sidelong grin. "If only Freya had been more like you, I think you mean. If she'd been anything like you at all, we wouldn't be here now. But then she wouldn't have been Freya."

"I wish I'd known her," I said quietly.

"I'm glad I did."

We sat in silence for another couple of minutes, at the end of which Will stood up.

"What are you doing?"

"Getting out of here. You're shivering again and I'm getting cold too. It's not going to do us any good to hang around."

"Remember what I was saying about wearing stupid clothes?" I stuck out my foot. "I am not going to be able to climb up there in these."

"I'm not suggesting we go up."

"It's closer."

"And much more difficult. You aren't strong enough to haul yourself up and I'm not going to make you try."

"Couldn't you just get a rope and pull me up?"

He shook his head. "I wouldn't want to risk it. I'd do it that way if the coast guard were here but we don't have the right equipment. It would be bad if we dropped you."

Bad was an understatement, I gathered. "So what then? Down?" I fought hard to keep my voice casual but Will was too perceptive not to notice the terror.

"It'll be fine. It's an easy one."

"For you, I can imagine it is. But for me . . ."

"You can do it. I know you can." He crouched down in front of me. "I'll be there the whole way. I'll talk you through every move you have to make."

"What if I fall?" I whispered.

"That's why God invented ropes." He grinned. "I'm not taking any unnecessary risks, believe me. I just think it's more dangerous to stay where we are and get hypothermia."

"I can't feel my feet. But that's probably good because otherwise they would be killing me."

"If a few blisters are your only damage from tonight, you're seriously lucky."

"Not as lucky as Coco." I sounded bitter because I was. "She should buy a lottery ticket tomorrow morning."

"She'll get what's coming to her, one way or another. Now stop thinking about it and concentrate on this." Will put his hands on my shoulders and shook me gently. "Are you going to do what I tell you to do?"

"If the alternative is plummeting to my doom, yes."

"Good to know." He stood up and took out his phone again. "Let's get these ropes."

It didn't take a huge amount of time to organize the things we needed, so I didn't have long to start worrying about how I was going to cope with the climb. From somewhere or other, Dan Henderson had managed to get ropes. More remarkable still, he sent down a bag containing a pair of jeans and a jumper for me.

"How did he know this was what I wanted?" I could barely wait to take off the loathsome dress.

"No one in their right mind would go climbing wearing that sort of thing. But don't get too excited. These clothes will be too big for you. They're Dad's."

"They've got to be better than this." I plucked at the skirt. "The next time I want to get dressed up as Sandy from *Grease*, this is absolutely what I'm wearing. Otherwise, never again."

"Better take it off, then." Will was grinning at me again. I folded my arms and waited until he turned round, very slowly. I was smiling myself as I struggled into the clothes. As Will had predicted, I had to roll up the sleeves and trouser-legs. I was still stuck with the hateful shoes but it was beyond brilliant to have trousers instead of a flouncy skirt, and I could breathe again. Or I could until Will started to sort out my harness and ropes. He manhandled me with a business-like detachment that I tried to copy, but I was intensely aware of his hands on my body.

"Are you ready?" he said at last.

"I don't think it's possible to be ready, but I want to get away from here."

"That'll do. You know what they always say, don't you? Don't look down."

"Will . . ." I swallowed. "I'm scared."

"I know." He put out his hand and I held onto it. "It's going to be fine."

He sounded like he meant it, so I chose to believe it, or I would never have moved an inch off the rock ledge. I would never have stepped into space, trusting my life to a surprisingly thin rope and Will's knowledge of the cliffs. But I did it. I eased myself off the ledge that had saved my life and clung to the rock where he told me to hold on, finding a toehold with his help. And almost before I realized it, I was three meters below the ledge, moving slowly but steadily toward safety.

In truth, I don't remember a lot of the details of the climb. Will was doing the thinking for me. I was like a robot, letting him dictate every single move I made. He was brilliant at finding the easy way down, guiding me around difficult patches of rock to take advantage of a gentler slope, or finding another place where we could stop and take a breather. He was encouraging and stern and funny in turn, never stopping the flow of advice and praise that prevented me from panicking about what I was attempting. I concentrated on every movement I made at each individual moment, not allowing myself to think about what I had done already or what I still had to do.

And I didn't look down once.

I have no idea how long it all took, but by the end of it my muscles were quivering and I was barely able to hold on.

"You're doing really well. Almost there. You can do it. Come on, Jess. Right hand here."

I reached for the place he had indicated and my hand slipped on the stone, so I fell sideways with a gasp, swinging on the rope. Will caught me and held me tightly.

"It's OK. You're OK. You've only got about three meters to go."

"I just can't," I said, bursting into tears of sheer exhaustion. I was angry with myself for being so pathetic, which made me sob all the harder.

As if he recognized that I'd nothing left to give, he didn't bother trying to cajole me into trying. He more or less carried me down the last part, setting me down on a flattish bit of rock. He kept his arms around me and I was glad of it, because my knees were shaking so much I could barely stand.

"There. You're on the ground. You did it."

I looked up at the great wall of rock above us and wiped my eyes, sniffing. "I did, didn't I?"

"What do you think? Want to take up climbing?"

I looked at my fingertips, which were seriously battered. I didn't even want to think about the state of my feet. "Not a chance." I sniffed again. "How embarrassing. Sorry."

"Don't be silly." Will set about detaching us from the ropes. "I hate to mention it, but we've still got a walk to get to the beach."

I looked around, taking in for the first time that we were in the middle of the piled-up rocks at the base of the cliff. They were jumbled together like giant building blocks at all sorts of crazy angles, and slick with seaweed or spray from the waves that broke not very far away at all. The water surged in under our feet, bursting through gaps in the rock here and there.

"Don't worry. This I can do."

"Statistically this is the most dangerous bit," Will said.

"We are literally at sea level. I'm no longer scared."

"You should be. People get washed off the rocks all the time."

"Aren't you the little ray of sunshine?"

"Famously so." He paused. "Seriously, Jess. Be careful. We're not done yet."

We set off after Will had told his dad where we were and let him know we were finished with the ropes. I was too cold and my feet hurt too much to hurry, so I would have had to take my time even if Will hadn't been barking warnings at me every two minutes.

"I've got the message," I said. "Be careful."

"Yeah, but you still have to behave as if you've got it." He reached over and grabbed my arm as I wobbled on a perilously sharp bit of rock. "If you fall into the water I'm not going to dive in and rescue you."

"Yes, you will. You're that sort of person. You're a Saint Bernard in human form. Show you a damsel in distress and you can't help yourself." I was giggling to myself. It was hard to take anything seriously when I had looked death in the face and survived.

"Get a grip, Jess."

"I mean it. You need to be needed, don't you?"

He ignored me. "Just watch where you're going."

I quietened down and did as I was told, and with the exception of a big wave that would have taken us both out if we hadn't jumped out of the way, we made it round to the beach. I stepped off the last rock onto the soft sand at the same time as Will.

"Are we safe now?"

"Completely." He reached out and pulled me into his arms, holding on tightly.

I leaned in to him. "Not that I mind, but what's the hug for?"

"Just because." He was still holding me and I didn't feel any need to fight him off.

"Were you really worried? You didn't tell me you were worried."

"There wasn't any point in telling you."

"What happened to *It's going to be fine*?" I leaned back so I could see his face.

"Truthfully, it could have gone either way."

"I'm glad you didn't share that with me on the cliff."

"I'm not stupid. We'd still be sitting there waiting to be rescued, gradually turning into ice cubes." Will frowned, considering me. "You know, I like your hair. I think I did a good job."

"Don't you miss the old me?"

"Honestly? You could dye it blue and shave half of it off and I'd still think you were beautiful."

It felt as if I was blushing from my toes to the top of my head. I couldn't think of anything smart to say. I couldn't think of *anything* to say.

"Jess."

"Yes?"

Will took hold of me, his hands sliding into my hair, drawing me against him. I looked into his eyes, silver-gray in the moonlight, and there was nothing to stop me from falling this time, and falling hard. He leaned toward me and I forgot the pain in my feet, and the cold, and the bitter disappointment of not having done what I'd set out to do. None of it mattered. My heart was pounding, or maybe it was his. We were so close to one another I couldn't tell. I closed my eyes.

"Sorry to interrupt." The voice was deeply sarcastic.

I pulled back and squinted as, once again, a torch beam got me in the eyes. The same torch beam, in fact, that had blinded Ryan a few nights before. With a sinking feeling I realized that for the second time since I'd been in Port Sentinel, Dan Henderson had caught me kissing someone on the beach. Almost kissing someone, to be precise. And Will had dropped me as if I were red-hot the moment his father spoke. I risked a look in his direction and discovered he was staring into the middle distance, ignoring me and his dad. Which left me to do the chatting, I gathered.

"Hi." Not winning any prizes for originality, but at least I'd managed to say something.

"You made it down all right, then. Well done, Will." The torch played over me. "Any injuries?"

"No. Not really." I looked down at my feet, at the sad excuse for shoes that I was still wearing. They were ripped and filthy, and would never be the same again, which was fine by me because I was never going to try to wear them. The nicest part was the blood that had soaked through from my heels. The seawater had made it spread, so it looked as if my feet were cut to pieces. Which, in fact, they possibly had been. I flexed the right one and winced.

"That looks nasty," Dan said, his voice hard.

"It's not too bad." Even as I said it I was reassessing. My feet were actually in ribbons.

"You'd better come and get checked out by the paramedics."

"I'm fine." I glanced at Will, hoping he'd tell his dad to leave us alone. But instead he nodded.

"Sounds like a good idea." To his dad, he said, "I'm heading home."

"Good. Check on your mother."

Will glowered at his father, but didn't say anything. He turned to walk away without saying good-bye to me.

"Thanks," I called after him. "I'll see you around."

I might as well have said nothing for all the response I got.

Which left me with Dan. He took hold of my arm. "Come on, young lady. The ambulance is over there."

"No!" I pulled myself free and took two steps back. By the light of the moon, I could see him frown.

"What's the matter?"

"I don't need your help to walk over there."

He tilted his head to one side, considering me. "All right. No need for the dramatics."

"There's every need." My face was hot. "After the car the other night."

"What about the car?"

"You know what I'm talking about."

"I'm afraid I don't. Unless you mean"—and he broke off to laugh—"tidying up your lipstick. Sorry. Did I step on your dignity?"

"It was inappropriate."

"Oh, was it?" He laughed again. "It was a friendly gesture. Fatherly. I'm going to assume you don't get on well with yours, or you'd have recognized it for what it was. I always wanted a daughter, you know."

"Is that what you told Freya?" My nerves were stretched to breaking point, but I knew if I didn't confront him about it now, I never would. "You saw her as a daughter."

Dan shrugged, puzzled but not alarmed. "She's got nothing to do with this. Whatever this is."

"So you say."

"I mean it." He took a step closer to me. "This is what I was worried about, Jess. You start looking for mysteries everywhere and you get paranoid. You start throwing around wild accusations. You misjudge people."

I hadn't misjudged him. I was almost sure of it. But he seemed so confident, so unflustered, and I could hear myself telling my mother about it and not being able to convey how wrong his behavior had been and how uncomfortable it had made me, without sounding like a lunatic.

Dan held out his hands. "Look, I'm not going to *make* you take my arm. But the sand is difficult to walk on and your feet are injured. If you're sensible, you'll accept my help and we'll say no more about whether I should have helped you tidy yourself up after your little adventure with Ryan."

My face burned but I couldn't see what else to do. Forgetting about the whole thing was impossible, but making a fuss was even less likely to help. I'd been played, and I knew it. Defeated, I put my hand on Dan's arm and together we began to plow through the soft sand toward the promenade.

But if I thought that was the end of our awkward conversation, I was wrong. Dan had more to say. "Right. While we're walking, I want you to explain to me exactly why you thought that was a good idea."

"What?"

"Setting up your clifftop confrontation. What did you think I meant?"

Kissing your son, obviously. I didn't say that, though. I didn't say anything. I adopted Will's technique and kept completely silent while Dan told me what he thought of me and the unacceptable risks I'd taken and how angry my mother would be when she heard about it, which she would as soon as he had a chance to call her. He carried on all the way across the beach, and it seemed endless. By the time we got to the promenade I felt as if I'd walked across the Sahara accompanied by a really creepy, angry Bedouin.

The ambulance was parked by some steps, its lights twirling but the siren off. Both paramedics were standing by the back doors, which were open.

"I want to have a word with these guys." Dan steered me toward the steps. "You go in first and wait. I'm not letting you go anywhere until you get checked over."

I didn't dare argue. I limped up the steps and climbed into the back of the ambulance, which was full of unidentifiable bits of medical equipment I hoped I wouldn't need.

Also in the back of the ambulance: someone I hadn't expected to see, sitting on the edge of a stretcher, wrapped in a blanket. I stopped dead as Coco looked up at me. I don't know which of us was more shocked.

"You're alive!"

"No thanks to you," I pointed out. It wasn't my best ever comeback, but in the circumstances it was the best I could do.

Her face had gone completely white. "He told me you were dead. They said you were dead."

"Disappointing, isn't it?"

"You should have died." Her hands were clenched into

fists, her voice rising hysterically. "I was sure you were gone. I pushed you off the cliff, for God's sake. I saw you fall. You should be dead. Why aren't you dead?"

"Thanks, Jess. That'll do." For once I was glad of Dan's sense of timing, even though I was outraged that he hadn't warned me what he was planning. He'd used me, and there was nothing I could do about it. In the circumstances, I couldn't even really complain. He clambered into the ambulance, taking a pair of handcuffs off his belt. "Cordelia Golding, you're under arrest for the attempted murder of Jessica Tennant. You do not have to say anything . . ."

I turned and hobbled back down the steps. I didn't feel the need to watch him arrest her and take her away. It was enough to know it was going to happen. It was justice for Freya, at last. I'd done what I set out to do.

I couldn't have said why, but it made me feel like crying again.

18

I spent the next three days lying on the dingy sofa in the horrible holiday cottage while a procession of people came to thank me, or tell me off, or both. My feet had been properly bandaged at the hospital, along with a gash to my calf that I hadn't even noticed at the time, and I wasn't pretending to be an invalid. Walking was agony; I could barely hobble across the room. I ached from head to toe, as if I had been systematically beaten up. On the bright side, it was quite fun to lie there like Beth in *Little Women*, looking fragile, as Mum brought me cups of tea and made vast quantities of toast. Her other job was opening the door to let in a noisy collection of Leonards who all wanted to hug me at the same time, or Darcy, creeping in miserably like a dog that knows it's going to be told off, or once, memorably, Natasha.

"I didn't know she'd done it," she said without preamble, standing in front of me. "It wasn't my idea."

I looked up at her, curious. "What was your idea, as a matter of interest?"

"I wanted to scare Freya."

"You wanted to get a reaction, didn't you?"

The frustration showed on her face. "She never cared about anything. I couldn't get through to her."

"So you had to shout." I shook my head. "You might not have intended for it to happen, but you set it up. You bullied her and tricked her and frightened her to the point where she ran out of places to hide."

"I know."

"Do you?"

"Yes." She sat down abruptly and put her face in her hands. "I made a mistake."

"Understatement of the year." I really didn't want to prolong the conversation, but there was one thing I still wanted to know. "Did Ryan know what you did? Was he there that night?"

Natasha looked shocked. "No. He wouldn't have liked it at all. Someone told him about it afterward. The whole thing gave him the creeps. He had nightmares about it, even."

Which explained his strong reaction to being up there, I thought. Maybe it had reminded him of being bullied when he was younger too. Ryan was more sensitive than he looked.

Natasha was fiddling with her sleeves. "She didn't even like him, did she?"

"Ryan? No. She wasn't interested."

"And you don't like him either."

Involuntarily I glanced across at the huge bunch of velvety red roses on the windowsill and Natasha followed my gaze.

"Are they from him?"

"He brought them round yesterday." I didn't tell her that I'd been asleep and hadn't even spoken to him. "In answer to your previous question, I do like him." I let her suffer for a second. "But not like that. He's just a good person."

"He is," she said quickly. "That's just it. He's amazing."

She was never going to see him as anything but, no matter what I said. I gave a complicated half-shrug that could have been agreement.

Natasha pulled her sleeves down over her hands, the picture of misery. "Do you think he'll ever stop flirting with other girls?"

"Not really. That's how he's made." She flinched, and I felt the tiniest bit sorry for her. "But it's sort of up to you whether you mind or not. If you really can't stand it, maybe you should try going out with someone else. Get over him. Have some self-respect."

"I just love him so much."

"Which explains why we're talking about him again." I sat up, swinging my feet down to the floor, so I could face her. "You know, I have no idea what you're really like. All I know is that you're obsessed with him. And it's really, really boring."

"You're just jealous."

"No, I'm not," I said gently. "I know you're going to find this hard to believe, but I don't want to be like you in any way. And that includes whatever is going on between you and Ryan. I don't want to get involved."

Her face was hard again. "So don't."

"You came to talk to me, remember?"

"Not so you could give me advice. What would you know about it, anyway?"

"Absolutely nothing." A wave of tiredness swept over me and I just managed not to yawn. "Why are you here, anyway?"

"Darcy told me to come."

"Did she?"

"She said I had to explain my part in what happened. She said it made her feel better."

Darcy had skipped out of the cottage like a spring lamb after I'd told her I couldn't have tricked Coco without her, as if it overwrote her previous behavior completely. That was Darcy, though. She couldn't help being shallow.

To Natasha, I said, "I'm not really qualified to forgive you your sins, whatever Darcy thinks."

"I shouldn't have listened to her." She stood up abruptly. "I'm going to go."

"Probably for the best." I watched her go to the door, where she stopped, her head down.

"I'm sorry about what happened. That's why I came. To say I was sorry."

"OK."

"Not just about Freya. About what happened to you too."

"Fair enough."

She hesitated, then said in a rush, "I can't believe you cut your hair off."

"It will grow again."

"Don't you mind?"

"Nope," I lied. I minded a lot. I missed it like a limb. But I wasn't about to share that with Natasha. I wasn't ready for her to become a friend. Forgiving Darcy for having her head turned was one thing, but I couldn't forget about the campaign of bullying and intimidation that Natasha had organized to torment Freya, or the anger I'd seen in her on the cliffs. She wasn't someone I understood at all and I was wary of letting her get any closer to me than she was already.

She nodded, as if she'd heard what I was thinking. She left without trying any further friendly overtures, and I thought I wouldn't miss *her*, at least, when I was back in London. I was pretty sure the feeling was mutual.

Later on that day, Dan Henderson came to see me, much to my annoyance. Mum answered the door, of course, and blushed before he even said hello. She stood back to let him in, mumbled something incomprehensible and then disappeared into the kitchen. I found myself thinking she had absolutely no game whatsoever. It was a good thing on two counts. One: The very thought of my mother trying to pull anyone was squicky. Two: Dan Henderson was completely off-limits, or at least he should have been. And I couldn't tell exactly what Dan thought about Mum, but he watched her all the way into the kitchen, and stared after her for a little bit too long once she'd disappeared from view. I coughed, and he looked down at me as if he'd forgotten I existed. A second later he was smiling broadly at me, the charm switched on at maximum wattage. *Fake, fake, fake* was all I could think. But two could play at that game. I had decided the thing to do was treat him as if nothing had happened, as if I'd never accused him of anything. So I smiled back.

"How's the great detective doing?"

"I'm fine."

"Brave girl." He sat down in the armchair and stretched his legs out in front of him, thereby occupying most of the very small sitting room. "I wanted to thank you for your hard work."

"What's happening to Coco?"

"She's been charged with attempted murder and released on bail." He saw the look on my face. "She's not likely to be dangerous to you or anyone else. I spoke to her father. She's going to plead guilty so you won't even have to give evidence at a trial."

"She's pleading guilty? I expected her to put up a fight."

"She's got very little choice. I heard what she said to you in the ambulance and she admitted it in interview. Her parents are devastated, as you can imagine. But she's a minor, and she'll get a reduced sentence for pleading guilty at the earliest opportunity. She's looking at ten or twelve years, depending on the judge. Best-case scenario, she's out of prison in five or six years."

I shivered. "That's a long time to be in prison."

"It's a serious crime. And she's only sixteen. She'll still be young when she gets out. She can do her exams in prison, go to university when she's released—she'll still have a life at the end of it all."

"I suppose." I bit my lip.

"Don't feel guilty about it. You didn't force her to behave that way."

"I sort of did. If I hadn't made her come to the top of the cliffs, she'd never have thought of trying to kill me."

"She made her own choices. She has to live with the consequences." Dan stopped, abruptly, and looked down at his hands, as if what he'd said had some resonance for him that I couldn't understand. After a second or two he looked up, and again, the transformation was total, the cheerful mask back in place. "You must be tired. Have a decent rest, Jess. Then get on with enjoying yourself while you're down here. Don't spend the whole time in that dusty shop."

"I won't," I said, but I was actually missing it quite badly. My window display needed to be changed, and there was Sylvia's hoard of donations to work through. Sylvia herself had sent a Get Well Soon card and a gorgeous pair of jade earrings I had admired one day in the shop, and I wanted to say thank you. All in all, the sooner I got off the sofa and back to reality, the better.

I was just about to ask Dan how Will was when he stood up. "I want a quick word with your mother before I go."

I watched him walk over to the kitchen with a deep sense of unease. He knocked on the doorframe to get Mum's attention, then went out of my line of sight. It was a tiny room. They had to be standing very close to one another if I couldn't see him. His voice was low, so I couldn't pick out any words. All I heard from Mum was a laugh that she tried to smother. I didn't like it. I particularly didn't like the look on Mum's face when she followed him out of the kitchen and went to the door to see him out. It was very unguarded and somehow vulnerable, and I worried about it for the rest of the day. I didn't want her to get hurt. And I didn't want her to do something unforgivable, like flirting with a man whose wife was dying.

I thought I'd been doing a great job of looking unconcerned, but apparently not. I had just climbed into bed that night (slowly, carefully, wincing as I did so) when Mum tapped on the door.

"Is everything all right?"

"Of course." I switched on a smile. "Except that the pain-killers aren't doing it. Killing the pain, I mean. At best they're annoying it. Calling it names. Talking behind its back. Low-level stuff."

"Poor you."

"I'll live."

"You could have died." Mum said it in a very matter-of-fact way but I knew better. *Uh-oh* . . . She came and sat on the end of the bed, avoiding my poor bruised feet, for which I was grateful. "I haven't spoken to you about it before now because I was too upset."

"Upset?"

"You didn't trust me." There were tears standing in her eyes. "You should have come to me instead of putting yourself in harm's way. I could have talked to Dan. I could have—"

"Mum, *I* talked to Dan. He didn't want to know. He told me to mind my own business."

"Well, it wasn't your business."

"Mum!"

"I'm sorry, Jess, but I can't say I'm happy about it. You risked your life to find out what happened to Freya."

"So Tilly and Jack and everyone know what really happened, and Coco isn't going to get away with it."

"That wouldn't makeup for you dying."

"I didn't die," I pointed out. "I'm here. I'll be back to normal in a couple of days."

"You were lucky. If Dan hadn't turned up when he did—"

"That was only because Will told him he had to. Dan was in a panic that I'd die and it would put off the tourists."

"Dan was worried about you," she snapped. "You should remember that."

"I remember that he didn't care about finding out the truth until I forced his hand."

Mum stood up, and I realized she was properly angry. "You know, you think you know everything, but you don't. You're not invincible. You're a child."

"Age has nothing to do with it."

"Didn't you think Dan had his reasons for not encouraging you to interfere?"

"Yeah, I did, but they were bad reasons."

"He wanted to make sure you were safe."

"Is that what he told you?" I really wished I wasn't lying down. It made it so much harder to look Mum in the eye. "Did he tell you about his wife too?"

She blushed, which told me all I wanted to know. "That has nothing to do with our discussion, Jessica."

"You know she's dying, though, don't you?"

A nod.

"And?"

"And nothing. It's very sad. I'm sorry for Will, and for Dan."

"And for her," I prompted.

"Of course."

I had a reckless, now-or-never feeling. "Do you know her? Did you know her when you lived here?"

Mum rubbed her eyes, looking exhausted. All the fight had gone out of her. She never could stay angry, with me or anyone else. "Do we have to talk about this now?"

"Please, Mum."

She sat down again and jammed her hands between her knees. "This all happened such a long time ago, Jess."

"I know. It's ancient history. But, Mum . . . I've seen the way you look at Dan. And I've seen the way he looks at you."

She was blushing again. "He doesn't look at me in any way at all. Don't be ridiculous, Jess."

"You know what I'm talking about." I sat up. "Look, I've worked a lot of it out for myself. I can probably guess the whole story. But I'd rather hear it from you. Dan was the reason you left Port Sentinel, wasn't he?"

"Oh." Mum swallowed, keeping her composure, but I could see she was on the verge of tears. "You're right. But I've never regretted it."

I flapped a hand. "Taken as read. Go on."

"I started going out with Dan when I was fifteen. Even younger than you are now." She shook her head. "We were such babies, but we thought it was true love. We thought it was going to last forever. And it felt like forever."

"Three years?"

"Two and a half," Mum corrected. "Because after two and a half years we had a fight."

"About what?"

"Nothing. Nothing important." Nothing she was going to tell me about, I realized, knowing better than to try wheedling it out of her. "And we broke up."

"That must have been awful."

"I saw him every day. I was waitressing in one of the cafés in town and he was working on a building site, getting some money together to go traveling. He came in for lunch with his mates all the time." She had a faraway look in her eyes, lost in her memories. "It was horrible. But I was stubborn. He wanted me to admit I was wrong, and I wouldn't."

"And?"

"And I met your father."

"I always knew Dad was a rebound," I said wisely. "Such a bad choice."

"Not that again." Mum reached out and shook my knee, amused. "I thought your dad was so funny and clever. He was so different. He went after me from the moment he first saw me. I told him I was in love with someone else but it didn't put him off."

"He wore you down."

"No. I chose to go out with him." Her voice was sharp. "I know you think I'm a total doormat, but I really liked him, and I was flattered, and I knew it would upset Dan. I was fed up with him pushing me around."

"He's that sort of person."

"He hasn't changed. Anyway. Where was I?"

"Dad. And Dan. I bet he wasn't thrilled."

"He decided to teach me a lesson. Karen had been in love with him forever and a day. So he called her up and asked her out. Just like that." She clicked her fingers. "It was that easy. I knew what he was doing, and so did he. Talking to Dan this week—he was the same as me. He was sure we would end up together. Your father and Karen were just diversions on the way."

"Except not."

"No."

"Because . . ." I prompted.

"Karen got pregnant." Mum's face was bleak as she remembered. "Dan came and told me. Then he went and asked her to marry him, because he thought it was the right thing to do. And she said yes."

"Oh. My. God."

"Yeah." Mum gave me a crooked smile. "I had to get out of Port Sentinel. I couldn't bear to stay and watch them settling down to married life. I called up the only person I knew in London."

"Dad."

"One and the same. He met me off the train and that was it. We were together from then on."

I was trying to do the sums. "So Karen was pregnant with Will."

Mum nodded. "He was born five months after they got married. Dan had wanted to be a doctor but he joined the police because it was a steady job, he didn't need to go to university to do it and he would be earning decent enough money from the start. It changed his life."

"No wonder he hates Will."

"Hates him? No." Mum sounded definite. "He's proud of him."

"He has a funny way of showing it."

"He's a complicated person." She turned away but I saw the smile on her face and it sent a chill through me.

"Mum, what happens when Karen dies?"

"Jess!" She whipped back. "I hope you're not suggesting what I think you're suggesting."

"It's a valid question. He was the love of your life."

"No. He was my first love. That's different."

"But—"

"No." She sounded very definite. "What's done is done."

"Are you sorry?" I had to know. "Do you wish you had ended up together?"

"We talked about this before, remember?" I did, but it felt as if that conversation had taken place a million years ago, not just a few days. "If it hadn't worked out that way, I wouldn't have you." She touched my cheek briefly. "I wouldn't want things any other way."

I believed her, completely. But I was still glad we were leaving town, and soon, so we could leave Dan Henderson behind us too.

The last visitor of note was Tilly, who came in the evening on the third day and sat in the armchair, with Mum leaning over the back. Her face looked different, as if some of the fine lines had been smoothed away.

"I've come to thank you."

"Don't thank me," I said quickly.

"But I have to. Without you, I'd never have known for certain that Freya didn't kill herself. I thought I'd let her down, you see."

"I never thought she'd wanted to die. She was happy."

"Yes, she was. And I can remember her like that now, instead of wondering if she'd been hiding secrets from me."

"Everyone hides secrets from their parents. That's our job." *And some parents hide things from their children.* I caught Mum's eye and smiled to hide what I was thinking. Oh, the irony.

"Maybe so." Tilly hugged herself. "I still miss her. Of course I do—I always will. But I'm starting to feel more like me."

"Are you going to start painting again?"

"Soon." I could see her considering it. "Not yet. But definitely soon."

"I'd love to see you work."

She glanced up at Mum for a second, then looked back at me. "I'm sure you will."

"What she means is, you're going to be around for longer than a few weeks. If you like, that is." Mum was looking seriously nervous, I realized.

"What do you mean?"

"I want us to stay in Port Sentinel."

I couldn't believe what I was hearing. "Forever?"

"For a year, anyway."

"A year," I repeated. "A whole year. What about school? What about your job?"

"You can go to school here, Jess—I've already found out about it. The local school has an excellent reputation, far better than Cranway College."

"Well, that wouldn't be hard," I said, thinking of the dingy buildings and chaotic classes in my very under-resourced London school. But there were other things there that mattered, such as my friends. Such as my life.

Mum breezed on. "And I don't care about my job. You know I've been taking pictures while I've been here. Dan showed some of them to Nick Trabbet, who runs the Sentinel Gallery on Fore Street, and he wants to sell them. He's already sold two, actually." She was glowing with excitement and I hoped it was because of the pictures and not Dan. Bloody Dan, making her dreams come true and giving her a reason to stay.

"That's lovely, Mum, and I'm very proud of you, but we're

not going to be able to live off the sales from your photos and my charity-shop money."

"I know that—but I've been offered a job. I'd be working in the gallery."

"Wow. Nick must owe Dan money or something."

"Don't be so cynical." Mum looked hurt. "Nick really believes in my talent. He wanted to help me. He said it would be a shame if I went back to London and lost this opportunity."

"Right." This wasn't a spur-of-the-moment thing, I was starting to realize. This had taken planning. "And you didn't say anything to me about any of this."

"Not until I knew it was all going to work out. Besides, you were busy not saying anything to me about cutting your hair and trying to find out what happened to your cousin and putting your life in danger."

Moving swiftly on . . . "Where are we going to live?"

"With us," Tilly said promptly. "For as long as you like. The whole year, preferably."

"Really?"

"Sandhayes is a huge house. It's your family home. And we'd love to have you."

"It's perfect. You know, Jack turned one of the outhouses into a proper dark room for Freya, so I can use that too." Mum sounded truly excited.

Tilly smiled at her, and then back at me. "Please say yes. Your mother won't commit to any of this until you say yes. Don't you want to stay and get to know your cousins a bit better? I think you'll enjoy it if you do."

I ached to be a part of the Leonards' family. I had always

longed for siblings, and Hugo, Petra, and Tom were as close as I was going to get to that. And Mum looked so wistful, but at the same time determined not to show her disappointment if I said no.

Plus, there were all the other reasons for wanting to stay around, which I wouldn't think about because at the top of the list was Will, and I hadn't seen him since the beach, and I really wondered what I had done wrong. But he was still the main reason I wanted to stay.

Against that, Dan. And missing my life in London—my friends too. And missing Dad.

Who hadn't been in touch, it occurred to me, since we'd arrived.

"Does Dad know what happened to me?"

Mum looked surprised, as well she might because it wasn't an obvious response to what I'd been asked, but she answered anyway. "Yes. I called him on Saturday night when I heard you were at the hospital."

"He hasn't called me."

"I'm sure he will. He's probably busy."

I deserved more than that, I thought, just as Mum had deserved more than he'd given her. If she had a chance to be happy now, I shouldn't take it away from her. She'd waited long enough to be a success. I just had to hope that her vision of the future didn't include comforting a certain police inspector after his wife passed away. I forced that thought out of my mind and smiled at her.

"OK. Let's stay."

"Are you sure?"

"Absolutely," I said, sounding confident even as I worried about what might happen.

Mum and Tilly both jumped up to hug each other then turned on me, and it was beyond alarming to see the two of them coming at me like double vision from delayed concussion. They were so happy, the two of them, and it made me happy even though there was still a little voice whispering doubts in the back of my mind. I thought, on balance, that I'd made the right choice for both of us.

At least, I hoped so.

There was one more surprise for me when we went to Sand-hayes the following day for a celebratory lunch. The Leonards lined up in the hall to welcome us—except for Hugo, who was sprawling on the stairs, reading. Petra more than made up for his detached attitude by jumping up and down.

"Can I tell her? Can I tell her?"

"Say yes, Mum, or she won't stop," Tom said.

Tilly laughed. "Go on."

"You're going to have Freya's room!"

I gasped. "I couldn't."

"You must," Tilly said. "I don't want to leave it as it is. I want someone else to use it. Live in it."

I turned to Petra. "What about you?"

She wrinkled her nose. "I like my room. I don't want to change. Besides, it would suit you, I think."

"It's that or the other one upstairs—the one with the sea view," Jack said with a grin as his family snorted at the idea that five square centimeters of sea counted as a view. "I'd take the nicer one of the two if I were you."

"Go up and have another look at it," Tilly suggested. "You can makeup your own mind."

I did as I was told, skirting Hugo carefully as I went. On the top floor I put my head into the other room first, seeing a small space with a single bed in it and a chest of drawers and nothing else. Even the floorboards were bare. The window was small and overlooked the town so the view was crowded with houses. The sun glittered on the tiny patch of sea that was visible, as if to emphasize how small it was.

And on the other side, the room I loved with its two big windows. The pair of tabbies were curled up on the bed like a stripy yin and yang symbol. I walked in and shut the door and waited to feel as if I was intruding, to see if Freya minded me moving in on her territory. There was no sign of it. I stood with my back to the door and looked around, thinking about what I would leave as it was and what I would change if I did decide to stay there. I could move the desk. And I'd have to clear out the wardrobe or there would be no room for my things. Unless someone had done it already. I went over and pulled open the wardrobe door to check, then stopped dead.

It was still full of Freya's clothes, but that wasn't a shock. What made me stand stock-still was the dress that was hanging at the front of the rail, the dress I had last seen when I peeled it off on the cliff. It was still dirty from the fall and ripped in a couple of places.

Will had brought it back. He'd got it from the ledge where I'd dumped it and returned it to where it belonged.

He'd sorted out the dress, but he hadn't come to see me.

I stared at it for a long time, feeling miserable and pathetic in equal measure. What did it matter? So what if he'd decided he had better things to do than visit me? I had rationalized it to my own satisfaction: the near-miss kiss on the beach had been his reaction to the relief of making it down the cliff safely. He hadn't meant anything serious by it and now he was scared I'd think he wanted to revisit the moment. Which I didn't, obviously. I hadn't even thought about it since. Not more than sixty times a minute, anyway.

I turned round and my eye fell on the photograph of his hands on the wall. I turned my back to it and found myself staring at the roof of his house above the trees at the end of the garden. There was no escape. Maybe the other room would be better after all.

I was halfway to convincing myself that was true when anger kicked in. I stopped. "This is ridiculous. If he won't come to see me, I'll just go to him. There's no reason not to."

Except the crushing fear that he wouldn't want to see me, of course. But it was better to know the truth either way than to live in hope.

I was fairly sure.

Without waiting to have second thoughts, I limped down the stairs and paused beside Hugo. "Are you sorry we're moving in?"

He shook his hair out of his eyes to look up at me. "Of course not."

"You're not acting as if you're very pleased about it."

"This is me being delighted."

"OK," I said. "As long as you're sure."

He waited until I'd reached the hall. "Jess."

I turned round. "Yes?"

"You have to promise me one thing."

"What's that?"

"Make friends with lots of pretty girls and invite them here."

"So you can pick them off one by one?"

"Exactly." He grinned at me lazily. "I knew you'd understand."

"No way. You'll have to do your own hunting, I'm afraid."

"You're in a fierce mood," he observed. "Where are you off to?"

"I'm going to see Will."

Hugo raised his eyebrows. "Good luck to him, then."

"Have you seen him since Saturday?"

"Of course. Haven't you?" The eyebrows went up again. "Oh. I see."

"There's nothing to see," I said, with as much dignity as I could manage. "I just want to thank him for helping me. That's all. Do you happen to know what number his house is?"

"Twenty-three. But you could just go through the garden. You can climb over the wall in the corner, on the left."

"On a first visit I think I should use the front door."

"That's what I'm looking forward to. Learning how they do things in London. Getting a bit of metropolitan sophistication."

"Shut up, Hugo," I said, for what was not going to be the last time, and I left.

19

It was a five-minute walk round to Will's house and I could see why going over the wall was a better, quicker option, but I was glad of the time to think about what I was going to say. I *did* want to thank him. I also wanted to know how he felt about me, but if just turning up wasn't enough to elicit a response, I didn't really know what I was going to do. I couldn't just *ask*. I could fling myself at him and hope he caught me. I could tell him how I felt about him.

Which depended on me knowing how I felt, obviously. *Confused* was the word that came to mind. Maybe he felt the same way. Maybe we could work it out together.

Number 23 was small and square, more of a cottage than a house. The paint was graying in places and peeling in others, the front garden was overgrown, and there was a general air of people being too busy with other things to care about keeping the place looking nice. It occurred to me shortly after I had knocked on the door that I might be about to meet

Will's mother and I froze, suddenly terrified. What would she say if she knew who I was—or rather, who my mother was? Did she know Mum was back in town? Would she care?

I was racking up the unanswerable questions at a rate, so I was almost glad when the door opened, even though it was Dan who stood there. He looked surprised to see me.

I nerved myself to speak to him as if he was a normal dad. "Sorry to bother you. Is Will in?"

He stared at me for a long moment, taking in the jade drops that hung from my ears—Sylvia's present—and the pretty top I was wearing for the family lunch, and the jeans Darcy had talked me into buying with my charity-shop wages. I looked as if I had made an effort, I realized, and restrained myself with difficulty from explaining that it wasn't for Will's sake. It was just a coincidence that I had got my nerve back when I was looking pretty. Honest, guv.

"Come in." He held the door open. "First on the left."

I went past him into the tiny hall and turned left, my heart racing at the thought that I was about to see Will again. It was a bit of a letdown to find myself in a study, which was empty. I turned round and found Dan standing right behind me, closing the door softly, and I stepped back, suddenly on edge.

"I want to talk to you and I don't want to disturb Karen." He went and sat down behind his desk. "She's not well."

"So I heard." *That doesn't make it all right for you to flirt with my mum.* I wished I could say it.

He fiddled with a paperweight. "I'm glad you've come round. I wanted to ask you something."

"OK," I said, sounding as wary as I felt.

The paperweight clattered on the desk. "I want you to stay away from my son."

"What?"

"Stay away from Will."

I shook my head, stunned. "You can't ask me to do that."

"He doesn't need any distractions. He's got enough to worry about at the moment."

"Because his mum is dying?"

He flinched. "Yes."

"Don't you think he might need some support? Don't you think now is exactly when he might need to have someone who cares about him?"

"Maybe." Dan looked down, then back up at me and I saw the hatred in his eyes again, the same look I'd seen the first time I met him. "But it shouldn't be you."

My knees had begun to tremble. "Why not me?"

"He doesn't need to make the same mistakes I made."

"Are you talking about Mum?" I shook my head, angry now. "It's not the same thing. And from what I understand, the mistake was yours anyway."

"Is that what she told you?"

"I'm not going to discuss a private conversation with you, Mr. Henderson. Besides, you were there. You know what happened."

He winced.

"I'm not my mother," I said softly. "And Will's not you."

"So you're not going to do as I ask."

"I don't know. I don't know how Will feels about me. I don't know if he wants me around or not. But if he does, as a friend or—or—or *whatever*, nothing you say or do will keep us apart." I could not say "girlfriend" to Dan Henderson, it turned out.

"Is that right?" A smile curved the corners of Dan's mouth, but there was nothing pleasant about it.

"Try me."

He stared at me for a long moment, then nodded. "Consider yourself warned."

"I do." I was still shaking but I hoped he couldn't see it. "But I came to see Will, and I'm not leaving until I do."

He was at the back of the house, in a dusty garage that housed a car I only just recognized as a Ford Capri, low-slung and with pure seventies style in every line. It was painted brown and seemed to be missing about half its bodywork. The bonnet was open. Will was fiddling with something deep inside the engine, concentrating on what he was doing so I was able to stand and watch him for a couple of minutes before he noticed me. When he did, he straightened up with a start.

"Hey."

"Sorry. Did I scare you?"

"Surprised me. What are you doing here?"

"Watching you. Being told off by your dad for coming round."

He had been wiping oil off his hands with a rag, but now he went very still and stared at me. "Seriously?"

"Am I laughing?"

"What did he say to you?"

"That I should leave you alone."

Will looked down at his hands and started to work on them again. "Oh. That must have been a pleasant conversation."

"It had its moments." I hesitated. "Did he speak to you too?"

"Yeah."

"Is that why you didn't come to see me?"

He didn't answer me for a minute. "Not exactly."

"Oh." My face started to burn. "I see. I thought—"

He interrupted. "How are you?"

"Fine."

"Great. I'm glad. Thanks for coming over."

"Well, I was at the Leonards' anyway," I said, gesturing in that general direction. This was horrible. This was the worst conversation ever. Will was like a stranger and I didn't seem to be able to find a way past the polite chit-chat to what I wanted to say. I tried a different angle. "Did you hear the news? Mum wants us to stay here for a year."

"I heard." Will turned back to the engine and his voice was muffled when he asked, "Are you?"

"That's the plan. We're staying at Sandhayes."

"Oh, right." He sounded vague, as if he wasn't listening properly.

"What's the matter?"

"What do you mean?"

"You know what I mean. You're being weird." I felt as if I was on a tightrope over Niagara Falls and I hadn't practiced. I was very much afraid of getting this wrong and there was nothing I could do but keep going. "I thought . . . when we were on the beach, it seemed . . . you were going to—" Was it actually possible to die of embarrassment?

Will straightened up again and looked at me, his expression completely unhelpful. "What are you trying to say, Jess?"

"I haven't seen you. I waited, and you didn't come." I knew there were tears in my eyes because he had gone blurry all of a sudden. "What did I do wrong?"

"Nothing. Absolutely nothing. It's not you. Or Dad." He couldn't even look at me. "It's just better if we don't get too close."

"In what way?"

"Jess, why do you think your mum wants to stay in Port Sentinel? And why do you think my dad doesn't want us to get involved with one another? They're just waiting for my mother to be gone so they can get together. If we were going out, it would make it a bit awkward."

"You're wrong."

"I wish I was."

"That may be your dad's plan, but it's not Mum's. At all."

"She knows what he wants and she's gone along with it so far," Will said. "Whose idea do you think it was for you to stay here? It didn't come from her."

"She told me she wouldn't go back to him. She said it was all in the past."

"Not very far back." Will kicked the tire nearest him, very gently. "Do you know what Dad said? I'd ruined their lives once before. If it hadn't been for me, they would never have split up. He said it was his turn to be happy for the first time in eighteen years and he wasn't going to miss out on it again."

I would kill him, I thought. I would kill Dan with my bare hands. Not because he'd made it impossible for me and Will to be together, but because he'd put that expression on his own son's face. "He's so completely wrong. You didn't believe him, did you?"

He shrugged. "It's not that big a deal."

"Don't say that." I went over to him and put my hand on his arm, trying to get him to look at me. "You don't really think that, do you?"

Will gave me a quick, awkward smile and moved back so my hand fell away. I recognized the technique. I'd used it myself on boys whose attentions were unwanted.

"OK. Fine. I'll go." I turned to walk away, the tears I'd suppressed earlier springing into my eyes so I could hardly see. "See you around."

"Jess." Somehow he managed to get a world of longing into the way he said my name, and I stopped, but I didn't turn round. "I'm sorry," he said at last.

"Me too."

I couldn't trust myself to say anything more. It took everything I had, but I walked away without looking back.

Never stage a big dramatic exit without knowing exactly how you're going to get away. I had no intention of going back through the house, where Dan would be waiting to see what had happened. There wasn't another way back to the road without returning to the garage and I had even less intention of seeing Will again. That left the wall at the back of the garden, the one that led straight to Sandhayes. If it was the left corner of the garden there, it was the right corner in Will's house. I headed in that general direction, taking deep quivery breaths to try and get my tears under control. The garden was big, much bigger than it would have been in London, considering the size of the house. I was out of sight of the garage and the house itself when I saw the wall.

I could see straight away how it was possible to climb it, as it was crumbling in places and therefore had plenty of helpful gaps where you could hold on. Whether it was possible for *me* to do it was another matter. It was high—two and a half meters at a guess—and I wasn't fully recovered from adventuring on the cliffs.

But it was the only way out without serious loss of face. There was no alternative I was prepared to consider.

What I *was* prepared to do, however, was improvise. I had noticed an old garden chair a couple of meters away and I dragged it across to the corner, where an impressive array of scuffmarks told me that was Will's route. The chair was rickety and wobbled alarmingly as I stood up on the seat, very slowly, and then balanced on the back, and stretched as high as I could to reach the top of the wall. Success. I held on and found somewhere for my right foot to go, remembering Will's voice in my ear on the cliff.

Take your time. You've got to feel safe before you move. If one toehold doesn't work for you, find another.

I wedged my toes in between the crumbling concrete blocks and levered myself up in two moves, managing to haul myself up to the top of the wall. I sat there, amazed that my plan had worked. The happy feeling faded as I realized I couldn't pull my leg up. I had wedged my foot right into the gap I'd chosen, and now I could neither move it nor get it out. I was stuck, with my leg at an awkward angle. I couldn't go forward or back.

"What are you doing?" Will's tone was conversational, as if there was nothing weird about finding me marooned on his garden wall.

I looked down, acutely aware that I had just been crying and probably looked dreadful. I took refuge in sarcasm. "Learning to play the guitar. What does it look like?"

"It looks like you shouldn't ever attempt to climb something without me." He reached up and pulled my foot. "Wow. That's properly stuck."

"Can you get it out?"

"If I take your foot out of your shoe." He started undoing my laces. "Your foot should slide out of the trainer. Then the shoe will collapse and I'll be able to pull it out."

"Thanks," I said shortly.

"Anytime."

"Hopefully not." I glanced at him, at the long eyelashes that were lowered in concentration as he worked to untangle a particularly resistant knot. "What are you doing here, anyway?"

"I was on my way to see you."

"Why?"

He was levering my foot out of the shoe and didn't answer straight away. "I thought of something else I wanted to say."

"OK."

My foot came free and a moment later he had my shoe in his hand. He reached up and gave it to me. "Here you go, Cinderella."

"Too kind."

With a lot more dignity than I'd managed, Will climbed up and sat astride the wall.

"What did you want to say?" I asked.

"I'll tell you when we're on the ground."

"Are you coming too?"

"I thought I'd help in case you ran into any trouble on the other side."

I looked over. "It doesn't look too complicated."

"It's not."

I frowned at him. "Are you saying the trouble would be my fault?"

"Consider the last five minutes and tell me what you think."

"Anyone could have got stuck on the wall."

"Anyone *could*, but you *did*." He didn't wait to hear what I thought about that, jumping down with practiced ease.

"You can see you've done that before."

"A million times." He looked up at me. "Are you coming down?"

"In a second."

"You're not scared."

It looked a long way down now that I was on top of the wall. "I could break an ankle," I pointed out.

"I'll catch you if you fall."

"I'll flatten you."

Will shook his head, laughing a little. "Come on. You can't stay up there forever."

He was right. I finished putting my shoe back on, turned round to sit on the wall, as he had, and launched myself into space, to be caught and set gently on the ground and held. I didn't move, and neither did he, and we were as close as we had been on the beach, if not closer. His breath stirred my hair when he spoke.

"Did you close your eyes before you jumped or after you landed?"

"Somewhere in the middle, I think. Should I open them now? Is it safe?"

"You could risk it."

I blinked up at him, leaning back so I could see him. "Rescuing me is getting to be a habit, isn't it?"

"You keep climbing things. I never feel completely relaxed when you're off the ground."

"Me neither," I confided. "And I'm terrible at swimming. Give me good solid dry land any day of the week."

"I'll keep it in mind." Will was showing no signs of letting go of me and I'd have stayed like that forever, but I was too curious.

"You were going to say something else."

"Yes, I was. Thank you for reminding me."

"Well?"

"I don't like leaving things half done."

"What do you mean?" I tried for normal, but I could barely breathe.

He took a second to answer me and I could see he was weighing up the consequences of whatever he did next. I waited. And I might always wait for Will Henderson, I thought hopelessly, even if he walked away now.

Even if he never came back.

His eyes met mine again, and I forgot everything else but him, standing there, holding on to me as if he never meant to let me go.

"I mean this." He leaned in and kissed me, properly this time, and I had spent days imagining what it would be like to kiss him but I hadn't even come close. He kissed me like it was the start of something, or the end, and I couldn't work out which it was but I didn't want to ask.

For once, I didn't want to know.

Acknowledgments

This book would not exist without the help and support of the following people:

Lauren Buckland, the most wonderful editor, Duran Duran fan, and tweeter a writer could wish for; Sophie Nelson, razor-sharp copy editor and fount of good suggestions; Simon Trewin and Ariella Feiner, superheroes in literary-agent form; Jane Willis—who has waited so patiently for this book to exist—and all her other colleagues at United Agents; the podettes, particularly Rachel Petty, who loves YA as much as I do; the legions of YA authors whom I have edited, read, and admired from afar—they have taught me so much along the way; my fellow crime writers, lovely people despite their dark, dark thoughts; the snakepit, especially Philippa, who read the first draft on her phone; Michael and Bridget, Gemma, Tim and Amber, who make visiting Devon such a pleasure; *na lads*—Edward, Patrick, and Fred—who help, hinder and always entertain; and James, who knows which character is based on him.

And last of all, thanks to you, the reader, because I wrote this book for you.

Read on for a sneak preview of
Jane Casey's next Jess Tennant novel,

BET YOUR LIFE

1

Most people go out for the night and expect to have fun. I hadn't counted on it, and I'd been right. That was a very tiny consolation.

Surrounded by people laughing and joking and enjoying life, I felt like the saddest, loneliest person on earth. As if that wasn't enough to deal with, it was the coldest night of the year so far, and I had no coat. I wrapped my arms around myself and tried to stop my teeth from chattering as my breath misted in front of my face. Luckily, there was something to distract me. Just like everyone around me, I tilted my head back and stared at the sky. It was pure black, with more pinprick stars scattered across it than I had ever seen in light-polluted London. The sky was spectacular enough on its own, but when the first fireworks streaked up and flowered into brief glory, I almost forgot I was freezing.

Almost.

I had started out the night with a coat, obviously, because a Halloween fireworks party meant a lot of standing around on Port Sentinel's muddy recreation ground, waiting for the fun to start. I'd worn my favorite coat of all time, my new but old coat, found in the backroom clutter of the charity shop where I worked part-time. Fine Feathers was wall-to-wall designer cast-offs, thanks to the rich, fashion-conscious residents of Port Sentinel, but this coat had no label, just a couple of threads that showed where one had been. Narrow across the shoulders and waist, it swirled out before it ended just below my knees. It was made from ultra-black woven tweed and had tiny black roses embroidered around the inside of the hem, as if it wanted to keep them a secret. It made me walk taller and I adored it. And when I had gone to retrieve it from the cloakroom after a good two hours of not-totally-ironic dancing at the disco in the recreation center, it had disappeared. Now the heat of dancing had completely worn off and my thin cotton dress was keeping out precisely none of the cold. I had tights on, and boots, but I was shaking with cold.

A skinny black cat elbowed me in the ribs as she sashayed past, waving her tail, her ears set at a jaunty angle. I tried to work out if I knew her but she disappeared into the crowd before I could see her face, and there were a lot of cats at the party. I'd been in Port Sentinel for four months and it didn't surprise me that the local girls had gone for tight-fitting costumes, preferably with plenty of cleavage on display. Any excuse, quite frankly. Top choice: ghost, featuring pale-blue lipstick and ashy foundation, because ghosts apparently wore almost nothing— sheer dresses rather than the traditional white sheet. Second:

vampire. Leather and red lipstick appealed to a certain kind of girl and, more importantly, a certain kind of boy. There were a lot of bitten necks on display along with the fireworks. Third: witches in short black dresses, high boots, and fishnet tights. Port Sentinel was full of witches, in my experience, but they usually didn't bother with the costume. Finally, there were the pirates, a nod to Port Sentinel's smuggling past. These pirates wore tiny skirts, half-buttoned shirts, knee-boots, and cheeky grins along with their eye-patches. And all of them, but all of them, had got their coats before they came to stand outside.

It was notable—and typical—that if any of the boys were wearing a costume, they had made a token effort at best. I wasn't really in a position to criticize. I hadn't spent a huge amount of time on my own outfit. I'd only decided to go at the last minute, having resisted every effort my cousin Petra made to persuade me.

"You don't understand. Everybody goes. It's always the Saturday closest to Halloween, which in this case is the first of November, and it's really the start of half-term. Everyone who's away at boarding school comes back, and all the holiday-home kids turn up. It's like summer all over again," she had said, sounding wistful. Almost fourteen, she was still too young to go to the over-sixteens disco, though she'd promised me she'd be there for the fireworks.

"Saying it's like summer is not the way to sell it to me," I'd pointed out.

"You know what I mean. It's not like nearly dying and everything," Petra said impatiently. "There's a buzz. It's fun. You see people you haven't seen for ages."

"That sounds great." I didn't manage to sound enthusiastic,

because I wasn't. I was determined to keep my distance from anything that might remind me of the summer. The everything Petra mentioned in passing had been a whole world of pain. Nearly dying had been the easy part.

Mind-reading as usual, my cousin Hugo looked up from his book and smirked. "Don't worry. He won't be there. Halloween parties and fireworks are not his thing."

He. Hugo meant his friend, my ex, Will Henderson. Will, who had been sent away to boarding school at the start of September, mainly because he'd been going out with me. I longed to see him and I hoped to avoid him. It was that sort of confused thinking that made my head hurt.

"I wouldn't have thought Halloween parties would have been your thing, either," I said.

The smirk had widened to a wicked grin. "I wouldn't miss it for anything." Now that I was surrounded by so many scantily clad girls, I understood the appeal.

It occurred to me that I hadn't seen Hugo for a while, or Petra at all. I stopped watching the fireworks bloom and fade so that I could scan the crowd. Everyone was packed tightly together and I wasn't tall enough to see very far, what with all the rugby players and surfing types who were standing shoulder to broad shoulder in front of me. I saw plenty of people I recognized, but no one I would call a friend. That wasn't altogether surprising. In any Port Sentinel gathering, I was likely to find more enemies than friends. It was no wonder I was looking forward to the following day, when one of my best friends from London was coming for a visit. I had missed Ella more than I'd even realized.

In the meantime, Hugo. I moved to my left, trying not to

step on any toes, and worked my way toward the front. A skeleton swore in my ear as I moved past her. Her face was a glowing skull that floated against the dark night and I couldn't tell who she really was, but I was absolutely sure I should keep my distance from her. Skirting a kissing couple, looking back over my shoulder, I skidded on the slick mud and almost fell. I put a hand out to stop myself and grabbed the nearest thing, which turned out to be Ryan Denton's arm.

Oh no.

"Hey, Jess. How's it going?" Because of the fireworks exploding above our heads he said it loudly enough that the guys standing nearest to us heard, and turned, and I saw the same look spread across their faces: amusement and anticipation. I could have done without turning into a running joke, but I hadn't been given much of a choice about it.

"Sorry," I said. "I was just falling over. Thanks for lending me your arm."

"Any time. Hey!" I'd already started to walk away, but he caught hold of my wrist and pulled me back. "Don't go. Watch the fireworks with me."

"I'm looking for someone."

His eyebrows drew together. "Who?"

"Just Hugo."

"Oh." A smile, like the sun coming out from behind clouds. Cousin, not competition. "It'll be easier to find him when the fireworks are over."

He was right. Everyone was packed together on the recreation ground, kept a safe distance away from the pyrotechnics behind a semicircle of barriers. Once the display was over I would be able to move around without colliding with people.

"OK. Good idea."

"Come here," he said, and drew me toward him. A small gold dot shot into the sky and transformed itself into a huge shimmering orb that hung for a few seconds before fading. The light slanted across Ryan's face, highlighting the line of his cheek, the edge of his jaw, the full curve of his lower lip. It struck sparks in his sea-blue eyes. God, he was cute.

So off-limits it was untrue, but cute.

While I'd been gazing at him and his perfect mouth, he'd been checking out my costume. "I like the ringlets. What are you supposed to be?"

I looked down at the dress my aunt had dug out from the very back of her wardrobe. It was pale pink, short, and covered in tiny flowers, and she said she'd worn it in the nineties with a striped top underneath, woolly tights, big boots, and a man's cardigan. I was wearing cowboy boots (to cope with the mud) and a frilly apron. I'd have given quite a lot for a thick woolly cardigan at that moment, whether grunge was back in fashion or not. "Isn't it obvious? I'm Little Bo-Peep."

"No sheep, though."

I couldn't prevent myself from smiling. "Well, exactly."

"Oh yeah." He grinned back. "Not what I'd call a typical Halloween costume. It's not exactly spooky."

"I know." It wasn't all that surprising I'd resisted the chance to dress up as a ghoul or a ghost. I'd had a gutful of death during the previous summer. Mocking it didn't seem like a wise thing to do.

As for Ryan's costume, he looked exactly the same as usual. Hot.

"And what did you come as?" I asked, hoping he wasn't good at mind-reading.

"My identical twin."

"How is that spooky?"

He leaned down so that his face was inches from mine. "My identical twin is evil. He's capable of anything."

"Good to know."

"My identical twin thinks you look stunning tonight."

"Also good to know." Playing it cool . . .

"So do I."

I felt myself blushing, not because he was flirting with me but because I could see Ryan's friends grinning ever more widely. The flirting happened a lot, and I still found it hard to cope with.

"I thought you'd be looking for Will."

I jumped, surprised he'd mentioned Will's name. Once they'd been friends, then sworn enemies from the age of nine. Then I'd come to town and ended up as the prize in the latest competition, which Will had won. Ryan wasn't giving up, though. "No, I'm not looking for him."

"He's coming back this week, isn't he? Not spending half-term at his fancy new school."

"He's back," I said. "But I don't have any plans to see him."

Ryan raised his eyebrows. "Not planning to pick up where you left off?"

"That is where we left off. We broke up. Just before Will left." And I wasn't going to think about that painful little scene for a minute more than I had to. "What about you? Is Natasha coming back this week?"

It was his turn to look unsettled. "No. No way. She's on lockdown. No taking breaks from rehab."

Natasha, my arch-enemy and Ryan's psycho ex-girlfriend, had been found out in a big way at the end of the summer, when I'd uncovered the truth about the part she played in my cousin Freya's death. Natasha's mother had shipped her off to an ultra-strict boarding school to get her under control. I wished her good luck, but I was pretty sure she wasn't going to change. She was as evil as they came, I thought.

"It's not rehab, though."

"In all but name."

I shrugged. "You'd know more about it than I do."

"Not really. I haven't been in touch with her."

"But she's been in touch with you, I bet."

"She might have been. Jealous?" He sounded hopeful.

"Not even a little bit. Wow." I leaned out to look past him as the sky turned crimson, then jade-green, then ice-white. "That really is amazing."

Ryan glanced over his shoulder. "They always spend a fortune on the fireworks."

"I'd heard it was a big deal. How much longer is it going to be?"

"A few minutes."

My heart sank. My teeth were actually chattering. I wasn't sure I could make it to the end.

"Are you all right?" Ryan asked.

"F-freezing. I lost my coat."

"Come here. I'll keep you warm."

I should have said no, but I was too cold to argue. I moved a step closer to him and he turned me round to face away from him. He unzipped his down-filled jacket and drew me back so I was leaning against him, then wrapped the jacket around both of us and held me, his chin on my head. I felt the heat from his body spreading to mine, and it was as comforting as sitting by a log fire. The fireworks were winding up for a big finish, which helped me to ignore the stares we were getting. I knew it looked as if he'd succeeded in wearing me down, but I didn't care. Damage to my reputation was survivable. Hypothermia was, potentially, not.

They kept the best for last: a flurry of hundreds of gold stars that hung against the sky for what felt like forever, then faded to black. I sighed and then applauded along with everyone else, genuinely impressed.

The crowd started to come apart, drifting away in twos and threes to seek further entertainment, or a quiet corner for some alone time, or the next party. Ryan still had his arms around my shoulders and didn't seem inclined to let go.

"I need to look for Hugo," I said, twisting so I could see his face.

"In a minute." He ran a hand into my hair and held onto it at the back of my neck.

"Hey," I said half-heartedly. "Let go."

"It's traditional to round off the fireworks with a kiss."

I leaned away from him as far as I could, which was not very. "I keep hearing about Port Sentinel's traditions but I've never heard that one."

"You're still new in town. Give it a year and you should be up to speed." He leaned toward me and I did a quick calculation: Was it more embarrassing to make a fuss or to allow it to happen?

"Jess!"

Saved. I wriggled free as soon as Ryan's grip loosened. Hugo was coming toward us.

"Where have you been?"

"I was going to ask you the same thing." Hugo had an odd expression on his face, I noted, and could guess why. My cousin was not a Ryan fan. You didn't have to be particularly sensitive to spot that, and Ryan was actually quite good at reading other people's reactions. He let go of me completely and nodded to Hugo.

"Glad you found each other."

"Ryan!" The shout came from across the recreation ground, where a figure stood, arms outstretched. A knot of people was milling around him but he was very definitely the center of attention. He was instantly recognizable, even to me, as Harry Knowles. His hair stood straight up from his head, adding an extra six or so inches to his already quite impressive height. "Are you coming or not?"

"In a minute," Ryan yelled back.

"Don't miss out, man. It's going to be big." He picked up a small witch and threw her over his shoulder, spinning around as she shrieked with laughter.

"I'll be there." Turning to me, Ryan said, "There's a party at Harry's house tonight. Come along if you can."

"I don't know Harry." I meant personally. Everyone in Port Sentinel knew who Harry was: the wild son of a genius city trader who had made his first million of the day before breakfast, every day, until the day he'd burned out. He'd quit, taken his money, and fled to Devon. Even in a town full of rich kids, Harry was renowned for being loaded, and spoiled rotten. He was a founding member of Ryan's group of friends, who were essentially the prettiest and richest teenagers around. And all this could have been mine as well, if I'd been prepared to indulge Ryan and go out with him.

"You don't need to know Harry. You know me." Ryan grinned down at me, ignoring Hugo. "Anyway, if you change your mind, let me know. Harry's folks are in Venezuela for half-term. He's aiming for a party a night."

"I'll keep it in mind."

Ryan's eyes narrowed a fraction, registering that I hadn't said yes. "It would be fun. You don't want to miss out."

"Definitely not. Thanks for asking me."

"Good luck with finding your coat," Ryan said, and then, as I was just about to reply, dropped a kiss on my mouth. My lips were parted and it was startlingly intimate, even if it was quick. I stared after him as he walked away, my mouth tingling. When Hugo spoke, I jumped. I had completely forgotten he was there.

"What were you doing with him?"

"Nothing. Keeping warm." I rubbed my arms, trying to generate some heat. "Have you seen my coat?"

He unwound his scarf and handed it to me. "Never mind about your coat."

"I do mind. Obviously. But thanks." I wrapped the scarf around my neck, watching him curiously. "Where were you during the show, anyway?"

For Hugo, he was oddly slow to respond. "Looking for you. Then looking at you."

"How fascinating for you. I'm surprised I was enough to distract you from the fireworks. You can stare at me any time."

"I can. Will can't."

I was knotting the scarf but I stopped dead. "What did you say?"

"Will can't." Two syllables. Perfect enunciation. Nothing confusing about it. Except . . .

"He was here?" My voice was very small.

"Yeah."

"And he saw me."

"With Ryan."

"Where is he?"

"He just left."

"Just now?"

"A minute ago." After Ryan had kissed me. He didn't have to say it. I knew.

"Which way did he go? Hugo!" I grabbed his arm and held onto it. "Tell me."

"When he got to the gate he turned left, so into town, I assume." He dragged himself free. "I wouldn't bother, Jess. Leave it for now. You can explain the next time you see him."

He was talking to cold, thin air. I was already sprinting for the gate. I dodged through the stragglers who were leaving, the mud clinging to my boots as I ran. I cut between two cars and snagged my tights on the front wing of one of them, where an accident had left it buckled and bent. I lost valuable seconds freeing myself, but once I hit the road I was able to go faster and I flew down the hill in the direction Hugo had indicated, keeping to the center of the streets because the pavements were wonky and narrow, and I would definitely, certainly trip. I liked my front teeth enough to want to keep them intact, but I wasn't going to slow down until I had to.

There was no sign of Will down any side street or round any corner—just little groups of costumed revellers and the occasional pumpkin grinning in a window or on a doorstep, eyes flickering as the candle inside guttered. I took a chance on him heading for the city center and did likewise, hoping I'd find him there, or near where I lived. His house backed onto my family's home, Sandhayes, so if I headed in that general direction I had a chance of finding him.

What I would say when and if I did find him was another question.

It was a long way to the center of town from the recreation ground and I started to feel it in my legs just around the time a wicked stitch skewered my side. I slowed and then stopped, my breathing ragged, one hand gripping my waist where the pain was worst. The chill in the air was nothing to the cold horror that was sending shivers over my skin.

Will had been there.

Will had seen me with Ryan.

Will had seen Ryan kiss me.

Will would have the wrong idea.

Will might even care.

The very thought jolted me back into action. I moved forward at a pace that was a long way from a sprint, limping and wincing, so wrapped up in my own misery that I turned down a narrow lane and saw a flashing blue light irradiating the side of some buildings in the distance and didn't even think that it might be something to concern me. I was closer to it when I started to hear the radio squawking, and another joining it, and a low throaty roar that was an engine turning over. I hurried round the corner into St. Laurence Square, a tiny paved

341

space in the heart of town in front of an old church. There was an oak tree in the center of it with a bench circling its trunk. In the summer it was a nice place to sit. Now, on a cold dark autumn night, the tree was shedding leaves with every breath of wind. An ambulance was parked beside it. Beside that, there were two police cars. Beside that, another car I recognized. It had a blue light on the top that swung and swirled and caught me in the eyes, but not before I'd noticed the figure on the ground, under a blanket, and the spreading pool of blood around his head. He was young, my age or so, and his face was battered beyond recognition. I stared for a long, horrified moment—short dark hair, and he'd be tall if he was standing—before a paramedic knelt down beside him and blocked my view. I went forward on wobbling legs, really, truly terrified that, somehow, it was Will who was lying on the paving slabs. As I edged sideways to see him, the boy on the ground moaned, and I felt a sting of relief as I realized it wasn't Will. I felt guilty for being glad.

Two policemen in uniform were crouching by a drain, trying to reach something that had been dropped in it, while another unrolled blue-and-white tape to cordon off the crime scene. I stood, unobserved for the moment. I couldn't take my eyes off the boy on the ground.

"It's all right," one of the paramedics said, holding his head steady while the other one prepared to put a neck brace on him. "Don't worry, mate. We'll look after you."

The boy groaned again and lifted a hand, as if he meant to push them away. His wrist was ringed with a red mark that was bleeding a little where the skin had been rubbed away. One of the paramedics gently pushed his arm back down by his side.

The effort seemed to have exhausted the boy and he lay completely still while they treated him. If I hadn't seen him move and heard him moan, I'd have thought he was dead. His skin was bleached white where it wasn't marked with purple bruises or streaked with darkening blood. The paramedics were talking in low voices, scrawling notes on the backs of their gloves as they assessed him. They were obviously worried about his condition and in a hurry to get him into the ambulance. I made myself concentrate on his face and realized, with a shiver, that under the blood, despite the swelling around his eyes and mouth, I recognized him. I had met him before.

The next minute I jumped out of my skin as someone grabbed my arm and held onto it, tightly enough to hurt.